The Essential
Tawfiq al-Hakim

The Essential
Tawfiq al-Hakim

GREAT EGYPTIAN WRITERS

Edited by
Denys Johnson-Davies

The American University in Cairo Press
Cairo   New York

Copyright © 2008, 2013 by
The American University in Cairo Press
113 Sharia Kasr el Aini, Cairo, Egypt
420 Fifth Avenue, New York, NY 10018
www.aucpress.com

First paperback edition 2013

Dar el Kutub No. 13836/12
ISBN 978 977 416 592 4

Dar el Kutub Cataloging-in-Publication Data

Johnson-Davies, Denys
      The Essential Tawfiq al-Hakim / edited by Denys Johnson-Davies.—Cairo: The American University in Cairo Press, 2013.
        p.   cm.
        ISBN 978 977 416 592 4
        1. Authors I. Johnson-Davies, Denys (ed.)
        928.1

1 2 3 4 5   17 16 15 14 13

Designed by Sally Boylan
Printed in Egypt

Contents

Introduction

—∿∿∿—

Had the committee for the Nobel Prize decided at an earlier date than 1988 that recognition should be given to the renaissance that was occurring in modern Arabic literature, the prize would surely have been awarded to Tawfiq al-Hakim (1898–1987). As with George Bernard Shaw in the west, Tawfiq al-Hakim's fame as a writer was not helped by being regarded in the main as a playwright, at a time when most readers found their preferred reading in the novel.

Even before going to Paris in 1925 to study law—his father was a judge, and no career was more highly esteemed in Egypt than the law—Tawfiq al-Hakim had from his earliest years been fascinated by the theater, and in particular by the dramatic art as it was being practiced in Paris at that time. So it is not surprising that the young man who was sent off to Paris to study law returned home with one single burning desire: to write plays and to establish for his country the foundations of a serious theater.

Up to this time in Egypt, the theater had been regarded as a place for entertainment pure and simple, with no links to literature. What put it outside the realm of literature for most intellectuals of the time was that theatrical performances were conducted in the colloquial language, and were thus placed within reach of the general populace. The classical language, in contrast, was employed for the writing of literature—which comprised, first of all, poetry, and included belles-lettres and history, but gave no recognition to

1

the purely imaginative genres of writing such as the novel and the short story. Thus while the *Arabian Nights*, for instance, has been regarded in the west as a masterpiece of storytelling, it does not even warrant a mention in Arabic books of literary criticism. Plays, like the novel and the short story, were certainly not part of Arabic literature, and it was Tawfiq al-Hakim who brought about the introduction of drama into the literary canon.

On returning from Paris, he wrote his first play, *Ahl al-kahf* (The People of the Cave), based on the legend of the Seven Sleepers of Ephesus, which is briefly referred to in the Qur'an. It tells the story of three men who, escaping the tyranny of a king, take refuge in a cave. There they fall asleep and awaken some three hundred years later in an obviously changed world, which, unfortunately they do not find to their liking—so they once again go back to the cave.

Al-Sultan al-ha'ir (The Sultan's Dilemma), published in 1960, is widely considered his most successful play (the translation of the play was later published in the expanded edition of the *Norton Anthology of World Masterpieces*). Before the coming of the Ottoman Empire, Egypt was ruled for two and a half centuries by the Mamluks, whose name means 'slave'; the sultans were slaves who had been manumitted. In *The Sultan's Dilemma*, a Mamluk who has acceded to the throne is found not to have been properly manumitted. He therefore has himself sold by auction, certain in the knowledge that his new owner will then set him free. The result is a drama that, as one critic put it, manages to be serious without being solemn. One of the playwright's great contributions to modern literature was to create a form of literary Arabic that was acceptable to the educated reader but would at the same time allow the playwright to indulge in comic exchanges between the characters. For many years, though, his plays were available only in print, and were first staged only in the late 1940s, when a professional theater began to be established in Egypt. From then on his plays found a ready audience in Cairo and in other capitals of the Arab world.

In all, Tawfiq al-Hakim wrote some seventy full-length plays, deriving his material from sources both Arabic and foreign. The years he spent in Paris meant that he was well-read in French literature. Thus his familiarity with such authors as Ionesco and Samuel Beckett made him aware of such innovative movements as the theater of the absurd, and he even wrote an absurdist play, *The Tree Climber*, the other full-length play included in this volume.

Our playwright also drew on traditional sources for some of his work, employing with great success the highly expressive Egyptian vernacular and making of it an acceptable tool in the armory of the modern Arabic writer. His skill in dealing with such material is shown in his one-act play *The Donkey Market*. Borrowing the basic plot from a well-known tale told about the wise fool Goha, who has long been a part of traditional Egyptian folklore, the play shows Tawfiq al-Hakim at his most skillful in producing a highly amusing play yet with serious undertones.

The other one-act play in this volume, *The Song of Death*, is in complete contrast to the delightful comedy about donkeys. It nevertheless also deals with the Egyptian countryside and one of the darker elements that is still part of life among its peasant population: blood revenge. The play, treated in a highly dramatized, almost Grand Guignol manner, was later made into a film.

While known primarily as the writer who introduced the theater into modern Arabic writing, Tawfiq al-Hakim also practiced all the other genres of writing that had emerged in Egypt at that time. In his autobiography, *The Prison of Life*, he gives a commendably frank account of his relationship with his parents, in particular his father.

Al-Hakim wrote a number of short stories, of which a volume has been published in English translation. Three examples are included in this book. However, in this genre he was outstripped by the younger Egyptian writer, Yusuf Idris (1927–91), who specialized in the short story and also played a role in making the colloquial language an acceptable part of serious literature.

He was also the author of several novels. Of these, the best known, and the one that has stood the test of time, is *Diary of a Country Prosecutor*. It was through this novel that I first came to know the writer. On arriving in Cairo in 1945, I had sought a meeting with him to ask his permission to translate this novel, but Abba Eban had beaten me to it and produced his translation, under the title *The Maze of Justice*, in 1947. The fact that this novel has been republished several times, and is still in print, speaks much for it. I can do no better than quote a part of the foreword to the novel by P.H. Newby, one of the earliest winners of the Booker Prize: "Tawfik al-Hakim's comedy is blacker than anything Gogol or Dickens wrote because life for the Egyptian peasantry, the fellahin, was blacker than for the nineteenth-century Russian serf or English pauper. It must also be said that the first readers of Gogol and Dickens would not have been prepared to look at unwelcome facts with the honesty Tawfik al-Hakim expected of his readers. The Egyptian reading public all those years ago (the novel was first published in 1937) was, in its cynical way, more realistic than the reading public in Tsarist Russia or Victorian England. The savage satire of the book is, as a result—and by general consent—on target."

Tawfiq al-Hakim certainly earned himself a worthy place alongside Naguib Mahfouz as one of the pillars upon which the renaissance of Arabic literature has been built.

The cover photograph was given to me by the author after I had completed my translation of *The Donkey Market*.

I was able to compile this volume through the generous sponsorship of the British Council.

The Sultan's Dilemma

—⟋⟍—

Cast

the SULTAN	UNKNOWN MAN
the VIZIER	1ST LEADING CITIZEN
the CHIEF CADI	2ND LEADING CITIZEN
a BEAUTIFUL LADY	3RD LEADING CITIZEN
her MAIDSERVANT	1ST MAN IN CROWD
an EMINENT SLAVE TRADER	2ND MAN IN CROWD
the CONDEMNED MAN	MOTHER
the EXECUTIONER	CHILD
the WINE MERCHANT	TOWNSPEOPLE
the MUEZZIN	GUARDS
the SHOEMAKER	SULTAN'S RETINUE

ACT ONE

An open space in the city during the time of the Mamluk Sultans. On one side there is a mosque with a minaret; on the other, a tavern. In the center is a house with a balcony. Dawn is about to break and silence reigns. A stake has been set up to which a MAN, *condemned to death, has been tied. His* EXECUTIONER *is nearby trying to fight off sleep.*

CONDEMNED MAN [*contemplating the* EXECUTIONER]: Getting sleepy? Of course you are. Congratulations. Sleep well. You're not awaiting something that will spoil *your* peace of mind.

EXECUTIONER: Quiet!

CONDEMNED MAN: And so—when is it to be?

EXECUTIONER: I told you to be quiet.

CONDEMNED MAN [*pleadingly*]: Tell me truly when it's to be? When?

EXECUTIONER: When are you going to stop disturbing me?

CONDEMNED MAN: Sorry. It is, though, something that particularly concerns me. When does this event—a joyous one for you—take place?

EXECUTIONER: At dawn. I've told you this more than ten times. At dawn I'll carry out the sentence on you. Now do you understand? So let me enjoy a moment's peace.

CONDEMNED MAN: Dawn? It's still far off, isn't it, Executioner?

EXECUTIONER: I don't know.

CONDEMNED MAN: You don't know?

EXECUTIONER: It's the Muezzin who knows. When he goes up to the minaret of this mosque and gives the call to the dawn prayer, I'll raise my sword and swipe off your head—those are the orders. Happy now?

CONDEMNED MAN: Without a trial? I haven't yet been put on trial, I haven't yet appeared before a judge.

EXECUTIONER: That's nothing to do with me.

CONDEMNED MAN: For sure, you have nothing to do with anything except my execution.

EXECUTIONER: At dawn, in furtherance of the Sultan's orders.

CONDEMNED MAN: For what crime?

EXECUTIONER: That's not my affair.

CONDEMNED MAN: Because I said . . . .

EXECUTIONER: Quiet! Quiet! Shut your mouth—I have been ordered to cut off your head right away if you utter a word about your crime.

CONDEMNED MAN: Don't be upset, I'll shut my mouth.

EXECUTIONER: You've done well to shut your mouth and leave me to enjoy my sleep. It's in your interest that I should enjoy a quiet and peaceful sleep.

CONDEMNED MAN: In my interest?

EXECUTIONER: Certainly, it's in your interest that I should be completely rested and in excellent health, both in body and mind; because when I'm tired, depressed, and strung up, my hand shakes, and when it shakes I perform my work badly.

CONDEMNED MAN: And what's your work to me?

EXECUTIONER: Fool! My work has to do with your neck. Poor performance means your neck will not be cleanly cut, because a clean cut requires a steady hand and calm mind so that the head may fly off at a single blow, allowing you no time to feel any sensation of pain. Do you understand now?

CONDEMNED MAN: Of course, that's quite right.

EXECUTIONER: You see! Now you must be quite convinced why it is necessary that you should let me rest; also, to bring joy to my heart and raise my morale.

CONDEMNED MAN: Your morale? *Yours?*

EXECUTIONER: Naturally, if I were in your shoes . . . .

CONDEMNED MAN: O God, take him at his word! I wish you *were* in my shoes.

EXECUTIONER: What are you saying?

CONDEMNED MAN: Carry on. What would you do if you had the honor and good fortune to be in my shoes?

EXECUTIONER: I'll tell you what I'd do—have you any money?

CONDEMNED MAN: Ah, money! Yes, yes, yes! Money! An apposite thought. As for money, my friend, you may say what you like about that. The whole city knows—and you among them—that I'm one of the very richest of merchants and slave-traders.

EXECUTIONER: No, you have misunderstood me—I'm not talking of a bribe. It's impossible to bribe me—not because of my honesty and integrity, but because, quite frankly, I am unable to save you. All I wanted was to accept your invitation to have a drink—if you should happen to do so. A glass of wine is not a bribe. It would be impolite of me to refuse your invitation. Look! There's a Wine Merchant a stone's throw away from you—his tavern is open all night, because he has customers who visit that whore who lives in the house opposite.

CONDEMNED MAN: A drink? Is that all?

EXECUTIONER: That's all.

CONDEMNED MAN: I've got a better and more attractive idea. Let's go up together, you and I, to that beautiful woman. I know her and if we went to her we'd spend the most marvelous night of our lives—a night to fill your heart with joy and gaiety and raise your morale. What do you say?

EXECUTIONER: No, gracious sir.

CONDEMNED MAN: You would accept my invitation to a drink, but refuse my invitation to a party of drinking and fun, beauty and merriment?

EXECUTIONER: In that house? No, my dear condemned friend, I prefer for you to stay as you are: fettered with chains till dawn.

CONDEMNED MAN: What a pity you don't trust me! What if I were to promise you that before the call to dawn prayers I would be back again in chains?

EXECUTIONER: Does a bird return to the snare?

CONDEMNED MAN: Yes, I swear to you on my honor.

EXECUTIONER: *Your* honor? What an oath!

CONDEMNED MAN: You don't believe me.

EXECUTIONER: I believe you so long as you are where you are—and in handcuffs.

CONDEMNED MAN: How can I invite you to have a drink then?

EXECUTIONER: That's easy. I'll go to the tavern and ask him to bring two glasses of his best wine and when he brings them we'll drink them right here. What do you say?

CONDEMNED MAN: But . . . .

EXECUTIONER: We're agreed. I'll go—there's no need for you to trouble your-self. Just a minute, with your permission.

The EXECUTIONER *goes to the tavern at the corner of the square and knocks at the door. The* WINE MERCHANT *comes out to him, he whispers something in his ear, and returns to his place.*

EXECUTIONER [*to the* CONDEMNED MAN]: Everything necessary has been arranged, and you will see, my dear condemned man, the good result shortly.

CONDEMNED MAN: What good result?

EXECUTIONER: My masterful work. When I drink I'm very precise in my work, but, if I haven't drunk, my work goes all to hell. By way of example I'll tell you what happened the other day. I was charged with the job of executing someone, and I hadn't drunk a thing all that day. Do you know what I did? I gave that poor fellow's neck such a blow that his head flew off into the air and landed far away—not in this basket of mine, but in another basket over there, the basket belonging to the Shoemaker next door to the tavern. God alone knows the trouble we had getting the missing head out of the heaps of shoes and soles.

CONDEMNED MAN: The Shoemaker's basket! What a shameful thing to happen! I beseech you by God not to let my head suffer such a fate.

EXECUTIONER: Don't be afraid. Things are different where you are concerned. The other head belonged to a horribly stingy fellow.

The WINE MERCHANT *appears from his shop carrying two glasses.*

WINE MERCHANT [*moving toward the* CONDEMNED MAN]: This is of course for you—your last wish.

CONDEMNED MAN: No, for the Executioner—it's his cherished wish.

EXECUTIONER [*to the* WINE MERCHANT]: To bring calm and contentment to my heart.

WINE MERCHANT: And from whom shall I receive payment?

CONDEMNED MAN: From me of course—to bring joy and gladness to his heart.

EXECUTIONER: It is incumbent upon me to accept his warm invitation.

CONDEMNED MAN: And it is incumbent upon me to raise his morale.

WINE MERCHANT: What very good friends you two are!

EXECUTIONER: It is a reciprocated affection.

CONDEMNED MAN: Until dawn breaks.

EXECUTIONER: Don't worry about the dawn now—it is still far off. Come, let's touch glasses.

The EXECUTIONER *snatches up the two glasses and strikes one against the other, turns, raises a glass, and drinks to the* CONDEMNED MAN.

EXECUTIONER: Your health!

CONDEMNED MAN: Thank you.

EXECUTIONER [*after he has drained his glass he holds the other glass up to the* CONDEMNED MAN*'s mouth*]: And now it's your turn, my dear fellow.

CONDEMNED MAN [*taking a gulp and coughing*]: Enough. You drink the rest for me.

EXECUTIONER: Is that your wish?

CONDEMNED MAN: The last!

EXECUTIONER [*raising the second glass*]: Then I raise my glass to . . . .

CONDEMNED MAN: Your masterful work.

EXECUTIONER: God willing! Also to your generosity and kindness, my friend.

WINE MERCHANT [*taking the two empty glasses from the* EXECUTIONER]: What's this old slave-trader done? What's his crime? All of us in the city know him—he's no murderer or thief.

CONDEMNED MAN: And yet my head will fall at dawn, just like that of any murderer or thief.

WINE MERCHANT: Why? For what crime?

CONDEMNED MAN: For no reason except that I said . . . .

EXECUTIONER: Quiet! Don't utter a word! Shut your mouth!

CONDEMNED MAN: I've shut my mouth.

EXECUTIONER: And you, Wine Merchant, you've got your glasses, so off with you!

WINE MERCHANT: And my money?

EXECUTIONER: It's he who invited me—and only a dastardly fellow refuses an invitation.

CONDEMNED MAN: To be sure I invited him, and he was good enough to accept my invitation. Your money, Tavern Owner, is here in a purse in my belt. Approach and take what you want.

EXECUTIONER: Allow me to approach on his behalf.

He approaches and takes some money from the CONDEMNED MAN*'s purse and pays the* WINE MERCHANT.

EXECUTIONER: Take what you're owed and a bit more that you may know we're generous people.

The WINE MERCHANT *takes his money and returns to his shop. The* EXECU-
TIONER *begins humming in a low voice.*

CONDEMNED MAN [*anxiously*]: And now . . . .

EXECUTIONER: Now we begin our singing and merrymaking. Do you know,
my dear condemned man, that I'm very fond of good singing, a pleasant
tune, and fine lyrics? It fills the heart with contentment and joy, with gladness and a delight in life. Sing me something!

CONDEMNED MAN: I? Sing?

EXECUTIONER: Yes. Why not? What's to stop you? Your larynx—thanks be to
God—is perfectly free. All you have to do is raise your voice in song and
out will come a lovely tune to delight the ear. Come on, sing! Entertain me!

CONDEMNED MAN: God bless us! O God, bear witness!

EXECUTIONER: Come along! Sing to me!

CONDEMNED MAN: Do you really think I'm in the mood for singing at this time?

EXECUTIONER: Did you not just now promise me to bring gladness to my soul
and remove the depression from my heart?

CONDEMNED MAN: Are you the one to feel depressed?

EXECUTIONER: Yes, please remove my depression. Overwhelm me with joy!
Let me enjoy the strains of ballads and songs! Drown me with melodies
and sweet tunes! Listen—I've remembered something. I know by heart a
song I composed myself during one night of sleeplessness and woe.

CONDEMNED MAN: Then sing it to me.

EXECUTIONER: I don't have a beautiful voice.

CONDEMNED MAN: And who told you that *my* voice was beautiful?

EXECUTIONER: To me all other people's voices are beautiful—because I don't
listen to them, especially if I'm drunk. All I'm concerned with is being
surrounded on all sides by singing: the feeling that there is singing all
around me soothes my nerves. Sometimes I feel as though I myself would
like to sing, but one condition must obtain: that I find someone to listen to
me. And if there is someone to listen, let him beware if he does not show
admiration and appreciation, for if not . . . if not I become shy and embarrassed and begin to tremble, after which I get very angry. Now, having
drawn your attention to the condition, shall I sing?

CONDEMNED MAN: Sing!

EXECUTIONER: And will you admire me and show your appreciation?

CONDEMNED MAN: Yes.

EXECUTIONER: You promise faithfully?

CONDEMNED MAN: Faithfully.

EXECUTIONER: Then I'll sing you my tender song. Are you listening?

CONDEMNED MAN: I'm listening and appreciating.

EXECUTIONER: The appreciation comes at the end. As for now, all you're asked to do is merely to listen.

CONDEMNED MAN: I'm merely listening.

EXECUTIONER: Good. Are you ready?

CONDEMNED MAN: Why? Isn't it you who're going to sing?

EXECUTIONER: Yes, but it's necessary for you to be ready to listen.

CONDEMNED MAN: And am I capable of doing anything else? You have left my ears free—no doubt for that purpose.

EXECUTIONER: Then let's start. This tender song, called "The Flower and the Gardener," was composed by me. Yes, I composed it myself.

CONDEMNED MAN: I know that.

EXECUTIONER: How odd! Who told you?

CONDEMNED MAN: You told me so yourself just a moment ago.

EXECUTIONER: Really? Really? And now, do you want me to begin?

CONDEMNED MAN: Go ahead.

EXECUTIONER: I'm just about to begin. Listen—but you're not listening.

CONDEMNED MAN: I am listening.

EXECUTIONER: The listening must be done with superlative attention.

CONDEMNED MAN: With superlative attention!

EXECUTIONER: Be careful not to upset me by letting your mind wander and not paying attention.

CONDEMNED MAN: I am paying attention.

EXECUTIONER: Are you ready?

CONDEMNED MAN: Yes.

EXECUTIONER: I don't find you excessively enthusiastic.

CONDEMNED MAN: And how should I behave?

EXECUTIONER: I want you to be burning with enthusiasm. Tell me you absolutely insist that you listen to my singing.

CONDEMNED MAN: I absolutely insist. . . .

EXECUTIONER: You say it coldly, with indifference.

CONDEMNED MAN: Coldly?

EXECUTIONER: I want the insistence to issue forth from the depths of your heart.

CONDEMNED MAN: It comes from the depths of my heart.

EXECUTIONER: I don't sense the warmth of sincerity in your voice.

CONDEMNED MAN: Sincerity?

EXECUTIONER: Yes, it's not apparent from the tone of your voice; it is the tone and timbre of the voice that reveals a person's true feelings, and your voice is cold and indifferent.

CONDEMNED MAN: And so—are you going to sing or aren't you?

EXECUTIONER: I shan't sing.

CONDEMNED MAN: Thanks be to God!

EXECUTIONER: You thank God for my not singing?

CONDEMNED MAN: No, I shall always thank God for your singing and your not singing alike. I don't believe there's anyone who'd object to praising God in all circumstances.

EXECUTIONER: Deep down you're wishing that I won't sing.

CONDEMNED MAN: Deep down? Who but God knows a man's inner thoughts?

EXECUTIONER: Then you want me to sing?

CONDEMNED MAN: If you like.

EXECUTIONER: I'll sing.

CONDEMNED MAN: Sing!

EXECUTIONER: No, I have a condition: implore me first of all to sing. Plead with me.

CONDEMNED MAN: I plead with you.

EXECUTIONER: Say it sensitively, entreatingly.

CONDEMNED MAN: Please—I implore you—by your Lord, by the Lord of all creation. I ask of God, the One, the Conqueror, the Strong and Mighty, to soften your cruel heart and to listen to my request and to be so good and gracious as to sing.

EXECUTIONER: Again!

CONDEMNED MAN: What?

EXECUTIONER: Repeat this pleading!

CONDEMNED MAN: God Almighty! Have mercy upon me! You've killed me with all this resistance and coyness. Sing if you want to; if not, then, for God's sake let me be and I'll have nothing to do with it.

EXECUTIONER: Are you angry? I don't want you to be angry. I'll sing so as to calm you down and remove your feeling of distress. I'll start right away. [*He coughs, then hums softly preparatory to singing.*]

CONDEMNED MAN: At last!

EXECUTIONER [*standing up suddenly*]: If you'd prefer me not to sing, say so frankly.

CONDEMNED MAN: Heavens above! He's going to start all over again.

EXECUTIONER: Is your patience exhausted?

CONDEMNED MAN: And how!

EXECUTIONER: Am I making you suffer?

CONDEMNED MAN: And how!

EXECUTIONER: Just be patient, my dear fellow. Be patient.

CONDEMNED MAN: This Executioner is really killing me!

EXECUTIONER: What are you saying?

CONDEMNED MAN: I can't stand any more.

EXECUTIONER: You can't stand the waiting. What a poor, pining creature you are, so consumed with wanting to hear my singing! I'll begin then. I shan't make you wait any longer. I'll start right away. Listen! Here's my tender song.

He clears his throat, hums, and then sings in a drunken voice:

O flower whose life is but a night,
Greetings from your admirers!
Plucked at dawn of day tomorrow,
The robe of dew from you will fall.
In a firewood basket you will lie
And all around my tunes will die.
In the air the deadly blade will flash

Shining bright in gardener's hand.
O flower, whose life is but a night!
On you be peace, on you be peace!

Silence.

EXECUTIONER: Why are you silent? Didn't you like it? This is the time to show admiration and appreciation.

CONDEMNED MAN: Is this your tender song, you ill-omened Executioner?

EXECUTIONER: Please—I'm no Executioner.

CONDEMNED MAN: What do you think you are then?

EXECUTIONER: I'm a gardener.

CONDEMNED MAN: A gardener?

EXECUTIONER: Yes, a gardener. Do you understand? A gardener. I'm a gar—den—er.

A window is opened in the beautiful lady's house, and the MAID *looks out.*

MAID: What's all this now? What's this uproar when people are asleep? My mistress has a headache and wishes to sleep undisturbed.

EXECUTIONER [*sarcastically*]: Your mistress! [*He laughs derisively.*] Her mistress!

MAID: I told you to stop that noise.

EXECUTIONER: Take yourself off, server of vice and obscenity.

MAID: Don't insult my mistress! If she wanted to she could have twenty sweepers like you to sweep the dust from under her shoes.

EXECUTIONER: Hold your tongue and take yourself off, you filthiest of creatures!

The LADY *appears at the window behind her servant.*

LADY: What's happening?

MAID: This drunken Executioner is raising a din and hurling abuse at us.

LADY: How dare he!

EXECUTIONER [*pointing at the window*]: That's her, in all her splendor—her famous mistress!

LADY: Show a little respect, man!

EXECUTIONER [*laughing sarcastically*]: Respect!

LADY: Yes, and don't force me to teach you how to respect ladies.

EXECUTIONER: Ladies? [*He laughs.*] Ladies! She says ladies! Listen and marvel!

LADY [*to her* MAID]: Go down and give him a lesson in manners.

MAID [*to the* EXECUTIONER]: Wait for me—if you're a man!

The two women disappear from the window.

EXECUTIONER [*to the* CONDEMNED MAN]: What does this . . . this she-devil intend to do? Do you know? She's capable of anything. Good God, did you see how she threatened me?

MAID [*emerging from the door of the house, a shoe held high in her hand*]: Come here!

EXECUTIONER: What are you going to do with that shoe?

MAID: This shoe is the oldest and filthiest thing I could find in the house—do you understand? I came across nothing older or filthier befitting that dirty, ugly face of yours.

EXECUTIONER: Now the effect of the glass of lovely wine has really flown from my head. Did you hear the nice polite things she was saying, oh condemned man?

CONDEMNED MAN: Yes.

EXECUTIONER: And you utter not a word?

CONDEMNED MAN: I?

EXECUTIONER: And you remain unmoved?

CONDEMNED MAN: How?

EXECUTIONER: You let her insult me like this and remain silent?

CONDEMNED MAN: And what do you want me to do?

EXECUTIONER: Do something! At least say something!

CONDEMNED MAN: What's it got to do with me?

EXECUTIONER: What lack of gallantry, what flagging resolution! You see her raising the shoe in her hand like someone brandishing a sword and you don't make a move to defend me. You just stand there with shackled hands. You just look on without caring. You listen without concern to my being insulted, humiliated, and abused? By God, this is no way to show chivalry.

CONDEMNED MAN: Truly!

MAID [*shaking the shoe in her hand*]: Listen here, man! Leave this poor fellow alone. You face up to me if you've got any courage. Your reckoning is with me. You've behaved very rudely toward us and it's up to you to apologize and ask our forgiveness. Otherwise, by the Lord of Hosts, by the Almighty, by the Omnipotent . . . .

EXECUTIONER [*gently*]: Steady! Steady!

MAID: Speak! What's your answer?

EXECUTIONER: Let's come to an understanding.

MAID: First, ask for forgiveness.

EXECUTIONER: From whom should I ask for forgiveness? From you?

MAID: From my mistress.

EXECUTIONER: Where is she?

LADY [*appearing on the threshold of her house*]: Here I am. Has he apologized?

MAID: He will do so, milady.

EXECUTIONER: Yes, milady.

LADY: Good. Then I accept your apology.

EXECUTIONER: Only, milady — would it not be best for the waters to flow back to their usual channels and for things to be as before?

LADY: They are.

EXECUTIONER: I meant for the wine to flow back into the channels of my head.

LADY: What do you mean?

EXECUTIONER: I mean that there is a certain damage that requires repairing. Your efficient servant has removed the intoxication from my head. From where shall I fill the void?

LADY: I shall take upon myself the filling of your head. Take as much drink as you wish from the Wine Merchant at my expense.

EXECUTIONER: Thank you, O bountiful lady. [*The* EXECUTIONER *signals to the* WINE MERCHANT *who is standing by the door of his tavern to bring him a glass.*]

CONDEMNED MAN [*to the* LADY]: Do you not know me, beautiful lady?

LADY: Of course I know you. From the first instant when they brought you here at nightfall. I caught sight of you from my window and recognized you and it saddened me to see you in shackles, but—but what crime have you committed?

CONDEMNED MAN: Nothing much. All that happened was that I said . . . .

EXECUTIONER [*shouting*]: Careful! Careful! Shut your mouth!

CONDEMNED MAN: I've shut my mouth.

LADY: Naturally they gave you a trial?

CONDEMNED MAN: No.

LADY: What are you saying? Weren't you given a trial?

CONDEMNED MAN: I wasn't taken to court. I sent a complaint to the Sultan asking that I be given the right to appear before the Chief Cadi, the most just of those who judge by conscience, the most scrupulous adherent to the canonical law, and the most loyal defender of the sanctity of the law. But—here dawn approaches and the Executioner has had his orders to cut off my head when the call to dawn prayers is given.

LADY [*looking up at the sky*]: The dawn? The dawn's almost breaking. Look at the sky!

EXECUTIONER [*in his hand a glass taken from the* WINE MERCHANT]: It's not the sky, my dear lady, that will decide the moment of fate for this condemned man but the minaret of this mosque. I am waiting for the Muezzin.

LADY: The Muezzin. He is surely on his way. Sometimes I stay awake in the morning and I see him at this very moment making for the mosque.

CONDEMNED MAN: Then my hour has come.

LADY: No—not so long as your complaint has not been examined.

CONDEMNED MAN: This Executioner will not await the result of the complaint. Isn't that so, Executioner?

EXECUTIONER: I shall await only the Muezzin. Those are my orders.

LADY: Whose orders? The Sultan's?

EXECUTIONER: Roughly.

CONDEMNED MAN [*shouting*]: Roughly? Is it not then the Sultan?

EXECUTIONER: The Vizier—the orders of the Vizier are the orders of the Sultan.

CONDEMNED MAN: Then I am irretrievably lost.

EXECUTIONER: Just so. No sooner does the Muezzin's call to prayer rise up to the sky than your soul rises with it. This causes me great sadness and distress but work is work. A job's a job.

LADY [*turning toward the street*]: Oh disaster! Here is the Muezzin—he has arrived.

CONDEMNED MAN: The die is cast.

The MUEZZIN *makes his appearance.*

EXECUTIONER: Hurry, O Muezzin—we're waiting for you.

MUEZZIN: Waiting for me? Why?

EXECUTIONER: To give the call to the dawn prayer.

MUEZZIN: Do you want to pray?

EXECUTIONER: I want to carry out my work.

MUEZZIN: What have I to do with your work?

EXECUTIONER: When your voice rises up to the sky the soul of this man will rise with it.

MUEZZIN: God forbid!

EXECUTIONER: Those are the orders.

MUEZZIN: The life of this man hangs on my vocal chords?

EXECUTIONER: Yes.

MUEZZIN: There is no power and no strength save in God!

EXECUTIONER: O Muezzin, hasten to your work so that I may do mine.

LADY: And what's the hurry, kind Executioner? The Muezzin's voice has been affected by the night cold and he is in need of a hot drink. Come into my house, Muezzin. I shall prepare you something which will put your voice to rights.

EXECUTIONER: And the dawn?

LADY: The dawn is in no danger and the Muezzin knows best as to its time.

EXECUTIONER: And my work?

LADY: Your work is in no danger—so long as the Muezzin has not yet called for the dawn prayers.

EXECUTIONER: Do you agree, oh Muezzin?

LADY: He agrees to accepting my little invitation for a short while, for he is among my best friends in the quarter.

EXECUTIONER: And those who have gone to pray in the mosque?

MUEZZIN: There are only two men there. One of them is a stranger to this city and has taken up his abode in the mosque, whilst the other is a beggar who has sought shelter in it from the night cold. All are now deep in sleep and seldom do people pay attention to the call to dawn prayers. Only those get up whom I wake with a kick so that they may perform their religious duties.

LADY: Most of the people of the quarter live a life of ease and sleep well on into the forenoon.

EXECUTIONER: Are you both meaning to say that the call to dawn prayers won't be given today?

LADY: What we mean is . . . there's no hurry. There is safety in proceeding slowly, remorse in proceeding hastily. Don't worry yourself! The call to the dawn prayer will be given in good time, and in any event you are all right and are not answerable. The Muezzin alone is responsible. Let us go then, oh Muezzin! A cup of coffee will restore your voice.

MUEZZIN: There's no harm in just a little time and just a small cup.

The LADY *enters her house with the* MUEZZIN.

EXECUTIONER [*to the* CONDEMNED MAN]: Did you see? Instead of going up into the minaret he went up to the house of the . . . the honored lady. There's the Muezzin for you!

CONDEMNED MAN: A gallant man! He risks everything. As for you, you against whom no censure or blame will be directed, you who are safely covered by your excuse, who bear no liability, possessed as you are of a pretext, it's you who's raging and storming and becoming alarmed. Calm down a little, my friend! Be forbearing and patient! Put your trust in God! Listen, I've got an idea—an excellent, a brilliant idea. It will calm your nerves and bring joy to your soul. Sing me your tender song once again with that sweet, melodious voice of yours, and I swear to you I'll listen to it with a heart palpitating with enthusiasm and admiration. Come along—sing! I'm listening to you with my very being.

EXECUTIONER: I no longer have any desire to.

CONDEMNED MAN: Why? What's upset you? Is it because you didn't lop off my head?

EXECUTIONER: It's because I failed to carry out my duty.

CONDEMNED MAN: Your duty is to carry out the sentence at the time of the call to the dawn prayer. Yet who gives the call to the dawn prayer? You or the Muezzin?

EXECUTIONER: The Muezzin.

CONDEMNED MAN: And has he done so?

EXECUTIONER: No.

CONDEMNED MAN: Then what fault is it of yours?

EXECUTIONER: Truly it is not my fault.

CONDEMNED MAN: This is what we're all saying.

EXECUTIONER: You're comforting me and making light of things for me.

CONDEMNED MAN: I'm telling the truth.

EXECUTIONER [looking up and down the street and shouting]: What are these crowds? Good God! It's the Vizier's retinue! It's the Vizier!

CONDEMNED MAN: Don't tremble like that! Calm yourself!

EXECUTIONER: It won't be held against me . . . I'm covered, aren't I?

CONDEMNED MAN: Set your mind at rest! You are covered with a thousand blankets of arguments and excuses.

EXECUTIONER: It's the accursed Muezzin who will pay the harsh reckoning.

The VIZIER *appears surrounded by his* GUARDS.

VIZIER [shouting]: How strange! Has this criminal not been executed yet?

EXECUTIONER: We are awaiting the dawn prayer, milord Vizier, in accordance with your orders.

VIZIER: The dawn prayer? We have performed it at the palace mosque in the presence of Our Majesty the Sultan and the Chief Cadi.

EXECUTIONER: It's not my fault, milord Vizier. The Muezzin of this mosque has not yet gone up to the minaret.

VIZIER: How's that? This is unbelievable. Where is this Muezzin?

The MUEZZIN *comes out drunk from the door of the house and tries to hide himself behind the* LADY *and her* MAID.

EXECUTIONER [*catching sight of him and shouting*]: That's him! There he is!

VIZIER [*to the* GUARDS]: Bring him here! [*They bring him before the* VIZIER.] Are you the Muezzin of this mosque?

MUEZZIN: Yes, milord Vizier.

VIZIER: Why have you not yet given the call to the dawn prayer?

MUEZZIN: Who told you that, milord Vizier? I gave the call to the dawn prayer some time ago. . . .

VIZIER: To the dawn prayer?

MUEZZIN: At its due time, just like every day, and there are those who heard me.

LADY: Truly we all heard him give the call to the dawn prayer from up in the minaret.

MAID: Yes, today as is his habit every day at the same time.

VIZIER: But this Executioner claims . . . .

LADY: This Executioner was drunk and fast asleep.

MAID: And the sound of his snoring rose up to us and woke us from our sweet slumbers.

VIZIER [*in astonishment to the* EXECUTIONER]: Is it thus that you carry out my orders?

EXECUTIONER: I swear, I swear, milord Vizier. . . .

VIZIER: Enough of that!

The EXECUTIONER *is tongue-tied with bewilderment.*

CONDEMNED MAN: O Vizier, I would beg you to listen to me. I sent to His Majesty the Sultan a complaint. . . .

EXECUTIONER [*collecting his wits and shouting*]: I swear, milord Vizier, that I was awake. . . .

VIZIER: I told you to keep quiet. [*He turns to the* CONDEMNED MAN.] Yes, your complaint is known to His Majesty the Sultan and he ordered that you be turned over to the Chief Cadi. His Majesty the Sultan will himself attend your trial. This is his noble wish and his irrefutable command. Guards! Clear the square of people and let everyone go home. This trial must take place in complete secrecy.

The GUARDS *clear the square of people.*

EXECUTIONER: Milord Vizier . . . [*He tries to explain matters but the* VIZIER *dismisses him with a gesture.*]

The SULTAN *appears with his* RETINUE, *accompanied by the* CHIEF CADI.

CONDEMNED MAN [*shouting*]: Your Majesty! Justice! I beg for justice!
SULTAN: Is this the accused?
CONDEMNED MAN: Your Majesty! I have committed no fault or crime!
SULTAN: We shall see.
CONDEMNED MAN: And I haven't been tried yet! I haven't been tried!
SULTAN: You shall be given a fair trial in accordance with your wish, and the Chief Cadi shall be in charge of your trial in our presence. [*The* SULTAN *makes a sign to the* CHIEF CADI *to start the trial, then sits down in a chair which has been brought for him, while the* VIZIER *stands by his side.*]
CADI [*sitting on his chair*]: Remove the accused's chains. [*One of the* GUARDS *undoes the* CONDEMNED MAN*'s fetters.*] Approach, man! What is your crime?
CONDEMNED MAN: I have committed no crime.
CADI: What is the charge brought against you?
CONDEMNED MAN: Ask the Vizier that!
CADI: I am asking *you.*
CONDEMNED MAN: I did nothing at all except utter an innocent word in which there is neither danger nor harm.
VIZIER: It's a terrible and sinful word.
CADI [*to the* CONDEMNED MAN]: What is this word?
CONDEMNED MAN: I don't like to repeat it.
VIZIER: Now you don't like to, but in the middle of the market place and amongst throngs of people . . . .

CADI: What is this word?

VIZIER: He said that His Majesty, the great and noble Sultan, is a mere slave.

CONDEMNED MAN: Everyone knows this—it is common knowledge.

VIZIER: Don't interrupt me—and he claimed that he was the slave trader who undertook the sale of our Sultan in his youth to the former Sultan.

CONDEMNED MAN: That's true. I swear it by a sacred oath—and it is a matter of pride to me which I shall treasure for all time.

SULTAN [*to the* CONDEMNED MAN]: You? You sold me to the late Sultan?

CONDEMNED MAN: Yes.

SULTAN: When was that?

CONDEMNED MAN: Twenty-five years ago, Your Majesty. You were a small boy of six, lost and abandoned in a Circassian village raided by the Mongols. You were extremely intelligent and wise for one of your tender years. I rejoiced in you and carried you off to the Sultan of this country. As the price for you he made me a present of one thousand dinars.

SULTAN [*derisively*]: Only a thousand dinars!

CONDEMNED MAN: Of course you were worth more than that but I was new to the trade, not being more than twenty-six years of age. That deal was the beginning of my business—it opened for me the way to the future.

SULTAN: For you and for me!

CONDEMNED MAN: Thanks be to God!

SULTAN: Is it this that merits your death—bringing me to this country? I see the matter quite differently.

VIZIER: He deserves death for his babbling and indiscretion.

SULTAN: I see no great harm in his saying or bruiting abroad the fact that I was a slave. The late Sultan was just that—is not that right, Vizier?

VIZIER: That's right but . . . .

SULTAN: Is it not so, Chief Cadi?

VIZIER: Quite so, O Sultan.

SULTAN: The entire family comes from slaves since time immemorial. The Mamluk Sultans were all taken from earliest childhood to the palace, there to be given a strict and hardy upbringing; and later they became rulers, army leaders, and Sultans of countries. I am merely one of those, in no way different from them.

CONDEMNED MAN: Rather are you among the best of them in wisdom and sound judgment, may God preserve you for the good of your subjects.

SULTAN: Even so, I don't remember your face; in fact I don't clearly remember my childhood days in that Circassian village you talk about and in which you say you found me. All I remember is my childhood at the palace under the protection of the late Sultan. He used to treat me as though I were his real son, for he himself had no children. He brought me up and instructed me so that I might take over the rule. I knew for absolute certainty that he was not my father.

CONDEMNED MAN: Your parents were killed by the Mongols.

SULTAN: No one ever talked to me of my parents. I knew only that I had been brought to the palace at a young age.

CONDEMNED MAN: And it was I who brought you there.

SULTAN: Maybe.

CONDEMNED MAN: Therefore, Your Majesty, what is my crime?

SULTAN: By God, I know not. Ask him who accused you.

VIZIER: That's not his real crime.

SULTAN: Is there a real crime?

VIZIER: Yes, Your Majesty. To say that you had been a slave is truly not something shameful, no reason for guilt—all the Mamluk Sultans have been slaves. It's not there that the crime lies. However, a Mamluk Sultan is generally manumitted before ascending the throne.

SULTAN: So what?

VIZIER: So, Your Majesty, this man claims that you have not yet been manumitted, that you are still a slave and that a person bearing such a stigma is not entitled to rule over a free people.

SULTAN [to the CONDEMNED MAN]: Did you really say that?

CONDEMNED MAN: I did not say all that; however, people in the market place always enjoy such gossip and tittle-tattle.

SULTAN: And from where did you learn that I had not been manumitted?

CONDEMNED MAN: It is not I who said so. They ascribe to me every infamous word that is spoken.

SULTAN: But they are nevertheless indulging in gossip and tittle-tattle.

CONDEMNED MAN: Not I.

SULTAN: You or someone else—it no longer matters. The important thing now is that all the people everywhere know that it is all sheer lies—isn't that so, Chief Cadi?

CADI: The fact is, your Majesty . . . .

SULTAN: It's utter falsehood and slander. It's mere fabrication unsupported by logic or common sense. Not yet manumitted? I? I, who was a leader of armies and conquered the Mongols? I, the right-hand man of the late Sultan, whom he arranged to rule after him? All this, and the Sultan did not think about manumitting me before his death? Is it plausible? Listen, Cadi! All you now have to do is to let the town-criers announce an official denial in the city and publish to the people the text of the document registering my manumission, which is doubtless kept in your strongrooms, isn't that so?

CADI [*combing his fingers through his beard*]: You are saying, Your Majesty
. . . .

SULTAN: Didn't you hear what I said?

CADI: Yes, but . . . .

SULTAN: You were busy playing with your beard.

CADI: Your Majesty!

SULTAN: What? Your Majesty the Sultan is addressing you in clear and simple language requiring no long consideration or deep thought. All it amounts to is that it has become necessary to make public the document. Do you understand?

CADI: Yes.

SULTAN: You're still playing with your beard. Can't you leave it alone—just for a while?

VIZIER [*intervening*]: Your Majesty! Would you permit me . . . .

SULTAN: What's up with you? You too?

VIZIER: I would ask Your Majesty to . . . .

SULTAN: What's all this embarrassment? You and he are as bad as each other.

CADI: It is better to postpone this trial until some other time—when we are on our own, your Majesty.

VIZIER: Yes, that would be best.

SULTAN: I'm beginning to catch on.

The VIZIER, *by a sign, orders everyone to move off with the* CONDEMNED
MAN, *leaving only himself, the* SULTAN, *and the* CHIEF CADI *on stage.*

SULTAN: Now here we are on our own. What have you to say? I see from your
expressions that you have things to say.

CADI: Yes, Your Majesty. You have with your perspicacity realized . . . in
actual fact there is no document of your manumission in my strongrooms.

SULTAN: Perhaps you have not yet received it, though it must be somewhere.
Isn't that so, Vizier?

VIZIER: In truth, Your Majesty . . . .

SULTAN: What?

VIZIER: The truth is that . . . .

SULTAN: Speak!

VIZIER: There is no document to prove your having been manumitted.

SULTAN: What are you saying?

VIZIER: The late Sultan collapsed suddenly following a heart attack and
departed this life before manumitting you.

SULTAN: What's this you're alleging, you rogue?

VIZIER: I'm certainly a rogue, Your Majesty—and a criminal. I'm wicked, I
don't deny it. I should have arranged all this at the time, but this business of manumission did not occur to me. My head was filled with other
weighty matters. At that time, Your Majesty, you were far away—in the
thick of the fray. No one but myself was present by the dying Sultan's
bedside. I forgot this matter under the stress of the situation, the momen-
tous nature of the occasion, and the intensity of my grief. Nothing
occupied me at that moment save taking the oath, before the dying man,
that I would serve you, Your Majesty, with the very same devotion as
that with which I had served him for the whole of his life.

SULTAN: Truly, here and now you have really served me!

VIZIER: I deserve death—I know that. It is an unpardonable crime. The late
Sultan could not think of everything or remember everything. It was the
very essence of my work to think for him and to remind him of important matters. It was certainly my duty to put before him the matter of

manumission, because of its particular seriousness, and to do the necessary legal formalities. But your lofty position, Your Majesty, your influence, your prestige, your great place in people's hearts—all these high attributes caused us to overlook your being a slave; to overlook the necessity for someone of your stature to have such proofs and documents. I swear to God, this matter never occurred to me until after you had ascended the throne, Your Majesty. At that time the whole business became clear to me. I was seized with terror and almost went mad. I would surely have done so, had I not calmed down and pulled myself together, cherishing the hope that this matter would never arise or be revealed.

SULTAN: And now it has arisen and been revealed.

VIZIER: What a tragedy! I did not know that such a man would come along one day with his gossip and tittle-tattle.

SULTAN: For this reason you wanted to close his mouth by handing him over to the Executioner?

VIZIER: Yes.

SULTAN: And so bury your fault by burying the man himself?

VIZIER [*with head lowered*]: Yes.

SULTAN: And what's the point of that now? Everyone's gossiping now.

VIZIER: If this man's head were cut off and hung up in the square before the people, no tongue would thenceforth dare to utter.

SULTAN: Do you think so?

VIZIER: If the sword is not able to cut off tongues, then what can?

CADI: Will you allow me to say a word, Your Majesty?

SULTAN: I'm listening.

CADI: The sword certainly does away with heads and tongues; it does not, however, do away with difficulties and problems.

SULTAN: What do you mean?

CADI: I mean that the problem will still nevertheless remain, namely that the Sultan is ruling without having been manumitted, and that a slave is at the head of a free people.

VIZIER: Who dares to say this? Whoever does so will have his head cut off.

CADI: That's another question.

VIZIER: It is not necessary for the person ruling to be carrying around documents and proofs. We have the strongest and most striking example of this in the Fatimid dynasty. Every one of us remembers what Al-Mu'izz li-Din Allah Al-Fatimi did. One day he came along claiming he was descended from the Prophet (the prayers of God be upon him), and when the people did not believe him, he went at them with drawn sword and opened up his coffers of gold, saying "These are my forbears, these my ancestors." The people kept silent and he reigned and his children reigned after him quietly and peaceably for centuries long.

SULTAN: What do you say about this, Cadi?

CADI: I say that this is correct from the historical point of view but . . . .

SULTAN: But what?

CADI: Then, O illustrious Sultan, you would like to solve your problem by this method?

SULTAN: And why not?

VIZIER: Truly, why not? There is nothing easier than this, especially in this matter of ours. It is sufficient for us to announce publicly that Our Majesty the Sultan has been legally manumitted, that he was manumitted by the late Sultan before his death, and that the documents and proofs are recorded and kept with the Chief Cadi—and death to anyone who dares deny it!

CADI: There is a person who will so deny.

VIZIER: Who's that?

CADI: I.

VIZIER: You?

CADI: Yes, Your Majesty. I cannot take part in this conspiracy.

VIZIER: It is not a conspiracy—it's a plan for saving the situation.

CADI: It is a conspiracy against the law I represent.

SULTAN: The law?

CADI: Yes, Sultan—the law. In the eyes of the civil and religious codes you are only a slave, and a slave—by civil and religious law—is regarded as a thing, a chattel. As the late Sultan, who had the power of life and death over you, did not manumit you before his death, you are thus still a thing, a chattel, owned by someone else, and so you have forfeited the basic qualification for entering into the normal transactions exercised by the rest of free people.

SULTAN: Is this the law?

CADI: Yes.

VIZIER: Take it easy, Chief Cadi! We are not now discussing the view of the law but are looking for a way by which to be free of this law, and the way to be free of it is to assume that manumission has in fact taken place. So long as the matter is a secret between us three, with no one but ourselves knowing the truth, it will be easy to induce the people to believe . . . .

CADI: The lie.

VIZIER: The solution rather—it's a more appropriate and suitable word.

CADI: A solution through lying.

VIZIER: And what's the harm in that?

CADI: In relation to you two there is no harm.

VIZIER: And in relation to you?

CADI: In relation to me it's different, for I cannot fool myself and I cannot free myself from the law, being as I am the person who represents it; I cannot break an oath by which I took upon myself to be the trusted servant of the civil and religious law.

SULTAN: You took this upon yourself before me.

CADI: And before God and my conscience.

SULTAN: Which means that you won't go along with us?

CADI: Along this road, no.

SULTAN: You will not join hands with us?

CADI: In this instance, no.

SULTAN: Then in that case you can take yourself off to one side. Don't interfere in anything and leave us to act as we think fit. You thus keep your oath and satisfy your conscience.

CADI: I'm sorry, Your Majesty.

SULTAN: Why?

CADI: Because, having admitted that in the eyes of the law you are lacking the authority to make a contract, I find myself obliged to order that all your actions are null and void.

SULTAN: You're mad—that's impossible!

CADI: I'm sorry but I cannot do other than this so long as . . . .

SULTAN: So long as?

CADI: So long as you don't order me to be dismissed from my post, thrown out of the country, or have my head cut off. In this manner I would be freed from my oath and you could suit yourself and do as you pleased.

SULTAN: Is this a threat?

CADI: No, it's a solution.

VIZIER: You're complicating the problem for us, Chief Cadi.

CADI: I am helping you to get out of an impasse.

SULTAN: I've begun to weary of this man.

VIZIER: He knows that we are in his grasp in that he will divulge everything to the people if the least amount of coercion is used on him.

SULTAN [*to the* CADI]: The substance of what you say is that you don't want to assist us.

CADI: On the contrary, Your Majesty, I wish very greatly to be of assistance to you, but *not* in this manner.

SULTAN: What do you suggest then?

CADI: That the law be applied.

SULTAN: If *you* applied the law, *I'd* lose my throne.

CADI: Not only that.

SULTAN: Is there something even worse?

CADI: Yes.

SULTAN: What is there then?

CADI: Owing to the fact that in the eyes of the law you are a chattel owned by the late Sultan, you have become part of his inheritance, and as he died without leaving an heir, his estate reverts to the Exchequer. You are thus one of the chattels owned by the Exchequer—an unproductive chattel yielding no profit or return. I, in my additional capacity as Treasurer of the Exchequer, say: it is the custom in such cases to get rid of unprofitable chattels by putting them up for sale at auction, so that the good interest of the Exchequer be not harmed and so that it may utilize the proceeds of the sale in bringing benefit to the people generally and in particular to the poor.

SULTAN [*indignantly*]: An unproductive chattel? I?

CADI: I am speaking of course strictly from the legal point of view.

SULTAN: Up until now I have obtained no solutions from you. All I have had are insults.

CADI: Insults? I beg your pardon, illustrious Sultan. You know very well how much I revere and admire you and in what high esteem I hold you. You will recollect no doubt that it was I who from the first moment was the one to come forward to pay you homage and proclaim you as the Sultan to rule over our country. What I am doing now is merely to give a frank review of the situation from the point of view of civil and religious law.

SULTAN: The long and short of it is then that I'm a thing and a chattel and not a man or a human being?

CADI: Yes.

SULTAN: And that this thing or chattel is owned by the Exchequer?

CADI: Indeed.

SULTAN: And that the Exchequer disposes of unproductive chattels by putting them up for sale at auction for the public good?

CADI: Exactly.

SULTAN: Oh Chief Cadi, don't you feel, as I do, that this is all extraordinarily bizarre?

CADI: Yes, but . . . .

SULTAN: And that there's a great deal of undue exaggeration and extravagance in it all?

CADI: Maybe, but in my capacity as Cadi what concerns me is where the facts stand in relation to the processes of the law.

SULTAN: Listen, Cadi. This law of yours has brought me no solution, whereas a small movement of my sword will ensure that the knot of the problem is severed instantly.

CADI: Then do so.

SULTAN: I shall. What does the spilling of a little blood matter for the sake of the practicability of governing?

CADI: Then you must start by spilling my blood.

SULTAN: I shall do everything I think necessary for safeguarding the security of the State, and I shall in fact start with you. I shall cast you into prison. Vizier! Arrest the Cadi!

VIZIER: Your Majesty, you have not yet listened to his answer to your question.

SULTAN: What question?

VIZIER: The question about the solution he deems appropriate for the problem.

SULTAN: He has answered this question.

VIZIER: What he said was not the solution but a review of the situation.

SULTAN: Is that true, Cadi?

CADI: Yes.

SULTAN: Have you then a solution to this problem of ours?

CADI [*in the same tone*]: Yes.

SULTAN: Then speak! What is the solution?

CADI: There is only one solution

SULTAN: Say! What is it?

CADI: That the law be applied.

SULTAN: Again? Once more?

CADI: Yes—once more and always, for I see no other solution.

SULTAN: Do you hear, Vizier? After this, do you entertain any hope of co-operation with this stubborn old windbag?

VIZIER: Allow me, Your Majesty, to interrogate him a little.

SULTAN: Do as you like!

VIZIER: O Chief Cadi, the question is a subtle one and it requires of you to explain to us clearly and in detail your point of view.

CADI: My point of view is both clear and simple and I can propound it in two words: for the solution of this problem we have before us two alternatives, that of the sword and that of the law. As for the sword, that is none of my concern; as for the law, that is what it behooves me to recommend and on which I can give a legal opinion. The law says: it is only his master, the possessor of the power of life and death over him, who has the right to manumit a slave. In this instance, the master, the possessor of the power of life and death, died without leaving an heir and the ownership of the slave has reverted to the exchequer. The Exchequer may not manumit him without compensation in that no one has the right to dispose gratis of property or chattels belonging to the State. It is, however, permitted for the Exchequer to make a disposition by sale, and the selling of the property of the State is not valid by law other than by an auction carried out publicly. The legal solution, therefore, is that we should put up His Majesty the Sultan for sale by public auction and the person to whom he is knocked down thereafter manumits him. In this manner the Exchequer is not harmed or defrauded in respect of its property and the Sultan gains his manumission and release through the law.

SULTAN [*to the* VIZIER]: Do you hear all this?

VIZIER [*to the* CADI]: We put up Our Majesty, the illustrious Sultan, for sale by public auction! This is sheer madness!

CADI: This is the legal and legitimate solution.

SULTAN [*to the* VIZIER]: Don't waste time. No answer is left for this stupid and impudent fellow except to chop off his head—and let result what may! And it is I who shall perform this with my own hand. [*He draws his sword.*]

CADI: It is a great honor for me, Your Majesty, to die by your hand and for me to give up my life for the sake of truth and principles.

VIZIER: Patience, Your Majesty, patience! Don't make a martyr of this man! Such a broken-down old man could not hope for a more splendid death. It will be said that through him you destroyed the civil and religious laws; he will become the living symbol of the spirit of truth and principles—and many a glorious martyr has more effect and influence on the conscience of peoples than a tyrannical king.

SULTAN [*suppressing his anger*]: God's curse . . . .

VIZIER: Don't give him this glory, Your Majesty, at the expense of the situation.

SULTAN: Then what's to be done? This man puts us in a dilemma, he makes us choose between two alternatives, both of them painful: the law which shows me up as weak and makes a laughing-stock of me, or the sword which brands me with brutality and makes me loathed.

VIZIER [*turning to the* CADI]: O Chief Cadi! Be tractable and obliging! Don't be rigid and hard! Meet us half-way, find a compromise and work with us toward finding a reasonable solution.

CADI: There is no reasonable way out other than the law.

VIZIER: We put the Sultan up for sale by auction?

CADI: Yes.

VIZIER: And the person he's knocked down to buys him?

CADI: He manumits him immediately, at the session for drawing up the contract—that's the condition.

VIZIER: And who will accept to lose his money in this manner?

CADI: Many people —those who would ransom the Sultan's freedom with their money.

VIZIER: Then why don't we ourselves undertake this duty—you and I—and ransom our Sultan secretly with our own money and gain this honor? Is it not an appropriate idea?

CADI: I'm afraid not. It cannot be secret—the law is specific in that it lays down that every sale of the properties of the Exchequer must be carried out publicly and by general auction.

SULTAN [*to the* VIZIER]: Don't trouble yourself with him—he's determined to disgrace us.

VIZIER [*to the* CADI]: For the last time, Chief Cadi—is there no stratagem for extracting us from this impasse?

CADI: A stratagem? I am not the person to ask to look for stratagems.

SULTAN: Naturally! This man looks only for what will provoke and humiliate us.

CADI: Not I as a person, Your Majesty. I as a person am weak and have nothing to do with the whole matter. If the matter were in my hands and depended upon my wishes, I would like nothing better than to extricate you from this situation in the best manner you could wish.

SULTAN: Poor weak fellow! The matter's not in his hands—in whose hands then?

CADI: The law's.

SULTAN: Yes, the specter behind which he hides in order to subjugate me, impose his will upon me, and show me up before the people in that laughable, feeble, and ignominious guise.

CADI: I as a person would rather wish for you to appear in the guise of the glorious ruler.

SULTAN: Do you consider it as being among the characteristics of glory that a sultan be treated like goods or chattels to be sold in the market?

CADI: It is certainly a characteristic of glory that a sultan should submit to the law as do the rest of people.

VIZIER: It is truly laudable, Chief Cadi, that the ruler should obey the law as does the sentenced person, but this entails a great hazard. The politics of government have their procedures; the ruling of people has other methods.

CADI: I know nothing of politics or of the business of ruling people.

SULTAN: It's our business—allow us then to exercise it in our own way.

CADI: I have not fettered your hands, Your Majesty. You possess complete freedom to exercise your rule as you wish.

SULTAN: Fine! I now see what I must do.

VIZIER: What are you going to do, Your Majesty?

SULTAN: Look at this old man! Do you see him carrying a sword on his belt? Of course not. He carries nothing but a tongue in his mouth with which he turns words and phrases. He's good at using the acumen and skill he possesses, but I carry this [*and he indicates his sword*]. It's not made of wood, it's not a toy. It's a real sword and must be useful for something, must have some reason for its existence. Do you understand what I'm saying? Answer! Why was it ordained that I should carry it? Is it for decoration or for action?

VIZIER: For action.

SULTAN: And you, Cadi—why do you not answer? Answer! Is it for decoration or for action?

CADI: For one or the other.

SULTAN: What are you saying?

CADI: I am saying, for this or for that.

SULTAN: What do you mean?

CADI: I mean that you have a choice, Your Majesty. You can employ it for action, or you can employ it for decoration. I recognize the undoubted strength possessed by the sword, its swift action and decisive effect. But the sword gives right to the strongest, and who knows who will be the strongest tomorrow? There may appear some strong person who will tilt the balance of power against you. As for the law, it protects your rights from every aggression, because it does not recognize the strongest—it recognizes right. And now there's nothing for you to do, Your Majesty, but choose: between the sword which imposes and yet exposes you, and between the law which threatens and yet protects you.

SULTAN [*thinking a while*]: The sword which imposes and exposes me, and the law which threatens and protects me?

CADI: Yes.

SULTAN: What talk is this?

CADI: The frank truth.

SULTAN [*thinking and repeating over to himself*]: The sword which imposes and exposes? The law which threatens and protects?

CADI: Yes, Your Majesty.

SULTAN [*to the* VIZIER]: What an accursed old man he is! He's got a unique genius for always landing us in a spot.

CADI: I have done nothing, Your Majesty, except to present to you the two sides of the question; the choice is yours.

SULTAN: The choice? The choice? What is your opinion, Vizier?

VIZIER: It is for you to decide about this, Your Majesty.

SULTAN: As far as I can see, you don't know either.

VIZIER: Actually, Your Majesty, the . . . .

SULTAN: The choice is difficult?

VIZIER: Certainly.

SULTAN: The sword which imposes me on all and yet which exposes me to danger, or the law which threatens my wishes yet which protects my rights.

VIZIER: Yes.

SULTAN: You choose for me.

VIZIER: I? No, no, Your Majesty!

SULTAN: What are you frightened of?

VIZIER: Of the consequences—of the consequences of this choice. Should it one day become apparent that I had chosen the wrong course, then what a catastrophe there'd be!

SULTAN: You don't want to bear the responsibility?

VIZIER: I wouldn't dare—it's not my right.

SULTAN: In the end a decision must be made.

VIZIER: No one, Your Majesty, but yourself has the right to decide in this matter.

SULTAN: Truly, there is no one but myself. I cannot escape from that. It's I who must choose and bear the responsibility of the choice.

VIZIER: You are our master and our ruler.

SULTAN: Yes, this is my most fearful moment, the fearful moment for every ruler—the moment of giving the final decision, the decision that will change the course of things, the moment when is uttered that small word which will decide the inevitable choice, the choice that will decide fate.

He thinks hard as he walks up and down, with the other two waiting for him to speak. Silence reigns for a moment.

SULTAN [*with head lowered in thought*]: The sword or the law? The law or the sword?

VIZIER: Your Majesty, I appreciate the precariousness of your situation.

SULTAN: Yet you don't want to assist me with an opinion?

VIZIER: I cannot. In this situation you alone are the one to decide.

SULTAN: There is, therefore, no getting away from deciding all by myself?

VIZIER: That's so.

SULTAN: The sword or the law? The law or the sword? [*He thinks for a while, then raises his head sharply.*] Good—I've decided.

VIZIER: Let us have your orders, your Majesty.

SULTAN: I have decided to choose, to choose . . . .

VIZIER: What, Your Majesty?

SULTAN [*shouting decisively*]: The law! I have chosen the law!

ACT TWO

The same square. GUARDS *have started to arrange rows of people around a platform that has been set up there. The* WINE MERCHANT's *shop is closed and he is standing talking to the* SHOEMAKER, *who is engrossed in his work at the open door of his shop.*

WINE MERCHANT: How odd of you, Shoemaker! You open your shop and work when today every shop is closed, just like a feast day?

SHOEMAKER: And why should I close it? Is it because they're selling the Sultan?

WINE MERCHANT: You fool—because you'll be watching the most incredible sight in the world!

SHOEMAKER: I can see everything that goes on from here while I work.

WINE MERCHANT: It's up to you. As for me I've closed my shop so that I shan't miss the smallest detail of this wonderful spectacle.

SHOEMAKER: You're making the biggest mistake, my friend. Today's an excellent opportunity for attracting customers. It's not every day you get such crowds gathered outside your shop. It is certain that today many people will suffer from thirst and will yearn for a drop of your drink.

WINE MERCHANT: Do you think so?

SHOEMAKER: It's obvious. Look—here am I, for example, showing off my finest shoes today. [*He points to the shoes hanging up at the door of his shop.*]

WINE MERCHANT: My dear Shoemaker, those who come to buy today have come to buy the Sultan, not your shoes.

SHOEMAKER: Why not? Maybe there are some among the people who are in greater need of my shoes.

WINE MERCHANT: Shut up, say no more! It seems you don't understand what's so extraordinary about this happening, don't realize that it's unique. Do you find a sultan being put up for sale every day?

SHOEMAKER: Listen, friend. I'll talk to you frankly: even were I to have sufficient money to buy the Sultan, by God I wouldn't do it!

WINE MERCHANT: You wouldn't buy him?

SHOEMAKER: Never!

WINE MERCHANT: Allow me to say you're a fool!

SHOEMAKER: No, I'm intelligent and astute. Just tell me what you'd want me to do with a sultan in my shop? Can I teach him this trade of mine? Of course not! Can I entrust him with any work? Certainly not! Then, it's I who'll go on working doubly hard so as to feed him, look after him, and serve him. I swear that that is what would happen. I'd merely be buying a rod for my back, a sheer luxury I couldn't afford. My resources, friend, don't allow me to acquire works of art.

WINE MERCHANT: What nonsense!

SHOEMAKER: And you—would you buy him?

WINE MERCHANT: Can there be any doubt about that?

SHOEMAKER: What would you do with him?

WINE MERCHANT: Many things, very many things, my friend. His mere presence in my shop would be enough to bring along the whole city. It would be enough to ask him to recount to my customers every evening the stories of his battles against the Mongols, the strange things that have happened to him, his voyages and adventures, the countries he has seen, the places he's been to, the deserts he's crossed—wouldn't all that be valuable and enjoyable?

SHOEMAKER: Certainly, you could employ him in that manner but I . . . .

WINE MERCHANT: You too could do the same.

SHOEMAKER: How? He knows nothing about repairing shoes or making soles for him to be able to talk about them.

WINE MERCHANT: It's not necessary for him to talk in your shop.

SHOEMAKER: What would he do then?

WINE MERCHANT: If I were in your place I'd know how to employ him.

SHOEMAKER: How? Tell me.

WINE MERCHANT: I'd sit him down in front of the door of the shop in a comfortable chair, I'd put a new pair of shoes on his feet and a placard above his head reading: "Sultan Shoes Sold Here," and the next day you'd see how the people of the city would flock to your shop and demand your wares.

SHOEMAKER: What a great idea!

WINE MERCHANT: Isn't it?

SHOEMAKER: I'm beginning to admire your ingenuity.

WINE MERCHANT: What do you say then to thinking about buying him together and making him our joint property. I'd release him to you during the day and you could give him to me for the evening?

SHOEMAKER: A lovely dream! But all we own, you and I, isn't enough to buy one of his fingers.

WINE MERCHANT: That's true.

SHOEMAKER: Look! The crowds have begun to arrive and collect.

Groups of men, women and children gather together and chat among themselves.

FIRST MAN [*to another man*]: Is it here they'll be selling the Sultan?

SECOND MAN: Yes, don't you see the guards?

FIRST MAN: If only I had money!

SECOND MAN: Shut up! That's for the rich!

CHILD: Mother! Is that the Sultan?

MOTHER [*to the* CHILD]: No, child, that's one of the guards.

CHILD: Where is the Sultan then?

MOTHER: He hasn't come yet.

CHILD: Has the Sultan got a sword?

MOTHER: Yes, a large sword.

CHILD: And will they sell him here?

MOTHER: Yes, child.

CHILD: When, Mother?

MOTHER: Very soon.

CHILD: Mother! Buy him for me!

MOTHER: What?

CHILD: The Sultan! Buy me the Sultan!

MOTHER: Quiet! He's not a toy for you to play with.

CHILD: You said they'll sell him here. Buy him for me then.

MOTHER: Quiet, child. This is not a game for children.

CHILD: For whom then? For grown-ups?

MOTHER: Yes, it's for grown-ups.

The window of the LADY's *house is opened and the* MAIDSERVANT *looks out.*

MAID [*calling*]: Wine Merchant! Tavern Keeper! Have you closed your shop today?

WINE MERCHANT: Yes—haven't I done right? And your mistress? Where is she? Is she still in bed?

MAID: No, she has just got out of her bath to dress.

WINE MERCHANT: She was superb! Her trick with the Executioner worked well.

MAID: Quiet! He's there. I can see him in the crowd. Now he's spotted us.

EXECUTIONER [*approaching the* WINE MERCHANT]: God curse you and wine!

WINE MERCHANT: Why? What sin has my wine committed to justify your curse? Didn't it bring joy to your heart that night, stimulate you in your singing, and cause you to see everything around you clear and pure?

EXECUTIONER [*in tones of anger*]: Clear and pure! Certainly that night I saw everything clear and pure!

WINE MERCHANT: Certainly—do you doubt it?

EXECUTIONER: Shut up and don't remind me of that night.

WINE MERCHANT: I've shut up. Tell me: are you on holiday today?

EXECUTIONER: Yes.

WINE MERCHANT: And your friend the condemned man?

EXECUTIONER: He has been pardoned.

WINE MERCHANT: And you, naturally. No one asked you about that business at dawn?

EXECUTIONER: No.

WINE MERCHANT: Then everything has turned out for the best.

EXECUTIONER: Yes, but I don't like anyone to make a fool of me or play tricks on me.

MAID: Even when it means saving a man's head?

EXECUTIONER: Shut up, you vile woman—you and your mistress.

MAID: Are you continuing to insult us on such a day?

WINE MERCHANT [*to the* EXECUTIONER]: Don't upset yourself! This evening I'll bring you a large glass of the best wine—free.

EXECUTIONER: Free?

WINE MERCHANT: Yes, a present from me, to drink to the health . . . .

EXECUTIONER: Of whom?

WINE MERCHANT [*catching sight of the* MUEZZIN *approaching*]: To the health of the brave Muezzin!

EXECUTIONER: That most evil of liars!

MUEZZIN: A liar? Me?

EXECUTIONER: Yes, you claim that I was fast asleep at that hour.

MUEZZIN: And you were drunk!

EXECUTIONER: I'm absolutely convinced that I was awake and alert and that I hadn't slept for a moment up until then.

MUEZZIN: So long as you're absolutely convinced of that . . . .

EXECUTIONER: Yes, I didn't sleep at all up until then.

MUEZZIN: Fine!

EXECUTIONER: You mean you agree about that?

MUEZZIN: Yes.

EXECUTIONER: Then it's you who're lying.

MUEZZIN: No!

EXECUTIONER: Then I *was* sleeping?

MUEZZIN: Yes.

EXECUTIONER: How can you say yes?

MUEZZIN: No!

EXECUTIONER: Make your mind up! Is it yes or is it no?

MUEZZIN: Which do you want?

EXECUTIONER: I want to know whether I was asleep at that time or whether I was awake.

MUEZZIN: What does it matter to you? So long as everything has passed peacefully—your friend the condemned man has been issued with a pardon and no one has asked you about anything. As for me, no one has spoken to me about the matter of that dawn. The question in relation to us all has ended as well as we could hope, so why dig up the past?

EXECUTIONER: Yes, but the question still troubles me since that day. I haven't grasped the situation absolutely clearly. I want to know whether I really was asleep at that time and whether you really gave the call to the dawn prayer without my being aware of it. In the end you must divulge to me what actually happened for you doubtless know the whole truth. Tell me exactly what happened then. I was in truth a little drunk at the time but . . . .

MUEZZIN: Since the matter occupies your mind to such an extent, why should I put you at ease? I prefer to leave you like this, grilling away and turning on the fire of doubt.

EXECUTIONER: May you turn on Hell's Fire, you ruffian of a Muezzin!

MUEZZIN [*shouting*]: Look! Look! The Sultan's retinue has come!

The RETINUE *with the* SULTAN *at its head appears, followed by the* CHIEF CADI, *the* VIZIER, *and the condemned* SLAVE TRADER. *They walk toward the dais, where the* SULTAN *seats himself in the middle chair with all around him, while the* SLAVE TRADER *stands beside him to face the people.*

WINE MERCHANT [*to the* EXECUTIONER]: Extraordinary! This is your friend the condemned man. What has brought him here alongside the Sultan?

EXECUTIONER [*looking at him*]: Truly, by God, it's none other than he.

MUEZZIN: No doubt he is the person charged with making the sale—is he not one of the biggest slave traders?

WINE MERCHANT: Do you see, Executioner? His escape, therefore, from your hands was no accident.

EXECUTIONER: How extraordinary! Here he is selling the same sultan twice— once as a child and again now when he's grown up.

MUEZZIN: Quiet! He's about to talk.

SLAVE TRADER [*clapping his hands*]: Quiet, people! I announce to you, in my capacity of slave-trader and auctioneer, that I have been charged with carrying out this sale by public auction for the benefit of the Exchequer. It honors me, first of all, that the Chief Cadi will open these proceedings with a word explaining the conditions of this sale. Let our venerable Chief Cadi now speak.

CADI: O people! The sale to be held before you is not like any other sale: it is of a special kind and this fact has been previously announced to you. This sale must be accompanied by another contract, a contract of manumission whereby the person who is the highest bidder at the auction may not retain what he has bought but must proceed with the manumission at the same session as the contract of sale, that is to say at this present session of ours. There is no need for me to remind you of the law's provision which prevents State employees from participating in any sale by the State. Having said this I leave the Vizier to speak to you about the patriotic character of these proceedings.

SHOEMAKER [*whispering to the* WINE MERCHANT]: Did you hear? The buyer cannot keep what he has bought. This means throwing one's money into the sea.

WINE MERCHANT [*whispering*]: We'll now see what imbecile will come forward.

SLAVE TRADER: Silence! Silence!

VIZIER: Honorable people! You are today present at a great and unique occasion, one of the most important in our history: a glorious Sultan asks for his freedom and has recourse to his people instead of to his sword—that sharp and mighty sword by which he was victorious in battles against the Mongols and with which he could also have been victorious in gaining his freedom and liberating himself from slavery. But our just and triumphant Sultan has chosen to submit to the law like the lowliest individual amongst his subjects. Here he is seeking his freedom by the method laid down by law. Whoever of you wishes to redeem the freedom of his beloved Sultan, let him come forward to this auction, and whoever of you pays the highest price will have done a goodly act for his homeland and will be remembered for time immemorial.

Cheers from the crowd.

VOICE [*raised from amongst the people*]: Long live the Sultan!

ANOTHER VOICE: Long live the law!

SLAVE TRADER: Silence, O people!

VIZIER [*continuing*]: And now, O noble people, that you know the small and trivial sacrifice your country expects of you for the sake of this high and lofty purpose—the freeing of your Sultan with your money and the passing of that money to the Exchequer so that it may be spent on the poor and those in need—now that your dearly beloved and cherished Sultan has come to you so that you may compete in showing your appreciation of him and liberating him, I declare that the proceedings shall begin.

He indicates to the SLAVE TRADER *that he should begin, while the crowds cheer.*

SLAVE TRADER: Silence! Silence! O people of this city, the auction has commenced. I shall not resort to enumerating properties and attributes as is generally resorted to in the markets for the purpose of making people want to acquire the goods, for the subject of this sale is above every description or comment. It is no extravagance or exaggeration to say that he is worth his weight in gold. However, it is not the intention to make things difficult or to inhibit you, but to facilitate matters for you in gauging what is possible. I thus begin the auction with a sum both small and paltry in respect of a sultan: Ten thousand dinars! [*Uproar amongst the crowd.*]

SHOEMAKER [*to the* WINE MERCHANT]: Ten thousand? Only! What a trifling sum! Look at that great ruby in his turban! By God, it alone is worth a hundred thousand dinars!

WINE MERCHANT: Truly it's a paltry amount—especially when paid for a noble and patriotic end! Ten thousand dinars! It is not seemly. I'm a loyal citizen and this displeases me. [*shouts*] Eleven thousand dinars!

SLAVE TRADER: Eleven thousand dinars! Eleven thousand?

SHOEMAKER [*to the* WINE MERCHANT]: Only eleven thousand dinars? Is that all you have? Then I'll say [*shouting*]—twelve thousand dinars!

SLAVE TRADER: Twelve thousand dinars! Twelve thousand. . . .

WINE MERCHANT [*to the* SHOEMAKER]: Are you outbidding me? Then I'll say . . . thirteen thousand dinars!

SLAVE TRADER: Thirteen thousand dinars! Thirteen thousand. . . .

An UNKNOWN MAN *comes forward suddenly, forcing his way through the crowd.*

UNKNOWN MAN [*shouting*]: Fifteen thousand dinars!

SHOEMAKER: Good heavens! Who can this man be?

WINE MERCHANT: A joker of your own ilk without doubt.

SHOEMAKER: And of your ilk too.

SLAVE TRADER: Fifteen thousand dinars! Fifteen thousand! Fifteen thousand!

SHOEMAKER [*shouting*]: Sixteen thousand dinars!

SLAVE TRADER [*shouting*]: Sixteen thousand dinars! Sixteen!

UNKNOWN MAN: Eighteen thousand dinars!

SHOEMAKER [*to the* WINE MERCHANT]: In one fell swoop! This fellow's overdoing things!

SLAVE TRADER: Eighteen thousand dinars! Eighteen thousand!

WINE MERCHANT [*scrutinizing the* UNKNOWN MAN *closely*]: It seems to me I've seen this man somewhere. Yes, he's one of the well-to-do; he comes to my tavern from time to time and drinks a glass of wine before going up to that beautiful lady.

SHOEMAKER [*turning to her window*]: Look! There she is at the window! Glittering in all her cheap finery as though she were some sugar doll! [*shouts to her*] You pretty one up in your heights, are you too not a loyal citizen?

LADY: Shut up, you Shoemaker! I am not one to be made fun of in such circumstances. By God, if you don't keep quiet I'll tell on you and they'll put you into prison.

SLAVE TRADER [*calling out*]: Eighteen thousand dinars . . . at a sum of eighteen thousand. . . .

A LEADING CITIZEN *comes forward to the dais.*

CITIZEN [*shouting*]: Nineteen thousand dinars!

UNKNOWN MAN: I bid twenty thousand dinars!

SLAVE TRADER: Twenty thousand dinars! Twenty thousand dinars! Twenty!

CITIZEN: I bid twenty-one thousand dinars!

UNKNOWN MAN: Twenty-two thousand dinars!

SECOND LEADING CITIZEN *comes forward.*

SECOND CITIZEN: Twenty-three thousand dinars!

SLAVE TRADER: Twenty-three! Twenty-three!

UNKNOWN MAN: Twenty-five!

SLAVE TRADER: Twenty-five thousand dinars! Twenty-five!

A THIRD LEADING CITIZEN *comes forward.*

THIRD CITIZEN: Twenty-six!

SLAVE TRADER [*Shouting*]: Twenty-six thousand dinars! Twenty-six!

UNKNOWN MAN: Twenty-eight!

SLAVE TRADER [*shouting*]: Twenty-eight! Twenty-eight thousand dinars!

THIRD CITIZEN: Twenty-nine!

SHOEMAKER [*whispering to the* WINE MERCHANT]: Are these people really serious about all this?

WINE MERCHANT: It seems so.

SLAVE TRADER: Twenty-nine . . . twenty-nine thousand dinars! Twenty-nine!

UNKNOWN MAN [*shouting*]: Thirty! I bid thirty thousand dinars!

SLAVE TRADER: Thirty! At a sum of thirty! Thirty thousand dinars!

SHOEMAKER [*whispering*]: Thirty thousand dinars to be thrown into the sea! What a madman!

SLAVE TRADER [*shouting at the top of his voice*]: Thirty thousand dinars! Thirty! Any better bid? No one? No one bids more than thirty thousand dinars? Is this all I'm offered as a price for our great Sultan?

SULTAN [*to the* VIZIER]: So this is the height of noble, patriotic, appreciation!

VIZIER: Your Majesty, those present bidding here are mostly the miserly merchants and well-to-do, those whose nature is niggardly, whose one desire is profit, and who begrudge spending money for the sake of a lofty purpose.

SLAVE TRADER [*shouting*]: Thirty thousand dinars! Once again I say: Who bids more? No one? No? No? [*The* SLAVE TRADER *exchanges a glance with the* VIZIER, *then announces*] I shall count up to three: One—two—three! That's it! The final price is thirty thousand dinars. [*Cheering from the crowd.*]

WINE MERCHANT [*to the* SHOEMAKER]: He's a client of mine, the man who won the auction.

SLAVE TRADER: Come forward the winner! Accept congratulations for your good luck!

The crowds cheer him.

VIZIER: I congratulate you, good citizen, and salute you.

Cheering from the crowd.

SLAVE TRADER [*shouting*]: Silence! Silence!

VIZIER [*continuing what he has to say*]: I salute you, good citizen, in the name of the fatherland and in the name of this loyal and upright people from whom you have your origins, for buying and ransoming the freedom of our great Sultan. This sublime deed of yours will be inscribed for ever-more in the pages of the history of this noble people.

Cheering from the crowd.

SLAVE TRADER [*shouting*]: Silence! [*Turns to the* UNKNOWN MAN.] O good cit-izen, the sum is ready, is it not?

UNKNOWN MAN: Certainly—the sacks of gold are but a few paces away.

SLAVE TRADER: Good. Wait, then, for the venerable Chief Cadi to give his orders.

CADI: The question is decided. The judgment of the law has been carried out. The problem has been solved. Approach, good citizen. Are you able to sign your name?

UNKNOWN MAN: Yes, milord Cadi.

CADI: Sign, then, on these deeds.

UNKNOWN MAN: I hear and obey, milord Cadi.

CADI [*presenting him with a document*]: Here—sign here.

UNKNOWN MAN [*reading before signing*]: What's this? And that?

CADI: This is the contract of sale.

UNKNOWN MAN: Yes, I'll sign. [*He signs the document.*]

CADI: And this too. [*He presents him with the second document.*]

UNKNOWN MAN: This? What's this?

CADI: This is the deed of manumission.

UNKNOWN MAN [*taking a step backwards*]: I'm sorry.

CADI [*taken unawares*]: What are you saying?

UNKNOWN MAN: I can't sign this deed.

CADI: Who not? What's this you're saying?

UNKNOWN MAN: I'm saying it's not within my power.

CADI: What's not within your power?

UNKNOWN MAN: To sign the deed of manumission.

CADI [*in a daze*]: It's not within your power to sign?

UNKNOWN MAN: No, it's not within my power or authority.

CADI: What's the meaning of this? What do you mean by this? You're undoubt-edly mad. It's your bounden duty to sign the deed of manumission. That's the condition—the basic condition for the whole of these proceedings.

UNKNOWN MAN: I much regret that I am in no position to do this. This is beyond me, is outside the limits of my authority.

VIZIER: What's this man saying?

CADI: I don't understand.

VIZIER [*to the* UNKNOWN MAN]: Why do you refuse to sign the deed of manumission?

UNKNOWN MAN: Because I have not been given permission to do so.

VIZIER: Have not been given permission?

UNKNOWN MAN [*confirming what he has to say with nods of the head*]: I have not been given permission, having been empowered only in respect of the bidding and the contract of sale. Outside this sphere I have no authorization.

CADI: Authorization? Authorization from whom?

UNKNOWN MAN: From the person who appointed me to act for him.

CADI: You are the agent for another person?

UNKNOWN MAN: Yes, milord Cadi.

CADI: Who is this person?

UNKNOWN MAN: I can't say.

CADI: But you must say.

UNKNOWN MAN: No! No, I can't.

VIZIER: You are absolutely required to tell us the person who appointed you to act for him in signing the deed of sale.

UNKNOWN MAN: I cannot divulge his name.

VIZIER: Why?

UNKNOWN MAN: Because I swore an irrevocable oath that I would keep his name a secret.

VIZIER: And why should the person who appointed you be so careful about his name remaining secret?

UNKNOWN MAN: I don't know.

VIZIER: He obviously has a lot of money seeing that he is able to spend this vast sum all at once.

UNKNOWN MAN: These thirty thousand dinars are his whole life's savings.

VIZIER: And he empowered you to put them all into this auction?

UNKNOWN MAN: Yes.

VIZIER: That's the very acme of generosity, the height of noble feeling . . . but why hide his name? Is it modesty? Is it an urgent wish that his bounty should remain hidden and his good deed unknown?

UNKNOWN MAN: Perhaps.

CADI: In such an event he should have given permission to his agent to sign the manumission deed as well.

UNKNOWN MAN: No, he commissioned me to sign only the contract of sale.

CADI: This is evidence of evil intent.

VIZIER: Truly!

SULTAN [*in a sarcastic tone*]: It seems that things have become complicated.

CADI: A little, Your Majesty.

VIZIER: This man must speak, otherwise I'll force him to talk.

CADI: Gently, O Vizier, gently. He will talk of his own accord and will answer my questions in friendly fashion. Listen, good man—this person who appointed you, what things does he make in order to earn his living?

UNKNOWN MAN: He makes nothing.

CADI: Has he no trade?

UNKNOWN MAN: They claim he has.

CADI: They claim he has a trade but he does not make anything.

UNKNOWN MAN: That's so.

CADI: Then he's an employee.

UNKNOWN MAN: No.

CADI: He's rich?

UNKNOWN MAN: Fairly so.

CADI: And you're in charge of directing his affairs?

UNKNOWN MAN: That's about it.

CADI: Is he one of the notables?

UNKNOWN MAN: Better than that.

CADI: How's that?

UNKNOWN MAN: The notables visit him but he is unaffected by their visits.

CADI: He's a vizier then?

UNKNOWN MAN: No.

CADI: Has he influence?

UNKNOWN MAN: Yes, on his acquaintances.

CADI: Has he many acquaintances?

UNKNOWN MAN: Yes—many.

CADI [*thinking in silence as he passes his fingers through his beard*]: Yes. Yes.

SULTAN: Well finally, O Cadi—have you found a solution to these riddles? Or shall we now spend our time in games of riddles and conundrums?

VIZIER [*his patience exhausted*]: We must have resort to the use of force, Your Majesty. There is no other choice open to us. That person, cloaked in secrets and concealing his name, who storms into this auction like this must inevitably be planning some suspiciously dangerous plan of action. With your permission, Your Majesty, I shall act in the matter. [*Calling to the* GUARDS.] Take this man off and torture him till he reveals the name of the person who appointed him and connived with him.

UNKNOWN MAN [*shouting*]: No! No! No! Don't send me to be tortured! Please! Don't torture me, I implore you!

VIZIER: Then talk!

UNKNOWN MAN: I swore not to.

VIZIER [*to the* GUARDS]: Take him away!

The GUARDS *surround him.*

UNKNOWN MAN: No! No! No!

The door of the LADY*'s house is opened. She appears and approaches the dais, followed by her* MAID *and slave-girls carrying sacks.*

LADY: Leave him! Leave him! It is I who appointed him and here are your sacks of gold—full thirty thousand dinars in cash!

Commotion among the crowds.

SLAVE TRADER [*shouting*]: Be quiet! Silence!

VIZIER: Who's this woman?

CROWDS [*shouting*]: The whore whose house is before us.

VIZIER: Whore!

CROWDS: Yes, a whore well known in the district.

SULTAN: Bravo! Bravo! The crowning touch!

VIZIER: You, O woman, are you she who . . . .

LADY: Yes, I am the person who authorized this man to take part in the auction on my account. [*Turning to the* UNKNOWN MAN.] Is that not so?

UNKNOWN MAN: That's the truth, milady.

VIZIER: You? You dare to buy His Majesty?

LADY: And why not? Am I not a citizen and do I not have money? Why then should I not have exactly the same rights as the others?

CADI: Yes, you have this right. The law applies to all. You must also, however, make yourself acquainted with the conditions of this sale.

LADY: That's natural. I know it's a sale.

CADI: A sale with a particular characteristic.

LADY: A sale by public auction.

CADI: Yes, but . . . .

VIZIER: Before everything else it's a patriotic action. You are a citizen and I would think you are concerned with the well-being of the fatherland.

LADY: Without doubt.

VIZIER: Then sign this deed.

LADY: What does this deed contain?

VIZIER: Manumission.

LADY: What does that mean.

VIZIER: Don't you know the meaning of manumission?

LADY: Does it mean giving up what I am in possession of?

VIZIER: Yes.

LADY: Giving up the chattel I bought at the auction?

VIZIER: That's it.

LADY: No, I don't want to give it up.

SULTAN: That's just fine!

VIZIER: You shall give it up, woman!

LADY: No.

VIZIER: Don't force me to be tough. You know that I can force you.

LADY: By what means?

VIZIER [*pointing to his sword*]: By this.

SULTAN: Resort to the sword now? The time has passed.

VIZIER: She must yield.

LADY: I do yield, oh Vizier—I yield to the law. Is it not in pursuance of the law that I have signed the contract of sale with the State? Is this law therefore respected or not?

SULTAN: Reply, O Chief Cadi.

CADI: Truly, woman, you have signed a contract of sale but it is a conditional contract.

LADY: Meaning?

CADI: Meaning that it's a sale dependent upon a condition.

LADY: What condition?

CADI: Manumission—otherwise the sale itself becomes null and void.

LADY: You mean, O Cadi, that in order for the sale to become valid I must sign the manumission?

CADI: Yes.

LADY: And you likewise mean that I must sign the manumission so that the purchase may become effective?

CADI: Exactly.

LADY: But, milord Cadi, what is a purchase? Is it not owning a thing in return for a price?

CADI: That is so.

LADY: And what is manumission? Is it not the opposite of possession? Is it not yielding up possession?

CADI: Yes.

LADY: Then, O Cadi, you make manumission a condition of possession, that is to say that in order validly to possess the thing sold, the purchaser must yield up that very thing.

CADI: What? What?

LADY: You're saying, in other words, in order to possess something you must yield it up.

CADI: What are you saying? In order to possess you must yield up?

LADY: Or, if you like, in order to possess you must not possess.

CADI: What is this talk?

LADY: This is your condition: in order to buy you must manumit; in order for me to possess I must not possess. Do you find this reasonable?

SULTAN: She is right—neither common sense nor logic can accept this.

CADI: Who taught you this, woman? There is certainly someone learned in the law, some knowing, impudent debauchee who has taught her the things she is saying.

SULTAN: What does it matter? That changes nothing. This is *your* law, O Cadi. Now, you've seen for yourself! With the law there is always some argument that clashes with some other argument, and none is devoid of sense and logic.

CADI: But this is picking holes. This is sophistry. What this woman is saying is mere sophistry.

SULTAN: It's your condition that's sophistry. Selling is selling—that's self-evident. As for the rest, it is binding on no one.

CADI: Yes, Your Majesty. However, this woman took part in the auction being aware of the nature of it and knowing full well the whys and wherefores of it; for her to behave after that in this way is nothing but trickery, deceit, and double-dealing.

SULTAN: If you now want to give her a lesson in morals, that's your affair. As for the law, it no longer has a leg to stand on and you should desist from talking in its name.

CADI: Rather it is my duty, Your Majesty, to protect the law from such creatures who ridicule and make fun of it.

LADY: I would ask you, O Cadi, not to insult me.

CADI: And you, woman, should be ashamed of yourself—aren't you embarrassed at this behavior of yours?

LADY: Embarrassed and ashamed? Why? Because I bought something the State was selling? Because I refused to be robbed of the thing I bought, the thing I'd paid such a high price for? Here are the sacks of gold, count out what is owing to you and take it!

CADI: I refuse your money, and I thus invalidate this contract.

LADY: For what reason do you invalidate it?

CADI: Because you're a woman of bad reputation and wicked conduct. This money may well have been earned through immorality, so how can it be accepted as money to be paid to the Exchequer and the State?

LADY: This same money of mine has in fact been accepted as payment for dues and taxes, and are not dues and taxes paid to the Exchequer and the State? If that is your opinion, O Cadi, then I shall not pay a single tax to the State from now on.

SULTAN: Accept her money, O Cadi: it's a lot easier and simpler.

CADI: Then you insist on the stand you've taken, woman?

LADY: Certainly. I am not joking with these sacks of gold. I am paying in order to buy and I buy in order to possess. The law gives me this right. A sale is a sale. Possession is possession. Take your due and hand me over what is mine!

VIZIER: How can you want us to hand over to you the Sultan who rules this land, O woman?

LADY: Why then have you put the Sultan up for sale?

SULTAN: What she says is logical. What a woman!

LADY: I shall reply, for the reply is simple. You put him up for sale so that one of the people might buy him. Now I have bought him, having been the highest bidder at the auction—in public, in front of everyone. Here is the required price and all that remains for you to do is to hand over to me the goods purchased.

SULTAN: The goods?

LADY: Yes, and I demand that they be delivered to the house.

SULTAN: Which house?

LADY: My house of course—this house opposite.

SULTAN [to the CADI]: Do you hear?

CADI: There is no longer any use or point in arguing with a woman of this sort. Your Majesty, I wash my hands of it.

SULTAN: What an excellent solution, Chief Cadi! You land me in this mire and then wash your hands of it.

CADI: I admit my failure—I didn't know I'd be facing this sort of a person.

SULTAN: And then?

CADI: Punish me, Your Majesty. I deserve the most terrible punishment for my bad advice and lack of foresight. Order that my head be cut off!

SULTAN: What's the point of cutting off your head? That head of yours on your shoulders cast me into this plight—will your decapitated head get me out of it?

VIZIER: Leave the matter to me, Your Majesty! I now see clearly what must be done. [*He draws his sword.*]

SULTAN: No!

VIZIER: But, Your Majesty . . . .

SULTAN: I said no. Sheathe your sword!

VIZIER: Listen to me for a moment, Your Majesty.

SULTAN: Sheathe your sword! We have accepted this situation, so let's proceed.

VIZIER: Your Majesty, seeing that the Cadi has failed and is at a loss, let us go back to our own methods.

SULTAN: No, I shall not go back.

VIZIER: By the sword everything is easily accomplished and is solved in the twinkling of an eye.

SULTAN: No, I have chosen the law and I shall continue on that path whatever obstacles I may encounter.

VIZIER: The law?

SULTAN: Yes, and you yourself said so a while ago and expressed it in beautiful terms: "The Sultan has chosen to submit to the law just like the lowliest individual amongst his subjects." These fine words deserve that every effort be expended in implementing them.

VIZIER: Do you think, Your Majesty, that the lowliest individual amongst your subjects would agree to accept this situation? Here are the people standing before us; if you will permit me I shall ask them and seek their decision. Do you give me permission?

SULTAN: Do so and show me!

VIZIER [*addressing the crowd*]: O people! You see how this impudent woman treats your august Sultan, are you in agreement with what she has done?

THE PEOPLE [*shouting*]: No!

VIZIER: Are you happy with her insulting behavior toward our illustrious ruler?

THE PEOPLE: No!

VIZIER: Do you consider it merits punishment?

THE PEOPLE [*shouting*]: Yes!

VIZIER: What is the appropriate punishment for her?

THE PEOPLE [*shouting*]: Death!

VIZIER [*turning to the* SULTAN]: You see, Your Majesty—the people have given their verdict.

LADY [*turning to the people*]: Death for me? Why, O people, do you condemn me to death? What offence have I committed? Is buying an affront and a crime? Have I stolen this money? It is my life's savings. Am I grabbing and making off by force with the thing offered for sale? I have bought it with my own money at a public auction before your very eyes. For what offense do you seek to spill the blood of a weak woman who has bought something at an auction?

VOICES [*rising from amidst the crowd*]: Death to the whore!

OTHER VOICES [*from amongst the crowd*]: No, don't kill her!

SULTAN [*to the* VIZIER]: Do you see?

VIZIER [*to the people*]: O people, do you consider that the judgment against her should be put into effect?

VOICES [*shouting*]: Yes!

OTHER VOICES [*shouting*]: No!

SULTAN: Opinions are divided, Vizier.

VIZIER: But the majority, Your Majesty, are on the side of death.

SULTAN: For me that is no justification for killing this woman. You are wanting the excuse of a semi-legal justification for employing the sword.

VIZIER: The death of this woman is essential for getting us out of this predicament.

SULTAN: We now need a lifeless corpse to save us?

VIZIER: Yes, Your Majesty.

SULTAN: Once again I am forced to choose between the mire and blood.

VIZIER: We can no longer force a way out for ourselves other than by the sword.

SULTAN: He who proceeds forwards along a straight line always finds a way out.

VIZIER: Your Majesty means . . . .

SULTAN: I mean that there is no retreating, no turning back—do you understand?

VIZIER: I understand, Your Majesty. You wish to go on complying with the law.

SULTAN: Just so, I shall not swerve from what I have chosen, I shall not go back on what I have decided.

VIZIER: And how shall we go on complying with the law with which the Cadi himself has announced his defeat and inability to cope?

SULTAN: He is free to announce his defeat. As for me, I shall not retreat, so let us proceed along the road to its end.

VIZIER: And this woman who blocks the road for us?

SULTAN: Leave her to me. [*He turns to the woman.*] Come here, woman! Approach! Another step—here in front of me! I want to put a few questions to you. Do you permit me?

LADY: I hear and obey, Your Majesty.

SULTAN: First and foremost—who am I?

LADY: Who are you?

SULTAN: Yes, who am I?

LADY: You are the Sultan?

SULTAN: You admit I'm the Sultan?

LADY: Naturally.

SULTAN: Good—and what's the Sultan's job?

LADY: His job is to rule.

SULTAN: You agree that he rules?

LADY: Certainly.

SULTAN: Very good. In as much as you acknowledge all this, how can you demand that the Sultan be handed over to you?

LADY: Because he has become mine by right.

SULTAN: I do not dispute your right. However, I merely wonder at the possibility of your implementing this right. In as much as I am a sultan who rules, how can I carry out the functions of my office if I am handed over to you in your house?

LADY: Nothing is easier or simpler. You are a sultan during the day, therefore I shall lend you to the State for the whole of the day, and in the evening you will return to my house.

SULTAN: I'm afraid you don't understand my work correctly. A sultan is not the owner of a shop who keeps it open during the day and then locks it up at night. He is at the beck and call of the State at any moment. There are urgent and important questions that often require him to hold talks with his men of State in the middle of the night.

LADY: This too is an easy matter, for in my house there is a quiet secluded room where you can work with your men of State.

SULTAN: Do you regard such a set-up as acceptable?

LADY: More than acceptable, I regard it as marvelous!

SULTAN: It is indeed marvelous—a sultan who directs affairs of State from the house of a woman of whom it is said that she . . . please forgive me . . . my apologies.

LADY: Say it! Go on! The word no longer wounds me because of the many torments I have suffered—I have become immune. However, I assure you, O Sultan, that you will experience greater joy in my house than you do in yours.

SULTAN: Possibly, except that a ruler is not proficient in carrying out the functions of government when he does so from the houses of others.

LADY: That is if the ruler is free.

SULTAN: You have scored—I am not free. [*He lowers his head. A moment's silence.*]

LADY: What I admire in you, O Sultan, is your composed and calm attitude in the face of this catastrophe.

SULTAN [*raising his head*]: You are admitting then that it is a catastrophe?

LADY: It's self-evident—a great Sultan like you being badly treated in this way.

SULTAN: And is anyone but you badly treating me?

LADY: How right you are! What pride and joy it is to me to hear this from the mouth of a great sultan! It's an honor which merits the payment of all the world's gold. No one in the city after today will dare slight me, for I am treating sultans badly!

VIZIER [*in a rage*]: Enough, woman! Enough! This is unbearable. She has overstepped all limits of decency. The head of this mischievous and shameless woman must fall!

SULTAN: Calm yourself!

LADY: Yes, calm yourself, O Vizier—and don't interfere in what does not concern you.

VIZIER: How can all this be borne? Patience, Lord! Patience, Lord!

LADY: Yes, have patience, O Vizier, and let the Sultan and me talk. This matter concerns us alone.

SULTAN: That's true.

LADY: Where did we get to, Your Majesty?

SULTAN: I no longer know—it was you who were talking.

LADY: Oh yes, I remember now—we got to where I was saying that it was an honor . . . .

SULTAN: For you to treat me badly.

LADY: Rather that I should have the good fortune of enjoying talking to you. In fact, Your Majesty, it's the first time I have seen you at close quarters. People have talked about you so much but I didn't know you were so charming.

SULTAN: Thank you.

LADY: Truly, it's as though we'd been friends for a long time.

SULTAN: Is it your custom to subject your friends to humiliation and ridicule in this manner?

LADY: Not at all—just the opposite.

SULTAN: Then why make an exception of me?

LADY: This in fact is what has begun to upset me. How I would like to bring happiness to your heart and show you reverence and respect! But how? How can I do that! What's the way to do it?

SULTAN: The way's easy.

LADY: By signing this manumission deed?

SULTAN: I would have thought so.

LADY: No, I don't want to let you go. I don't want to give you up. You belong to me. You're mine—mine.

SULTAN: I belong to you and to all the rest of the people.

LADY: I want you to be mine alone.

SULTAN: And my people?

LADY: Your people have not paid gold in order to acquire you.

SULTAN: That's right, but you must know that it's absolutely impossible for me to be yours alone and for me to remain thereafter a sultan. There is only one situation in which it is in order for me to be yours alone.

LADY: What's that?

SULTAN: That I should not be a sultan, that I should give up the throne and relinquish power.

LADY: No, I don't wish that for you—I wish you to remain a sultan.

SULTAN: In that event there must be sacrifice.

LADY: From my side?

SULTAN: Or from my own.

LADY: I should give you up?

SULTAN: Or I should give up the throne?

LADY: It's for me to choose?

SULTAN: Of course it's for you to choose, because all the cards are in your hands.

LADY: Have I all that importance, all that weight?

SULTAN: At this moment, yes.

LADY: This is wonderful!

SULTAN: Certainly.

LADY: Then I now hold all the cards in my hands?

SULTAN: Yes.

LADY: At my pleasure I keep the Sultan in power?

SULTAN: Yes.

LADY: And by a word from me the removal of the Sultan is accomplished?

SULTAN: Yes.

LADY: This is truly wonderful!

SULTAN: Without doubt.

LADY: And who has given me all this authority—money?

SULTAN: The law.

LADY: A word from my mouth can change your destiny and channel your life either to slavery and bondage, or to freedom and sovereignty.

SULTAN: And it is up to you to choose.

LADY [thoughtfully]: Between bondage that bestows you upon me, and between freedom which retains you for your throne and your people.

SULTAN: It is up to you to choose.

LADY: The choice is difficult.

SULTAN: I know.

LADY: It is painful to let you go, to lose you for ever; but it is also painful to see you lose your throne, for our country has never had the good fortune to have a sultan with such courage and sense of justice. No, do not give up the rule, do not relinquish the throne! I want you to remain a sultan.

SULTAN: And so?

LADY: I shall sign the deed.

SULTAN: The manumission deed?

LADY: Yes.

CADI [*hurrying to present the deed*]: Here is the deed.

LADY: I have only a final request.

SULTAN: What is it?

LADY: That you give this night to me, Your Majesty—a single night. Honor me by accepting my invitation and be my guest until daybreak. And when the Muezzin gives the call to dawn prayers from this minaret here, I shall sign the deed of manumission and Your Majesty will be free.

CADI: If the Muezzin does give the call to dawn prayers!

LADY: Yes. Is this too much—that I buy with these sacks of gold not the Sultan himself but a single night with him as my guest?

SULTAN: I accept.

VIZIER: But, Your Majesty, who will guarantee that this promise will be kept by such a woman?

SULTAN: I shall. I am the guarantor, I trust what she says.

CADI: Do you take an oath on what you say, woman?

LADY: Yes, I swear. I swear a triple oath by Almighty God. I shall sign the deed of manumission when the Muezzin gives the call to dawn prayers from on top of this minaret.

CADI: I bear witness before God to that. All of us here are witnesses.

SULTAN: As for me, I believe her without an oath.

LADY: And now, O noble Sultan, will you be so good as to honor my humble house with your gracious presence?

SULTAN: With great pleasure!

The SULTAN *rises and follows the* LADY *into her house. Music.*

ACT THREE

The same square. One side of the mosque with its minaret is in view, also a side of the LADY's house, showing a portion of the room with the window over-looking the square. The time is night. Among the throng are the VIZIER, the SHOEMAKER, and the WINE MERCHANT.

VIZIER [*in the square, shouting to the* GUARDS]: What are all these crowds waiting for in the middle of the night? Turn the people away! Let everyone go to his home, to his bed!

GUARDS [*turning away the crowds*]: To your homes! To your houses!

CROWDS [*grumbling*]: No! No!

SHOEMAKER [*shouting*]: I want to stay here.

WINE MERCHANT: And I too shan't budge from here.

VIZIER [*to the* GUARDS]: What are they saying?

GUARDS: They refuse to go.

VIZIER [*shouting*]: Refuse? What's this nonsense? Make them!

GUARDS [*forcefully*]: Everyone to his home! Everyone to his house! Get along! Get along!

SHOEMAKER: I'm already at home. This is my shop.

WINE MERCHANT: I too have my tavern right here before you.

GUARDS: Will you not obey orders? Get going! Get going! [*They push the* WINE MERCHANT *and the* SHOEMAKER.]

SHOEMAKER: There's no reason for violence—please.

WINE MERCHANT: Don't push me about like this!

VIZIER [*to the* GUARDS]: Bring along those two trouble-makers! [*The* GUARDS *seize hold of the* SHOEMAKER *and the* WINE MERCHANT *and bring them before the* VIZIER.]

SHOEMAKER: By God, I haven't done anything, milord Vizier.

VIZIER: Why do you refuse to go home?

SHOEMAKER: I don't want to go to bed. I have a strong desire to stay here, milord Vizier—in order to watch.

VIZIER: To watch what?

SHOEMAKER: To watch Our Majesty the Sultan leaving this house.

WINE MERCHANT: I too, milord Vizier—let me watch it.

VIZIER: Really, what effrontery? Today everyone's effrontery has reached the bounds of impudence. Even you and your comrade have the nerve to talk in such terms.

WINE MERCHANT: It's not impudence, milord Vizier, it's a request.

VIZIER: A request?

SHOEMAKER: Yes, milord Vizier, we request that you give us permission to watch.

VIZIER: What insolence! And what have you to do with this matter?

SHOEMAKER: Are we not good citizens? The fate of our Sultan inevitably concerns us.

VIZIER: This does not give you both the right to disobey orders.

SHOEMAKER: We are not disobeying, we are requesting. How can we sleep a wink tonight with the fate of our Sultan in the balance?

VIZIER: In the balance?

SHOEMAKER: Yes, milord—the balance of capricious whims.

VIZIER: What do you mean?

SHOEMAKER: I mean that the outcome is not reassuring.

VIZIER: Why do you think so?

SHOEMAKER: With such a woman one can be certain of nothing.

WINE MERCHANT: We have made a bet between ourselves. He says this woman will break her promise, while I say she will honor it.

VIZIER: A fine thing, indeed—of an important event like this you make a game of having bets!

WINE MERCHANT: We are not alone in this, milord Vizier. Many such as we among these crowds are tonight making bets among themselves. Even the Muezzin and the Executioner have made a bet.

VIZIER: The Executioner: where is the Executioner?

WINE MERCHANT [*pointing*]: Over there, milord. He's trying to hide among the people.

VIZIER [*to the* GUARDS]: Bring him over here.

The GUARDS *bring the* EXECUTIONER *to the* VIZIER.

EXECUTIONER [*frightened*]: It's not my fault, milord Vizier. It's the Muezzin's mistake. It's he who's responsible, it's he who did not give the call to the dawn prayers.

VIZIER: Dawn? What dawn? We're no longer talking about dawn prayers, you idiot. [*The* WINE MERCHANT *and the* SHOEMAKER *laugh.*] Do you dare to laugh in my presence? Get out of my sight! Out! [*The* WINE MERCHANT *and the* SHOEMAKER *take to their heels.*] And now, Executioner—are you busy with bets?

EXECUTIONER: Bets? Who said so, milord?

VIZIER: I want a straight answer to my question.

EXECUTIONER: But, milord, I . . . .

VIZIER: Don't be frightened—tell me.

EXECUTIONER: But this bet, milord . . . .

VIZIER: I know, I know, and I shall not punish you. Answer this question frankly: will this woman in your opinion break her promise or will she honor it?

EXECUTIONER: But, milord Vizier, I . . . .

VIZIER: I told you not to be frightened but to express. . . your opinion without constraint. That's an order and you must obey it.

EXECUTIONER: Your order must be obeyed, milord—in truth I have no trust in this woman.

VIZIER: Why?

EXECUTIONER: Because she's a liar, a cheat, and a swindler!

VIZIER: Do you know her?

EXECUTIONER: I got to know some of her wiles when I was here that day waiting for the dawn in order to carry out the sentence of execution on the slave trader.

VIZIER: A liar, a cheat, and a swindler?

EXECUTIONER: Yes.

VIZIER: And what does such a woman deserve?

EXECUTIONER: Punishment of course.

VIZIER: And what is the punishment you deem suitable for her if she has tricked and lied to our exalted Sultan?

EXECUTIONER: Death, without doubt!

VIZIER: Good. Then be prepared to carry out this sentence at dawn.

EXECUTIONER [*as though talking to himself*]: Dawn? Yet again?

VIZIER: What are you saying?

EXECUTIONER: I am saying that at dawn I shall be ready to execute the order of milord Vizier.

VIZIER: Yes, if the Muezzin has given the call to the dawn prayer and our Sultan has not emerged from this house a free man . . . .

EXECUTIONER: Then I cut off the head of this woman.

VIZIER: Yes, as punishment for the crime of . . . .

EXECUTIONER: Lying and cheating.

VIZIER: No.

EXECUTIONER [*not understanding*]: No?

VIZIER [*as though talking to himself*]: No, that is not enough—it is not a crime that merits death. This woman is liable to find some high-sounding phrases in law and logic to justify her action. No, there must be some terrible and serious crime which she will not be able to justify or defend herself against—a crime that will earn her the universal opprobrium of the whole people. We could for instance say she is a spy.

EXECUTIONER: A spy?

VIZIER: Yes, that she's working for the Mongols. Then the people in their entirety will rise up and demand her head.

EXECUTIONER: Yes, an appropriate punishment.

VIZIER: Is that not your opinion?

EXECUTIONER: And I shall raise my voice crying "Death to the traitor!"

VIZIER: Your voice alone will not suffice. There must be other voices besides yours giving this cry.

EXECUTIONER: There will be other voices.

VIZIER: Do you know whose they'll be?

EXECUTIONER: It won't be difficult to find them.

VIZIER: Witnesses must be got ready.

EXECUTIONER: All that is easy, milord.

VIZIER: I think that such an arrangement can be successful. I'm relying on you if things go badly.

EXECUTIONER: I am your faithful servant, milord Vizier.

A part of the room in the LADY's *house is lit up.*

VIZIER: Quiet! A light in the window! Let's move away a little.

While the room is lit up, the square becomes dark; the LADY *appears and moves toward the sofa followed by the* SULTAN.

SULTAN [*sitting down*]: Your house is magnificent and your furnishings costly.

LADY [*sitting at his feet*]: Yes, I told you just now that my husband was a wealthy merchant who had taste and a passion for poetry and singing.

SULTAN: Were you one of his slave-girls?

LADY: Yes, he bought me when I was sixteen years of age, then gave me my freedom and married me several years before his death.

SULTAN: Your luck was better than mine. With you no one forgot to free you at the proper time.

LADY: My real good luck is your having honored my house with your presence tonight.

SULTAN: Here I am in your house—what do you intend doing with me tonight?

LADY: Nothing except to allow you to relax a little.

SULTAN: Is that all?

LADY: Nothing more than that. Previously I said to you that at my house there is more joy than at yours. I have beautiful slave-girls who excel at dancing and singing and playing on every musical instrument. Be assured, you will not be bored here tonight.

SULTAN: Until dawn breaks?

LADY: Think not of the dawn now. The dawn is still far off.

SULTAN: I shall do all you demand until dawn breaks.

LADY: I shall ask nothing of you except to converse, to take food, and to listen to singing.

SULTAN: Nothing but that?

LADY: But do you want me to ask of you more than that?

SULTAN: I don't know—you know best.

LADY: Let us then start with conversation—tell me about yourself.

SULTAN: About myself?

LADY: Yes, your story—tell me the story of your life.

SULTAN: You want me to tell you stories?

LADY: Yes, in truth you must have a store of wonderfully entertaining stories.

SULTAN: It is *I* now who must tell stories!

LADY: And why not?

SULTAN: Truly that's how it should be, seeing that it is I who am in the position of Shahrazad! She too had to tell stories throughout the whole night, awaiting the dawn that would decide her fate.

LADY [*laughing*]: And I, then, am the dreadful, awe-inspiring Shahriyar?

SULTAN: Yes—isn't it extraordinary? Today everything is upside down.

LADY: No, you are always the Sultan. As for me, I am she who plays the role of Shahrazad, always seated at your feet.

SULTAN: A Shahrazad having her apprehensive Shahriyar by the neck until the morning comes.

LADY: No, rather a Shahrazad who will bring joy and gladness to the heart of her sultan. You will see now how I shall deal with your anxiety and misgivings. [*She claps and soothing music issues forth from behind the screens.*]

SULTAN [*after listening for a while*]: A delightful performance!

LADY: And I myself shall dance for you. [*She rises and dances.*]

SULTAN [*after she has finished her dance*]: Delightful! It's all delightful! Do you do this every night?

LADY: No, Your Majesty. This is an exception. It's just for you, for I myself have not danced since being manumitted and married. On other nights it is the slave-girls who do the dancing and singing.

SULTAN: For your clients?

LADY: My guests, rather.

SULTAN: As you will—your guests. Doubtless these guests of yours pay you a high fee for all this. I now realize how it is you have such wealth.

LADY: My wealth I inherited from my husband. Sometimes I spend on these nights more than I get back.

SULTAN: Why? For nothing?

LADY: For the sake of art. I am a lover of art.

SULTAN [*sarcastically*]: Refined art to be sure!

LADY: You don't believe me. You don't take what I say seriously. So be it. Think as badly of me as you like—I am not in the habit of defending myself against other people's assumptions. In people's eyes I am a woman who behaves badly, and I have reached the stage where I have accepted this judgment. I have found this convenient—it is no longer in my interests to correct people's opinion. When one has crossed the ultimate boundaries of wickedness one becomes free, and I am in need of my freedom.

SULTAN: You too?

LADY: Yes, in order to do what I enjoy.

SULTAN: And what do you enjoy?

LADY: The company of men.

SULTAN: Understood!

LADY: No, you understand wrongly. It's not as you think.

SULTAN: How is it then?

LADY: Do you want lies or the truth?

SULTAN: The truth of course.

LADY: You won't believe the truth, so what's the point of my telling it? A truth that people don't believe is a useless truth.

SULTAN: Say it in any case.

LADY: I shall say it purely to amuse you. I enjoy the company of men for their souls, not for their bodies. Do you understand?

SULTAN: No, not exactly.

LADY: I shall elucidate. When I was a young slave-girl of the same age as the slave-girls I have with me now, my master brought me up to love poetry and singing and playing on musical instruments. He used to make me attend his banquets and converse with his guests, who were poets and singers; they also included intellectuals and men of wit and charm. We would spend the night reciting poetry, singing and playing music and conversing, quoting and capping quotations from the masterpieces of literature, and laughing from the depths of our hearts. Those were wonderfully enjoyable nights, but they were also innocent and chaste. Please believe that. My master was a good man and knew no pleasure in life other than these nights—a pleasure without sin, without vulgarity. In this way did he bring me up and educate me. And when I later became his wife he did not wish to deprive me of the pleasure of those nights which used so to enchant me; he therefore allowed me to continue to attend, though from behind silken curtains. That's the whole story.

SULTAN: And after his death?

LADY: After his death I was unable to give up this practice, so I continued to invite my husband's guests. At first I would receive them screened behind the silken curtains, but when the people of the district began spreading gossip at seeing men nightly entering the house of a woman with no husband I found it pointless to continue to be screened behind the curtains. I said to myself: seeing that the people's verdict has pronounced me guilty, let me make myself the judge of my own behavior.

SULTAN: It is truly extraordinary that your exterior should proclaim so loudly what is not to be found within; your shop window advertises goods that are not to be found inside.

LADY: It is for you to believe or not what I have said to you.

SULTAN: I prefer to believe—it is more conducive to peace of mind.

LADY: Be that as it may, I do not at all intend to change my life and habits. If the road I tread be filled with mire I shall continue to wade through it.

SULTAN: Mire! It's to be found on every road—be sure of that!

LADY: Now you remind me of what I did to you in front of the masses of people.

SULTAN: Truly you rolled me in it properly!

LADY: I was intentionally insolent to you, deliberately vulgar and impudent. Do you know why? Because I imagined you as being quite different. I imagined you as an arrogant sultan, strutting about haughtily and giving yourself airs—like most sultans. You could, in fact, well have been even more conceited and overbearing by reason of the wars you have waged and your victories. People always talk of that fabulous ruby which adorns your turban, that ruby that is without peer in the world, of which it is said that you seized it at sword-point from the head of the Mongol Chief. Yes, your deeds are wondrous and splendid. Thus the picture of you in my mind was synonymous with haughtiness, harshness, and cruelty. But as soon as you talked to me so pleasantly and modestly I was overcome by a certain bewilderment and confusion.

SULTAN: Don't be misled! I am not always so pleasant, nor so modest. There are times when I am more cruel and brutal than the worst of sultans.

LADY: I don't believe that.

SULTAN: That's because you've fallen under the influence of the present circumstances.

LADY: You mean that you are specially pleasant to me? This fills me with great pride, dear Majesty. But wait! Perhaps I have misunderstood. What is it that causes you to be so pleasant to me? Is it personal? Or is it the decision you await from me at daybreak?

SULTAN: I affect being pleasant with you, I put it on, in order to gain your sympathy—isn't that so?

LADY: And no sooner will you achieve your freedom than you'll revert to your true nature and will become the cruel Sultan who pursues revenge in order to atone to himself for his moments of humiliation—and then will come my hour of doom.

SULTAN: It would therefore be wise and far-sighted of you to keep me always in your grasp and power.

LADY: Is that so?

SULTAN: That is absolutely logical, seeing that you have your doubts.

LADY: Have I not the right to doubt?

SULTAN: I don't blame you if you do, for it is I who, quite simply and incautiously, have implanted in you the seeds of doubt by saying what I did about myself.

LADY [*regarding him searchingly*]: No.

SULTAN: No? Why?

LADY: I prefer to rely on the womanly instinct that is deep within me. It never deceives me.

SULTAN: And what does your womanly instinct tell you?

LADY: It tells me that you are not that type of man. You are different. I should have realized this from the moment I saw you renouncing the use of the sword.

SULTAN: If only you knew how easy things would have been had I used my sword!

LADY: Do you now regret it?

SULTAN: I am merely talking about how easy it would have been. However, the real victory is in solving the problem by sleight-of-hand.

LADY: And this is the path you are now pursuing?

SULTAN: Yes, but I am not confident about the result.

LADY: Let's suppose the result to be that your hopes are dashed—what will you do then?

SULTAN: I have already told you

LADY: Give up your throne?

SULTAN: Yes.

LADY: No, I do not believe you would really do that. I'm not so simple or stupid as to believe that or to take it seriously. Even if you wanted to do it not a single person in the country would accept it, or would permit you to embark upon such an action. You would bear a heavy burden by accepting the easy solution and would revert to using the simple expedient.

SULTAN: It has never happened that I have taken a step backwards—not even in the field of battle. I admit that this is wrong from the military point of view, for there are circumstances that make retreat necessary. However, I have never done so. Perhaps luck was on my side; in any event I have adopted this bad practice.

LADY: You're amazing!

SULTAN: The truth is rather that I'm an unimaginative man.

LADY: You?

SULTAN: The proof is that were I possessed of imagination and had envisaged what awaited me at the end of such a road, I would have been stunned.

LADY: Nothing stuns you. You have composure, self-confidence, control over your actions, the ability to do what you want with meticulous precision and resoluteness. You are far from being weak or wily—you're frank, natural, and courageous. There's no more to say.

SULTAN: Are you flattering me? Who should be flattering whom? Once again the situations have been reversed.

LADY: Will you permit me, my dear Sultan?

SULTAN: To do what?

LADY: To ask you a personal question?

SULTAN: Personal? Is not all this that we are engaged in personal?

LADY: I want to ask you about—about your heart, about love.

SULTAN: Love? What love?

LADY: Love—for a woman?

SULTAN: Do you imagine I have the time to occupy myself with such things?

LADY: How strange! Has your heart never opened to love a woman?

SULTAN: Why have you opened your large eyes like this in astonishment? Is it such an important matter?

LADY: But you have definitely known many women?

SULTAN: Certainly—that is the nature of military life. The leader of an army, as you know, every night has some female prisoner, some captive, brought to him. Sometimes there are beautiful women among them. That's all there is to it.

LADY: And not a single particular woman succeeded in attracting your glances?

SULTAN: My glances? You should know that at the end of the day I returned always to my tent with eyes filled with the dust of battle.

LADY: And on the following day? Did you not retain a single memory of those beautiful women?

SULTAN: On the following day I would again mount my steed and think of something else.

LADY: But now you're the Sultan. You certainly have sufficient time for love.

SULTAN: Do you believe so?

LADY: What prevents you?

SULTAN: The problems of government. And this is one of them—this problem that has descended upon my head today so unexpectedly and put me in this fix. Do you consider that such a problem allows one to be in the mood for love?

LADY [*laughing*]: You're right!

SULTAN: You laugh!

LADY: Another question—the last, be sure of that! A very serious question this time, because it relates to me.

SULTAN: To you?

LADY: Yes. Let us assume that I have manumitted you at dawn—you will of course return to your palace.

SULTAN: Of course, I have business awaiting me there.

LADY: And I?

SULTAN: And what about you?

LADY: Will you not think about me after that?

SULTAN: I don't understand.

LADY: You really don't understand what I mean?

SULTAN: You know the language of women is too subtle for me, it is very often obscure.

LADY: You understand me only too well, for you are exceedingly intelligent and astute, and also very sensitive, despite appearances and the impression you like to give. In any case I shall explain my words—here is what I want to know: Will you forget me altogether and erase me from your memory directly you have left here?

SULTAN: I do not think it is possible to erase you altogether from my memory.

LADY: And will you retain a pleasant memory of me?

SULTAN: Certainly!

LADY: Is that all? Does everything for me end just like that?

SULTAN: Are we going over the same ground as before?

LADY: No, I merely wish to ask you: Is this night our last night together?

SULTAN: That's a question which it's difficult to answer.

LADY: Good! Don't answer it now!

The MAIDSERVANT *appears.*

MAID: Dinner is served, milady.

LADY [*rising to her feet*]: If Your Majesty pleases.

SULTAN [*rising to his feet*]: You are a model of kindness and hospitality.

LADY: Rather is it you who do me a kindness.

She leads him into another room to the accompaniment of music. The light in the house is extinguished and a dim light comes on in the square.

SHOEMAKER [*to the* WINE MERCHANT *in a corner of the square*]: Look! They've put out the light.

WINE MERCHANT [*looking toward the window*]: That's a good sign!

SHOEMAKER: How?

WINE MERCHANT: Putting out the light means going to bed!

SHOEMAKER: And so?

WINE MERCHANT: And so agreement is complete.

SHOEMAKER: Over what?

WINE MERCHANT: Over everything.

SHOEMAKER: You mean that she'll accept to give him up at dawn?

WINE MERCHANT: Yes.

SHOEMAKER: And so you win the bet.

WINE MERCHANT: Without the slightest doubt.

SHOEMAKER: You're over-optimistic, my friend, to think that such a woman would easily accept throwing her money into the sea.

WINE MERCHANT: Who is to know? I say yes.

SHOEMAKER: And I say no.

WINE MERCHANT: Fine, let us await the dawn.

SHOEMAKER: What time is it now?

WINE MERCHANT [*looking at the sky*]: According to the stars it is now approximately midnight.

SHOEMAKER: Dawn is still far-off and I am beginning to feel sleepy.

WINE MERCHANT: Go to bed!

SHOEMAKER: I? Out of the question! The whole city is staying up tonight, so how can I be the only one to sleep? In fact I have more reason than anybody to stay up until dawn in order to witness your defeat.

WINE MERCHANT: My defeat?

SHOEMAKER: Without the slightest doubt.

WINE MERCHANT: We shall see which of us turns out to be the loser.

SHOEMAKER [*turning to a corner of the square*]: Look! Over there!

WINE MERCHANT: What?

SHOEMAKER [*whispering*]: The Vizier and the Executioner. They look as though they're hatching some plot.

WINE MERCHANT: Quiet!

The VIZIER *walks up and down as he questions the* EXECUTIONER.

VIZIER: What exactly did you hear from the guards?

EXECUTIONER: I heard them say, milord Vizier, that it was impossible to quell the people and force them to go to bed tonight. The crowds are still standing or squatting in the lanes and alleyways and all are whispering together and gossiping.

VIZIER: Gossiping?

EXECUTIONER: Yes.

VIZIER: And what's all this whispering and gossiping about?

EXECUTIONER: About the business of the Sultan of course and what he's doing tonight in this house.

VIZIER: And what, in your opinion, might he be doing in this house?

EXECUTIONER: Are you asking me, milord Vizier?

VIZIER: Yes, I'm asking you. Are you not one of the people, and does not your opinion represent public opinion? Answer me! What do you imagine the Sultan is doing in this house?

EXECUTIONER: Actually . . . well he's certainly not performing his prayers there!

VIZIER: Are you making fun? Are you being insolent?

EXECUTIONER: Pardon, milord Vizier. I merely wanted to say that this house is not . . . is no saintly place.

VIZIER: Then the gossip in the city is along these lines—that the Sultan is spending the night in a . . . .

EXECUTIONER: A brothel!

VIZIER: What are you saying?

EXECUTIONER: That's what they are saying, milord. I am reporting what I heard.

VIZIER: Is this all that people are mentioning about this important matter? They are forgetting the noble purport, the lofty aim, the sublime concept, the patriotic objective! Even you, as I see it, have forgotten all this.

EXECUTIONER: No, milord Vizier, I have forgotten nothing.

VIZIER: We shall see. Tell me then why the Sultan accepted to enter this house.

EXECUTIONER: In order to . . . to gratify the whore.

VIZIER: Is that all it's about? What a shallow way of looking at things!

EXECUTIONER: Milord Vizier, I was present and I saw and heard everything from the beginning.

VIZIER: And you didn't understand any of it, except for the insignificant and degrading side of the issue. Are there many like you among the people?

EXECUTIONER: Like me they were all present.

VIZIER: And they all made of it what you did as far as I can see. Their talk does not deal with the profound reason, the exalted meaning of all that has happened. Their talk deals merely with what you yourself say: the Sultan is spending the night in a brothel! What a catastrophe! It's this that's the real catastrophe!

The CHIEF CADI *appears.*

CADI: I haven't slept tonight.

VIZIER: You too?

CADI: Why I too?

VIZIER: The whole of the rest of the city hasn't slept tonight.

CADI: I know that.

VIZIER: And everyone's whispering and gossiping.

CADI: I know that as well.

VIZIER: And do you know what they're saying in the city?

CADI: The worst possible things. The point of interest and excitement for the people is the scandalous side of the affair.

VIZIER: Unfortunately so.

CADI: It's my fault.

VIZIER: And mine too. I should have been more resolute in the defense of my opinion.

CADI: But, on the other hand, how could we have anticipated that woman's intervention?

VIZIER: We should have anticipated everything.

CADI: You're right.

VIZIER: Now the die is cast and we have no power to do anything.

CADI: Yet it is in our power to snatch the Sultan away from this house.

VIZIER: We must wait for the dawn.

CADI: No, now . . . at once!

VIZIER: But the dawn is still far off.

CADI: It must be made to come now—at once!

VIZIER: Who? What?

CADI: The dawn!

VIZIER: My apologies—I don't understand.

CADI: You will shortly. Where's the Muezzin of this mosque?

VIZIER [*turning toward the* EXECUTIONER]: The Executioner must know.

EXECUTIONER: He's over there, among the crowds.

CADI: Go and bring him to me.

The EXECUTIONER *returns, and after some whispered conversation hurries off obediently.*

VIZIER [*to the* CADI]: It seems you have some plan or other?

CADI: Yes.

VIZIER: May I know it?

CADI: Shortly.

The MUEZZIN *appears, panting.*

MUEZZIN: Here I am, milord Cadi.

CADI: Come close! I want to talk to you regarding the dawn.

MUEZZIN: The dawn? Be sure, milord Cadi, that I have committed no wrong. This Executioner is accusing me falsely of . . . .

CADI: Listen to me well.

MUEZZIN: I swear to you, milord Cadi, that on that day . . . .

CADI: Will you stop this nonsensical chattering! I told you to listen to me well. I want you to carry out what I am going to say to the letter. Do you understand?

MUEZZIN: Yes.

CADI: Go and climb up into your minaret and give the call to the dawn prayer.

MUEZZIN: When?

CADI: Now!

MUEZZIN [*in surprise*]: Now?

CADI: Yes, immediately.

MUEZZIN: The dawn prayer?

CADI: Yes, the dawn prayer. Go and give the call to the dawn prayer. Is what I say clear or not?

MUEZZIN: It's clear, but it's now approximately . . . midnight.

CADI: Let it be!

MUEZZIN: Dawn at midnight?

CADI: Yes! Hurry!

MUEZZIN: Isn't this just a little . . . premature?

CADI: No.

MUEZZIN [*whispering to himself*]: I'm at a loss about this dawn—sometimes I'm asked to put it back and sometimes I'm asked to bring it forward.

CADI: What are you saying?

MUEZZIN: Nothing, milord Cadi. I shall go at once to carry out your order.

CADI: Listen! Make sure you tell no one that it was the Cadi who gave you this order.

MUEZZIN: Meaning, milord?

CADI: Meaning that it's you on your own initiative who have acted thus.

MUEZZIN: On my own initiative? I go up into the minaret to give the call to dawn prayers at midnight? Anyone behaving like that *must* be a crazy idiot.

CADI: Leave to me the task of explaining your behavior at the appropriate time.

MUEZZIN: But, milord, by this action I expose myself to the ridicule of the masses and they'll ask that I be punished.

CADI: And whom will you appear before to be tried? Won't it be before me, the Chief Cadi?

MUEZZIN: And if you disown and abandon me?

CADI: Do not be afraid, that will never happen.

MUEZZIN: And how can I be sure?

CADI: I promise you—have you no faith in my promise?

MUEZZIN [*whispering to himself*]: The promises tonight are many—and not a soul is sure of anything.

CADI: What are you saying?

MUEZZIN: Nothing. I'm just asking myself—why should I expose myself to all this danger?

CADI: It's a service you're rendering the State.

MUEZZIN [*in astonishment*]: The State?

CADI: Yes, I shall tell you about the matter so that you may rest assured. Listen! If you give the call to dawn prayers now, the Sultan will immediately leave this house a free man. That, in a couple of words, is what it's all about. Do you understand now?

MUEZZIN: It's a patriotic act!

CADI: It certainly is. What do you say then?

MUEZZIN: I shall do it immediately. I shall be proud of it the whole of my life. Permit me, milord Cadi, also to tell you something—what I say being strictly between ourselves—which is that I previously told you a small falsehood of this sort in order to save the head of someone who had been condemned to death; so why should I not commit a similar falsehood in order to gain the freedom of Our Majesty the beloved Sultan!

CADI: You're quite right, but I enjoin you to secrecy. Be careful not to let that tongue of yours wag! Hide this pride of yours in your soul, for if you begin to boast of what you have done in these present circumstances the whole business will be ruined. Shut your mouth well if you want your action to bear fruit and be appreciated.

MUEZZIN: I shall shut my mouth.

CADI: Good. Hurry off and do it.

MUEZZIN: As swift as the winds I'll be!

The MUEZZIN *leaves hurriedly.*

CADI [*to the* VIZIER]: What do you think?

VIZIER: Do you think a trick like this will put matters right?

CADI: Yes, in the best way possible. Tonight I set about considering every aspect of the matter. I no longer regard myself as having been defeated. I still have in my quiver—or, to be more exact, in the law's quiver— many tricks.

MUEZZIN: Let us pray to God to make your tricks successful this time. Your personal honor is at stake.

CADI: You will see.

The voice of the MUEZZIN *rings out.*

MUEZZIN [*from afar*]: God is great! God is great! Come to prayers! Come to prayers! Come to salvation! Come to salvation!

The crowd make their appearance in a state of agitation, astonishment, protest, and anger.

THE PEOPLE [*shouting*]: The dawn? Now? It's still night—we're in the middle of the night. He's mad! This madman—arrest him! Bring him down, bring him down from on top of the minaret! Bring him down!

VIZIER [*to the* CADI]: The crowds will fall upon this poor fellow.

CADI: Order your guards to disperse the crowds.

VIZIER [*shouting at the* GUARDS]: Clear the square! Clear everyone out of the square!

The GUARDS *chase the people away and clear the square, while the* MUEZZIN *continues with his call to prayer.*

The light goes on in the LADY*'s room. She appears at the window followed by the* SULTAN.

LADY: Is it really dawn?

CADI: It is the call to prayers. Come down here at once!

LADY: This is absurd—look at the stars in the sky.

SULTAN [*looking at the sky*]: Truly this is most strange.

CADI [*to the* LADY]: I told you to come down here immediately.

SULTAN [*to the* LADY]: Let us go down together to see what it's all about.

LADY: Let us go, Your Majesty. [*They leave the room, the light is extinguished, and they are seen coming out of the house.*]

SULTAN [*looking at the sky*]: The dawn? At this hour?

VIZIER: Yes, Your Majesty.

SULTAN: This is truly extraordinary. What do you say, Cadi?

CADI: No, Your Majesty, the dawn has not yet broken.

VIZIER [*taken aback*]: How's that?

CADI: It's quite obvious—it's still night.

VIZIER [*to the* CADI *in astonishment*]: But . . . .

CADI: But we have all heard the Muezzin give the call to dawn prayers. Did you hear it, woman?

LADY: Yes, I did.

CADI: You admit then that you heard the voice of the Muezzin giving the call to dawn prayers?

LADY: Yes, but . . . .

CADI: There is nothing more to be said. As you have admitted this, there is nothing left for you to do but keep your promise. Here is the deed of manumission—you have only to sign.

He presents her with the deed.

LADY: I promised to sign it at dawn and here you are admitting, O Cadi, that it's still night.

CADI: Not so fast, woman! Your promise is inscribed in my head, word for word. Your exact words were: "When the Muezzin gives the call to dawn prayers." The whole matter now comes down to this question: have you or have you not heard the voice of the Muezzin?

LADY: I heard it, but if the dawn's still far off . . . .

CADI: The dawn as such is not in question—the promise related to the voice of the Muezzin as he gave the call to the dawn prayer. If the Muezzin has made a mistake in his calculation or conduct, it is he who is responsible for his mistake—that's his business. It's not ours. You understand?

LADY: I understand—it's not a bad trick!

CADI: The Muezzin will of course be prosecuted for his mistake. This, however, doesn't change the facts, which are that we have all heard the Muezzin giving the call to the dawn prayers from on top of his minaret. And so all the legal consequences deriving therefrom must take their course—immediately! Come along then and sign!

LADY: Is it thus that you interpret my one condition before manumitting the Sultan?

CADI: In the same manner as you interpreted our condition when you purchased the Sultan!

VIZIER: You have fallen into the very same snares of the law. Therefore, submit and sign!

LADY: This is not honest! It's sheer trickery!

VIZIER: Trickery matched by trickery! You began it—and he who begins is the greater offender. You are the last person to object and protest.

SULTAN [*shouting*]: Shame! Enough! Enough! Stop this nonsense! Cease this pettiness! She shall not sign. I absolutely refuse that she should sign this way. And you, Chief Cadi, aren't you ashamed of yourself for fooling around with the law like this?

CADI: Milord Sultan . . . .

SULTAN: I am disappointed. I am disappointed in you, Chief Cadi. Is this, in your opinion, the law? The expenditure of effort and skill in trickery and fraud!

CADI: Your Majesty, I merely wanted . . . .

SULTAN: To rescue me, I know that, but did you think I'd accept being rescued by such methods?

CADI: With such a woman, Your Majesty, we have the right . . . .

SULTAN: No, you have no right at all to do this. You have no such right. Maybe it was the right of this woman to indulge in trickery—she cannot be blamed if she did so; maybe she should be the object of indulgence because of her intelligence and skill. As for the Chief Cadi, the representative of justice, the defender of the sanctity of the law, the upright servant of the canonical law, it is one of his most bounden duties to preserve the law's purity, integrity, and majesty, whatever the price. It was you yourself who first showed me the virtue of the law and the respect it must be shown, who told me that it was the supreme power before which I myself must bow. And I have bowed down right to the end in all humility. But did it ever occur to me that I would see you yourself eventually regarding the law in this manner; stripping it of its robe of sanctity so that it becomes in your hands no more than wiles, clauses, words—a mere plaything?

CADI: Let me explain to you, Your Majesty. . . .

SULTAN: No, explain nothing. Go now! It's better for you to go home and betake yourself to bed until the morning. As for me I shall respect this lady's situation—in the true sense in which we all understand it. Let us go, milady! Let us return to your house! I am at your disposal.

LADY: No, Your Majesty.

SULTAN: No?

LADY: No, your Chief Cadi wanted to rescue you, and I don't want to be any less loyal than him toward you. You are now free, Your Majesty.

SULTAN: Free?

LADY: Yes, bring the deed of manumission, Chief Cadi, so that I may sign it.

CADI: You'll sign it now?

LADY: Yes, now.

CADI [*presenting her with the deed*]: God grant she's telling the truth!

LADY [*signing the deed*]: Believe me this time! There's my signature!

CADI [*examining the signature*]: Yes, despite everything you're a good woman.

SULTAN: Rather is she one of the most outstanding of women! The people of the city must respect her. That's an order, O Vizier!

VIZIER: I hear and obey, Your Majesty!

CADI [*folding up the deed*]: Everything has now been completed, Your Majesty, in first-class fashion.

SULTAN: And without a drop of blood being spilt—that's the important thing.

VIZIER: Thanks to your courage, Your Majesty. Who would imagine that to proceed to the end of this road would require more courage than that of the sword?

CADI: Truly!

SULTAN: Let us give praise to the generosity of this noble lady. Allow me, milady, to address my thanks to you, and I ask that you accept the return of your money to you, for there is no longer any reason why you should lose it. Vizier! Pay her from my private purse the amount which she has lost.

LADY: No, no, Your Majesty. Don't take away this honor from me. There are no riches in the world, in my opinion, to equal this beautiful memory on which I shall live for the whole of my life. With something so paltry I have participated in one of the greatest of events.

SULTAN: Good—as the memory has such significance for you, then keep this memento of it. [*He takes the enormous ruby from his turban.*]

VIZIER [*whispering*]: The ruby? The one without peer in the world?

SULTAN: Compared with your goodness, this is accounted a petty thing.

[*He presents her with the ruby.*]

LADY: No, dear Majesty, I don't deserve, am not worthy of this . . . this . . . .

SULTAN [*starting to leave*]: Farewell, good lady!

LADY [*with tears in her eyes*]: Farewell, dear Sultan!

SULTAN [*noticing her tears*]: Are you crying?

LADY: With joy!

SULTAN: I shall never forget that I was your slave for a night.

LADY: For the sake of principles and the law, Your Majesty! [*She lowers her head to hide her tears.*]

Music. The sultan's cortège moves off.

CURTAIN

Translated by Denys Johnson-Davies

The Tree Climber

—⟋⟍⟍—

Cast

the DETECTIVE

the MAIDSERVANT

the WIFE

the HUSBAND

the ASSISTANT TICKET INSPECTOR

the DERVISH

ACT ONE

There are no sets in this play, neither are there divisions between times and places, the past, present, and future sometimes all being present at the same time and one person occasionally present in two place on the stage and talking in his own voice twice at the same time. Here everything interlocks with everything else. There are no fixed 'props:' every character in the play makes his appearance carrying his 'props' and accessories and taking them out with him when he has finished. Thus the DETECTIVE *appears carrying his chair and file in his right hand, while behind him the old* MAIDSERVANT *makes her appearance carrying a light table which she places in front of him and on which he spreads out his papers.*

DETECTIVE: When exactly did your mistress disappear?

MAID: Just as the lizard returned to its lair.

DETECTIVE: You mean at sunset?

MAID: I didn't see the sun set.

DETECTIVE: And when does the lizard return to its lair?

MAID: When my master makes his appearance from under the tree.

DETECTIVE: And when does your master make his appearance from under the tree?

MAID: When my mistress calls to him.

DETECTIVE: And when does your mistress call to him?

MAID: When it gets chilly in the garden.

DETECTIVE: And when does it get chilly in the garden?

MAID: When my mistress tells him so.

DETECTIVE: And when does your mistress tell him so?

MAID: When I finish my work here and get ready to return home.

DETECTIVE: And why do you return home?

MAID: Because I always spend the night there with my husband who is blind and decrepit and whom I support.

DETECTIVE: And when you prepared to return home the day of the incident, your mistress was here?

MAID: No, she wasn't.

DETECTIVE: Where was she then?

MAID: She'd gone out.

DETECTIVE: Before calling to her husband as usual?

MAID: Yes, before calling to him. She left him in the garden.

DETECTIVE: Why?

MAID: She said she wouldn't be away more than half an hour—just as long as it takes to go down the road to buy a skein of wool with which to knit a little dress for her daughter.

DETECTIVE: Her daughter?

MAID: Yes, her daughter Bahiyya.

DETECTIVE: And where's her daughter Bahiyya?

MAID: She hasn't been born.

DETECTIVE: Hasn't been born? And when is she going to be born?

MAID: She won't be born.

DETECTIVE: And how do you know she won't be born?

MAID: It's only too well known.

DETECTIVE: But I don't know—tell me.

MAID: She was going to be born forty years ago, but she wasn't.

DETECTIVE: And why wasn't she born?

MAID: She was aborted in the fourth month, at her husband's request.

DETECTIVE: This husband of hers who's in the garden?

MAID: No, her first husband who died.

DETECTIVE: And her present husband hasn't had any children by her?

MAID: This present husband of hers married her when she was over fifty. That was nine years ago and she was past child-bearing.

DETECTIVE: Seeing that she is past child-bearing, that she has not had any children and won't do so, why should she be making a dress for her daughter who hasn't been born and won't be born?

MAID: She believes she is being born every day—and she is born every day.

DETECTIVE: And does she go out very much?

MAID: Sometimes, very occasionally, to do some shopping.

DETECTIVE: And she always returns—on time?

MAID: Oh yes, she is only away for as long as it takes to go down the road.

DETECTIVE: And this time she went out and didn't return?

MAID: No, she didn't.

DETECTIVE: Three days ago, roughly just before sunset?

MAID: Yes, just before sunset.

DETECTIVE [looking at his watch]: In an hour's time it will be about three nights and four days since her disappearance.

MAID: It never happened to her before.

DETECTIVE: It never happened that she spent the night away from home?

MAID: Never, not even half a night.

DETECTIVE: And you have been in service here for a long time?

MAID: For nine years—ever since her marriage to Bahadir Effendi. At that time he was still working.

DETECTIVE: And what do you know about the missing lady herself?

MAID: Madame Behana is well known in the district. This little house of hers was one of the first to be built in the whole suburb of Zeitoun—she inherited it from her first husband who was a broker.

DETECTIVE: I want you to give me any personal observations you have about her.

MAID: Personal observations?

DETECTIVE: Yes, things you have personally noticed about her.

MAID: Her whole mind's on her daughter.

DETECTIVE: And your master? Bahadir Effendi? What do you think of him?

MAID: His whole mind's on his tree.

DETECTIVE [*looking in the direction of the garden*]: His tree? This one?

MAID: Is there any other?

DETECTIVE: Certainly there's no other in this span of ground you call the garden. I believe it's an orange tree?

MAID: Yes, it's an orange tree, and at the base of its trunk is the sanctuary.

DETECTIVE: The sanctuary?

MAID: Yes, the sanctuary of the venerable Lady Green.

DETECTIVE: Who's Lady Green?

MAID: This same lizard. That's what he calls her. I've never seen her, but he sees her every day.

DETECTIVE: And apart from the tree and the lizard, what does he do?

MAID: Nothing. He's retired now. He left the railways five years ago.

DETECTIVE: And your mistress? She has no relations to whom she could have gone?

MAID: No, none at all. She is, you might say, a tree without roots.

DETECTIVE: Not even any acquaintances?

MAID: None.

DETECTIVE: You're sure?

MAID: Absolutely. All the time I've been here I haven't seen anyone visit them, nor have they paid anyone a visit.

The telephone rings.

DETECTIVE: That's the call I've been waiting for.

MAID [*hurries off*]: Just a moment, I'll bring you the telephone.

A little later she returns with a telephone on a long lead.

DETECTIVE [*into the telephone*]: Hullo. . . . Hullo! Yes . . . me . . . . That's odd! Nothing whatsoever? At all the police stations? You're sure? All the hospitals? And the first aid posts? A thorough search . . . ? No trace . . . ? Thanks.

He places the receiver and the instrument on top of the table.

MAID: They've found no trace?

DETECTIVE: None.

MAID: Poor Madame Behana.

DETECTIVE: Did no one get in touch with her by telephone before her disappearance?

MAID: No one.

DETECTIVE: And she, didn't she get in touch with anyone?

MAID: No one. This telephone has seldom been used since Bahadir Effendi retired. He asked the telephone company to install it while he was in the service and they would call him at night to go on shift or during the day when he was off for some job of work that cropped up. Since those days I've seldom heard it ring.

DETECTIVE: And the relationship between the couple?

MAID: The relationship?

DETECTIVE: Yes, were there any arguments between them, for example, or squabbles or disagreements?

MAID: None at all. Since I've been here I've never once seen them disagree about anything.

DETECTIVE: They never disagreed?

MAID: Not once.

DETECTIVE: But the situation as between a man and wife is not devoid of . . . .

MAID: Except where this husband and wife are concerned.

DETECTIVE: Are they all that . . . .

MAID: Yes, in absolute harmony. Would you like to see with your own eyes how they live?

DETECTIVE: Naturally I would, but how can that be done?

MAID: It's simple—just look over there and you'll see them.

DETECTIVE: Where?

MAID [*pointing*]: There—in that corner near the window overlooking the garden. That's my mistress Behana in her green dress which she never changes, seated in her usual chair.

At that moment the WIFE *actually makes her appearance. She is about sixty; her hair is white and her dress is green. She carries her chair and sits down on it. She begins knitting at a dress.*

WIFE [*turning to where the window is supposed to be*]: Come on, Bahadir! Leave your tree now and come inside! It's chilly outside.

HUSBAND [*he enters carrying gardening tools*]: I know. When it begins to turn chilly the venerable Lady Green goes into her sanctuary. But what I don't understand is that though there is no wind today yet some of the oranges are falling. What could have brought them down?

WIFE [*busy with knitting*]: It was I who brought her down. She was the first fruit and it was I, with my own hand, who aborted her. At that time he didn't want her. It was because of poverty—he didn't yet own anything, apart from the small grocery shop. He hadn't yet worked as a commission agent for land in this area, which was waste at that time. He said to me: "Have patience! Don't involve me now in the worry of having children."

HUSBAND [*cleaning the gardening tools*]: What really worries me is that there was no wind today and yet . . . .

WIFE: And yet I listened to what he had to say, and I did it. I did it myself—to myself. Then, after that, the winds of fortune blew, money came along, and we built this little house and this garden.

HUSBAND: This garden is not exposed to the force of the winds. Yet when the orange tree flowered I was frightened for the blossom, but God was kind and gracious.

WIFE: Yes, God was kind and gracious. We passed through the days of poverty and when good times came we sought to have children. But not a bit of it! Without doubt it was because the first abortion had affected my womb.

Yes, the first abortion was the cause without a doubt.

HUSBAND: Without a doubt this falling of the fruit is of no consequence—it was no more than three or four small green oranges the size of hazelnuts.

WIFE: It was in the fourth month. The child had formed, she had become the size of one's hand. I'm certain of that. . . .

HUSBAND: Yes, I'm certain of that, because the branches were moving extremely slowly. . . .

WIFE: Yes, she was moving inside me. I felt her moving. They were the movements of a girl. One can tell the way a girl moves, also I wanted her to be a girl. . . .

HUSBAND: I also wanted this slow movement, or no movement at all, because motionless branches stop any damage happening to the flowers and fruit in the early stage. . . .

WIFE: Yes, in the early stage of pregnancy I knew the name I'd give her: Bahiyya. And I knew she would be wonderfully good-looking and sturdily built. That's something one can know about, isn't it?

HUSBAND: Naturally, that's something one can know from the look of the fruit tightly clustered together at the stop of the branches like bunches of grapes—strong and hanging firmly together as though determined to survive, and grow.

WIFE: Grow . . . . Yes, how I wish I'd left her to grow. Do you know, my dear, had I left her to grow, what would have happened?

HUSBAND: I know exactly what happens: as growth increases so does the need for nourishment.

WIFE: Yes, good nourishment—that's what used to worry us at the time.

HUSBAND: And that's what worries me now. For the fruit to have really strong growth you've got to fertilize the tree with good fertilizer, and where can I find the money for good fertilizer? As you know, my pension is scarcely sufficient for our expenses—an inspector on the railways for forty years and I came out with no more than will shield us from the evils of destitution. Were it not for this little house of yours that gives us shelter, and this beautiful garden which is large enough for only one tree, our life would have no flavor. Yet, thanks to God and His blessings, there are no oranges on any other tree which can have such fine growth.

WIFE: I'm quite confident about that fine growth.

HUSBAND: Isn't it so? Look! Look! [*He points at the tree.*]

WIFE: Yes, I know. I'm quite confident about her fine growth. If only I had let her be. Look! Look! Here she is on her seventh day—just like a child a year old. This is the celebration of the seventh day after her birth. Look! Look! The candles! The candles! Listen! Listen! The pounding of the mortar! The pounding of the mortar! Do you hear the way they are singing?

Bargalatak . . . bargalatak.
Gold rings in your ears.
O Lord, our Lord, may you grow up
And become as big as us.
Bargalatak . . . bargalatak.

The sounds of the special party given on the seventh day after birth are heard: the words, the hubbub, and the pounding of the mortar.

HUSBAND [*after the sounds of the party have died away*]: The station bells . . . the clamor of the passengers . . . the din of the train! Always they are in my ears!

WIFE: Yes, in her ears. Did you see the gold rings in her ears?

HUSBAND: There's always that din in my ears. And I who thought I'd be at rest when I retired!

WIFE: Now I'm really at rest as I watch her seventh day party. What do you think of her green dress, the one I knitted for her with my own hands? Didn't it look lovely on her little body?

HUSBAND: Her little body is always attired in this green dress, summer and winter. Even when the tree is denuded of its green leaves she remains radiant in her greenness as she goes down to her sanctuary at the foot of the tree.

WIFE: Yes, yes, my dear, how beautiful Bahiyya is with the green dress over her little body!

HUSBAND: I always find her beautiful with her little body attired in perpetual greenness and that extraordinary brightness in her brilliant eyes. She's truly wonderful is Lady Green!

WIFE: Yes, she's truly wonderful is my daughter Bahiyya!

HUSBAND: Oh, yes.

WIFE: Oh, yes.

A deep silence reigns between the couple.

DETECTIVE [*to the* MAID]: Do they always talk together like that?

MAID: Oh, yes.

DETECTIVE: Oh, yes. [*to the* MAID] Thank you. Thank you.

MAID: May I go?

The MAID *leaves and the* DETECTIVE *turns toward the garden.*

DETECTIVE [*calling*]: Bahadir Effendi!

HUSBAND [*from outside*]: Yes.

DETECTIVE: Would you spare me a moment please?

HUSBAND [*appears wiping garden earth from his hands*]: Again?

DETECTIVE: Yes, a few more questions.

HUSBAND: First and foremost, I've got something to say, something strange
and extraordinary, utterly extraordinary.

DETECTIVE: Something, naturally, to do with the incident of the disappearance?

HUSBAND: Yes, the disappearance.

DETECTIVE: Please go ahead and tell me.

HUSBAND: She's disappeared. Can you imagine it?

DETECTIVE: We've know that for days.

HUSBAND: But I noticed it only today.

DETECTIVE: You only noticed your wife's disappearance today?

HUSBAND: I'm not talking about my wife.

DETECTIVE: About whom then?

HUSBAND: About the venerable Lady Green.

DETECTIVE: Ah, the lizard!

HUSBAND: She too has disappeared. Disappeared!

DETECTIVE: How do you know?

HUSBAND: She's nowhere in the garden.

DETECTIVE: Are you certain?

HUSBAND: Absolutely.

DETECTIVE: How can you be sure?

HUSBAND: I haven't seen her all day. I've kept watch on her sanctuary and she hasn't been in or out. She's positively not to be found there, nor in the whole of the garden. This is the first time it's happened to her in . . . nine years.

DETECTIVE: You've known this lizard for nine years?

HUSBAND: Yes, for nine years, ever since I set foot in this house . . . in this garden.

DETECTIVE: The very same one?

HUSBAND: Yes, the very same.

DETECTIVE: And can such a small lizard live for nine years?

HUSBAND: She has done so. I know her and have seen her every day for years.

DETECTIVE: Perhaps it was another lizard.

HUSBAND: There is no other lizard. It's her all right—I've never seen another lizard here.

DETECTIVE: But it's quite possible for you to see another lizard here.

HUSBAND: It has never happened. I have seen no other lizard. I've never seen another lizard with her. I've never seen two together. She's always on her own. Just she—unchanged. I'm sure of that. It's her all right. I know the way she moves, the way she glances about her, her gestures—also her features.

DETECTIVE: Her features?

HUSBAND: Yes, her features. For nine years I've been watching her every day. How, then, should I not know her features, how should I not have become her friend? I've got used to her presence, her proximity . . . I love her.

DETECTIVE: You love her?

HUSBAND: Yes, now I do. When you see something near to you every day over a period of nine years you inevitably get to know it, to love it, isn't that so? I don't deny that things weren't like this when I first set eyes on her. At that time I found her ugly-looking, horrible . . . abhorrent. I was about to kill her, then shelved the idea and let her live—temporarily.

Then I began to see her every day leaving her sanctuary and returning to it at regular times. I quickly got used to this and so I became attached to her—I arranged my life in the garden in accordance with her life, her ways and habits.

DETECTIVE: This is truly extraordinary.

HUSBAND: Yes, she has become a creature connected to me by the ties of kinship. Don't be surprised therefore that her disappearance is painful to me.

DETECTIVE: No, I'm not.

HUSBAND: No, when I think nowadays that I was going to kill her one day . . . . But it's natural that I should have wanted to kill her at that time, for I didn't know her properly.

DETECTIVE: The idea of killing did, then, occur to you?

HUSBAND: Certainly it did.

DETECTIVE: And with what would you have carried out the murder?

HUSBAND: Whose murder? My wife's?

DETECTIVE: Your wife? Did I so much as mention your wife? Oh, so be it! Your wife, then. Yes, your wife?

HUSBAND: But we were talking about the lizard.

DETECTIVE: That's enough talk for now about lizards. Let's talk about your wife. Have you ever felt a desire to kill her?

HUSBAND: Naturally.

DETECTIVE: What are you saying?

HUSBAND: I'm saying that this feeling is natural. Haven't you ever thought of killing your wife?

DETECTIVE: And you? You've thought of doing so?

HUSBAND: I'm asking you.

DETECTIVE: No, it's I who am asking you.

HUSBAND: You answer me first.

DETECTIVE: It's I who ask and you who answer—please. Don't reverse the roles!

HUSBAND: I am interested in knowing your feelings.

DETECTIVE: And I, by reason of my official position, am even more interested in knowing yours. Please, answer me. Haven't you ever thought of killing your wife?

HUSBAND: Why do you want me to kill my wife?

DETECTIVE: I don't want you to, it's you who said . . . .

HUSBAND: What did I say?

DETECTIVE: You said it was natural that you should think of killing your wife.

HUSBAND: Yes, it's natural in relation to me and to you.

DETECTIVE: Leave me out of this for now. Speak for yourself.

HUSBAND: Well, my opinion is that such thinking is natural when something about my wife annoys me.

DETECTIVE: And naturally something about her has annoyed you?

HUSBAND: No, it hasn't.

DETECTIVE: I have my doubts about that.

HUSBAND: And why should you?

DETECTIVE: Because I've just seen you both with my own eyes and heard you talking to each other.

HUSBAND: Don't you want a husband and wife to talk to each other?

DETECTIVE: Not that brand of talk!

HUSBAND: And what was wrong with it?

DETECTIVE: What was wrong was that this is something that cannot happen. . . .

HUSBAND: On the contrary, this is something which always happens between every husband and wife, in every household . . . with everyone . . . with you for example.

DETECTIVE: With me? No, my dear sir.

HUSBAND: Doesn't it happen with you?

DETECTIVE: Were that to happen with me I would have . . . .

HUSBAND: You'd have killed your wife?

DETECTIVE: I didn't say that.

HUSBAND: Do so! Say it openly—you'd have killed her.

DETECTIVE: Killed whom?

HUSBAND: Your wife, of course.

DETECTIVE: Please—we're now dealing with your wife.

HUSBAND: And yours?

DETECTIVE: I beg you, my dear sir! You've got nothing to do with my wife. My wife is still safe and sound at home.

HUSBAND: Fair enough! Then you excuse me—at least!

DETECTIVE: Excuse you?

HUSBAND: That's in effect what you've been saying.

DETECTIVE: You actually killed her then?

HUSBAND: Are you sure?

DETECTIVE: Almost.

HUSBAND: And do you know where her body is?

DETECTIVE: That's something you're naturally better informed about.

HUSBAND: It isn't difficult for you to find out.

DETECTIVE: It's better if you were to tell me.

HUSBAND: The place is very easy and ordinary—I'm surprised you haven't found out about it!

DETECTIVE: Where?

HUSBAND: Guess!

DETECTIVE: How can I?

HUSBAND: Can't you think of a suitable place to put her body?

DETECTIVE [*looking around him*]: Where? You tell me!

HUSBAND: Make a guess?

DETECTIVE: Guess?

HUSBAND: Yes, can't you guess?

DETECTIVE: I beseech you! We're not in the domain of riddles.

HUSBAND: Give up?

DETECTIVE: Yes.

HUSBAND [*pointing to the garden*]: Under the tree.

DETECTIVE [*turning in the direction of the tree*]: The orange tree?

HUSBAND: There is no doubt that this pleased her—that her whole body should be turned into fertilizer, fertilizer of an excellent quality with which to nourish this tree so that it will produce sturdily growing oranges . . . she who cares so much about sturdy growth.

DETECTIVE: I really should have thought of that.

HUSBAND: I told you to guess and probe around a bit and you'd have hit upon it yourself.

DETECTIVE: Then you confess?

HUSBAND: Confess to what?

DETECTIVE: That her body is buried under this tree?

HUSBAND: Don't you agree with me that this is the best place to put it?

DETECTIVE: As far as place is concerned, it is, doubtless, a beautiful one.

HUSBAND: And there she will be turned into splendid blossom and ripening fruit. Could a human body wish for anything better or more profitable?

DETECTIVE: In that respect you're right.

HUSBAND: Then you're of my opinion?

DETECTIVE: In so far as this poetical fancy is concerned, fair enough.

HUSBAND: We are in agreement then?

DETECTIVE: As good luck would have it!

HUSBAND: It's certainly lucky we have such similar views on things.

DETECTIVE: And thanks to this mutual understanding we have been able to arrive at quick results we'd have been unlikely to achieve for weeks or perhaps months.

HUSBAND: Thanks be to God!

DETECTIVE: However, the credit for the greater part of this success is due to your help!

HUSBAND: My help?

DETECTIVE: Without doubt. Would it have been possible for anyone by himself to find out the whereabouts of the body with such speed? [*He gets up.*]

HUSBAND: Are you going?

DETECTIVE: I want a spade. Bring me a spade!

HUSBAND: A spade? What'll you do with it?

DETECTIVE: We'll dig with it, of course.

HUSBAND: You'll dig?

DETECTIVE: Yes, under this tree.

HUSBAND: You'll dig under my orange tree? Have you gone mad, Detective-Inspector?

DETECTIVE: I'm sorry, but it's necessary.

HUSBAND: What's necessary about it?

DETECTIVE: We can't carry out our job of work without digging, that's obvious.

HUSBAND: Do you wish to destroy my tree? Do you know what this tree means to me?

DETECTIVE: I do.

HUSBAND: To my whole life in fact?

DETECTIVE: I do, but it's a question of a body and a case of murder.

HUSBAND: It's my body . . . my own body, and the spade which strikes at the trunk of the tree will be striking at my neck. Do you understand that? Do you understand?

DETECTIVE [*gruffly*]: The spade! Where's the spade?

HUSBAND [*attempting to seat him*]: You're killing me. You'll kill me—you're committing murder!

DETECTIVE: It's you who's committed murder, the murder of your wife.

HUSBAND: Murder of my wife? What's this madness, Detective-Inspector?

DETECTIVE: Haven't you just confessed to it?

HUSBAND: I confessed?

DETECTIVE: Didn't you just say you'd buried her under the tree after having killed her?

HUSBAND: I talked about burying but I didn't say anything about killing.

DETECTIVE: You mean you buried her but you didn't kill her?

HUSBAND: I didn't kill her.

DETECTIVE: But you buried her?

HUSBAND: That's another matter—one between her and me. However, I didn't kill her.

DETECTIVE: And who did?

HUSBAND: Has she been killed?

DETECTIVE: You know best, seeing as how you've buried her.

HUSBAND: Has she really been buried?

DETECTIVE: Listen! I've been more patient with you than I ought—and more open with you too—but I'm not going to go on putting up with being made a fool of. Do you understand?

HUSBAND: Calm yourself, Inspector, and have confidence in my good intentions. Let's talk, as we were doing a moment ago, in a spirit of mutual understanding. I'm ready to speak frankly with you about everything.

DETECTIVE: That's fine, then tell me everything.

HUSBAND: Tell me first. Why do you accuse me of killing my wife?

DETECTIVE: All the circumstances point to it.

HUSBAND: And why should I kill her?

DETECTIVE: For a very obvious reason. Your life with her was unbearable.

HUSBAND: My life with her unbearable?

DETECTIVE: Without a doubt—life with such a woman would be unbearable.

HUSBAND: That's your opinion.

DETECTIVE: That's everyone's opinion. There's not a person who could bear life with such a woman.

HUSBAND: But I've been living with her happily and comfortably for nine years. We didn't have a disagreement about anything.

DETECTIVE: Nor an agreement about anything.

HUSBAND: I didn't notice that.

DETECTIVE: But I did.

HUSBAND: Yet I don't complain of anything.

DETECTIVE: The fact that you don't complain isn't evidence of contentment.

HUSBAND: Then what is it evidence of?

DETECTIVE: Of despair.

HUSBAND: Quite the contrary—I live only in hope.

DETECTIVE: Hope of getting rid of your wife?

HUSBAND: Be sure I haven't even thought of getting rid of her.

DETECTIVE: It isn't necessary for you to have frankly and directly thought about it. It's sufficient that the idea should momentarily pass through your mind.

HUSBAND: Possibly, but I quickly forget my fleeting thoughts.

DETECTIVE: It seems so to you, but the idea remains for ever secretly working away, like a seed.

HUSBAND: And what does it work away at secretly?

DETECTIVE: At searching for a way in which to be rid of her.

HUSBAND: Be rid of my wife? But that's not what I want.

DETECTIVE: You do, and you strive for what you want without realizing it or voicing it.

HUSBAND: And why should I do that?

DETECTIVE: Because you're an unhappy husband.

HUSBAND: No, I'm a happy one.

DETECTIVE: That's not true.

HUSBAND: I assure you I'm happy.

DETECTIVE: And I assure you you're not.

HUSBAND: How can you assure me? Are you the husband or am I?

DETECTIVE: It's of no consequence—there's a barometer for marital happiness that doesn't tell lies.

HUSBAND: What's that?

DETECTIVE: Mutual understanding.

HUSBAND: And we have mutual understanding?

DETECTIVE: What I saw and heard occurring between the two of you a moment ago, can that be called mutual understanding?

HUSBAND: What then would you call it?

DETECTIVE: I would call it, quite simply, lack of understanding.

HUSBAND: And I call it understanding.

DETECTIVE: This cannot be understanding.

HUSBAND: Then you and I have no mutual understanding about understanding.

DETECTIVE: Because you call things by their wrong name.

HUSBAND: Names are of no importance to me. My wife and I have mutual understanding and our home is founded upon it.

DETECTIVE: That's falsifying the meaning of things.

HUSBAND: The meaning of things? What are these meanings? You want me to regard understanding and happiness as you comprehend them and not as I do.

DETECTIVE: As everyone comprehends them.

HUSBAND: And what business of mine is everyone? I'm talking about myself. Everyone isn't a husband to my wife—I alone am the husband.

DETECTIVE: You're a happy husband, then?

HUSBAND: Very.

DETECTIVE: And she—she's a happy wife?

HUSBAND: Very.

DETECTIVE: Then why has she left the matrimonial home and disappeared?

HUSBAND: That's what I don't know.

DETECTIVE: There are, I tell you, many possibilities: either she's been hurt in an accident—and the reports from hospitals and police stations rule that out; or she's been kidnapped, which is improbable as who in their right mind would kidnap a poor old woman who's not worth anything? Or else she's gone to one of her friends or relatives, which is also improbable as it's been shown she's out of touch with friends and relatives. Or else it's murder, which you now deny.

HUSBAND: Of course I deny it.

DETECTIVE: Of course. Then what's your explanation of the disappearance?

HUSBAND: I know of no explanation.

DETECTIVE: There must be an explanation.

HUSBAND: And what's the explanation of the disappearance of the venerable Lady Green?

DETECTIVE: Enough of that lizard for now!

HUSBAND: It's very important. If we find the explanation for her disappearance, we'll find the explanation for my wife's disappearance.

DETECTIVE: What's the connection?

HUSBAND: That would take too long to explain.

DETECTIVE: Please do so.

HUSBAND: That would be useless—you wouldn't understand me. You only understand what you find comprehensible, and your job is to ask clearly defined questions to which you want to receive clearly defined answers. I, for a long time, have directed no questions at anyone—nor expected answers from anyone.

DETECTIVE: Indeed, I didn't see you ask a single direct question of your wife—or ask her for an answer to a question.

HUSBAND: From this you'll realize the headache that afflicts me now that I'm involved in questions and answers.

DETECTIVE: I'm sorry to place you in this position, but how do you want a detective to detect and investigate without asking questions and expecting answers?

HUSBAND: Indeed, I feel sorry for you and the job of work you have to do.

DETECTIVE: Is there another method of arriving at the truth?

HUSBAND: What truth?

DETECTIVE: The truth of this disappearance, for instance?

HUSBAND: It's for you to arrive at that. That's your business—I'm merely the husband.

DETECTIVE: The husband of the woman who's disappeared. Yes, but isn't it natural for the husband of the woman who's disappeared to be concerned about knowing the truth as to his wife's disappearance?

HUSBAND: I am concerned.

DETECTIVE: You don't look it.

HUSBAND: How do you want me to look?

DETECTIVE: Worried . . . disturbed.

HUSBAND: I lost that habit a long time ago.

DETECTIVE: Can someone lose the habit of being worried and disturbed?

HUSBAND: Yes, when you've been an inspector on the railways for thirty or forty years.

DETECTIVE: What do you mean?

HUSBAND: I mean that an inspector on a train is the only one among the passengers who is neither worried nor disturbed about the train being late or whether or not it will arrive.

DETECTIVE: But there must be something that can make you worried and disturbed?

HUSBAND: Occasionally the station bell and the whistle of a train upset me a little—especially when I'm asleep or half asleep.

DETECTIVE: Only the station bell and the whistle of a train?

HUSBAND: Especially the whistle of a train.

DETECTIVE: That's odd!

HUSBAND [cupping his ear to listen]: Listen! It's the train's whistle! Do you hear it?

DETECTIVE: No.

HUSBAND: How is it you can't hear it? The train's approaching. There—don't you see it?

DETECTIVE: Where?

HUSBAND [pointing to a part of the stage]: There! Look! Look!

DETECTIVE [looking in the direction in which the other is pointing]: Oh, yes.

HUSBAND: You've seen it!

DETECTIVE [looking]: Yes, it really is the train.

The whistle and sound of the train is heard.

HUSBAND: Soon I shall begin checking the tickets.

DETECTIVE [*looking at where the other is pointing*]: I don't see you.

HUSBAND: I haven't put in an appearance yet. You'll see me soon enough.

A uniformed employee makes his appearance on that side of the stage. He is carrying part of a carriage window which he sets up. He then brings a chair, places it by the window and seats himself on it. He begins yawning.

DETECTIVE [*looking at the* HUSBAND]: Who's that?

HUSBAND: That's the Inspector's assistant—my assistant. He's a lazy fellow, as you can see. He likes to sit and sleep by the window. Were it not for the strict watch I keep on him he'd be even more negligent in the performance of his duties.

DETECTIVE: Where are you then?

HUSBAND: Going about my job, of course.

DETECTIVE: Where?

HUSBAND: In the train itself—in some other carriage no doubt. My responsibilities are formidable and require my being constantly on the alert.

DETECTIVE: Of course.

HUSBAND [*pointing at the train*]: Here I am coming along to surprise Mr. Assistant snoring away fast asleep!

DETECTIVE [*looking*]: That's right, there you are in your uniform!

The INSPECTOR, *Bahadir Effendi, appears dressed in uniform. Only his back is seen. It is necessary that his voice should be identical, though emanating from two different parts of the stage.*

INSPECTOR [*rapping his clippers on the back of the chair*]: Asleep, Mr. Assistant?

ASSISTANT [*starting up*]: Mr. Inspector?

INSPECTOR: Did I wake you from pleasant dreams?

ASSISTANT: I wasn't dreaming.

INSPECTOR: That's your affair: to dream or not to dream. The important thing is you were asleep.

ASSISTANT: I wasn't asleep. Just a moment ago I sat down to have a rest.

INSPECTOR: It's of no consequence, let's leave that for now. Have you checked through all the carriages?

ASSISTANT: Yes, all of them, sir.

INSPECTOR: And did you inform me of the result?

ASSISTANT: I did, sir.

INSPECTOR: At what time was this?

ASSISTANT: A quarter of an hour ago.

INSPECTOR: And where was I?

ASSISTANT: In an empty compartment in the first class.

INSPECTOR: And did I give you my signature?

ASSISTANT: No, sir.

INSPECTOR: And the reason?

ASSISTANT: I was frightened of rousing you.

INSPECTOR: Rousing me! Was I . . . asleep?

ASSISTANT: You were looking out of the window.

INSPECTOR: Then I wasn't asleep?

ASSISTANT: You were counting the trees in flight from the train.

INSPECTOR: Did you hear me?

ASSISTANT: Yes. You were saying: I want this tree . . . and this one . . . and this one . . . and this one. Catch me one of these trees in flight from the train. This is one . . . this the second . . . this the third . . . this the fourth . . . this the fifth . . . and this . . . and this . . . and so on.

INSPECTOR: You heard all that?

ASSISTANT: Not only today, Mr. Inspector.

INSPECTOR: You mean I do this every day?

ASSISTANT: Yes, every day.

INSPECTOR: Then you're spying on me?

ASSISTANT: I don't do so on purpose.

INSPECTOR: Why didn't you bring it to my attention?

ASSISTANT: I tried to, but you were in a state of . . . .

INSPECTOR: A state of what?

ASSISTANT: Of inner harmony . . . I mean of absorption.

INSPECTOR: It's no matter! Let's have your report.

The ASSISTANT *presents the report to the* INSPECTOR. *As he does so the sound of children singing is heard from afar.*

CHILDREN'S VOICES: *Oh tree climber bring me a cow with you. Make it and feed me with a china spoon.*

INSPECTOR [*to the* ASSISTANT]: What's that?

ASSISTANT: A school outing in the second class.

INSPECTOR: How many are there?

ASSISTANT: A hundred pupils—the number's recorded exactly on the paper here.

INSPECTOR [*going through the paper*]: Is this last figure the total number of passengers?

ASSISTANT: Yes, all the passengers on the train.

INSPECTOR: All of them have tickets?

ASSISTANT: Yes.

INSPECTOR: You didn't catch any passenger without one?

ASSISTANT: No, apart from . . . .

INSPECTOR: Apart from?

ASSISTANT: Apart from that dervish.

INSPECTOR: Dervish?

ASSISTANT: Yes, I found a dervish man who didn't have a ticket.

INSPECTOR: And you took the appropriate procedures against him?

ASSISTANT: No.

INSPECTOR: And the reason?

ASSISTANT: He spoke of things I didn't understand.

INSPECTOR: And is that a reason for not taking the appropriate procedures against him?

ASSISTANT: I waited till I could refer the case to you.

INSPECTOR: And why didn't you refer his case to me?

ASSISTANT: I was on the point of doing so.

INSPECTOR: When? After you woke up?

ASSISTANT: Not after *I* woke up.

INSPECTOR: I would ask you to take the trouble to go off and bring him to me right away.

ASSISTANT: Right away. [*He departs.*]

INSPECTOR: What a cheek! [*He sits himself in the chair and looks out of the carriage window and sings.*]

Oh tree climber bring me a cow with you.
Oh cow climber bring me a tree with you.
Bring me a tree with you. Bring me a tree with you.

The DETECTIVE *whispers to the* HUSBAND.

DETECTIVE: You turn the words upside down to suit yourself.

HUSBAND: The words come out of my mouth to suit themselves.

DETECTIVE: Without your being conscious of them?

HUSBAND: As you see, I look out of the window and think about nothing.

DETECTIVE: But you are looking at the trees.

HUSBAND: Indeed.

DETECTIVE: Here's your assistant returning with the man.

HUSBAND: Yes.

The ASSISTANT *appears with the* DERVISH.

ASSISTANT: I've brought him, Mr. Inspector.

INSPECTOR [*to the* DERVISH]: What station did you get on at, reverend sir?

DERVISH: I didn't get on at any station.

INSPECTOR: You mean you got on between stations?

DERVISH: Of course.

INSPECTOR: Was the train stationary or proceeding at a slow pace?

DERVISH: It was going along at its usual speed.

INSPECTOR: Extraordinary! You were able to get on while it was going?

DERVISH: Naturally, like everyone else.

INSPECTOR: Like everyone? Does everyone get on while it's going?

DERVISH: And get off while it's going, too.

INSPECTOR: What sort of people are these?

DERVISH: Everyone.

INSPECTOR: And where's your ticket?

DERVISH: To hand.

INSPECTOR [*stretching out his hand*]: May I have it?

DERVISH [*producing a piece of paper*]: Here you are.

INSPECTOR [*examining it*]: This is a birth certificate.

DERVISH: My birth certificate.

INSPECTOR: But I want your ticket for the journey.

DERVISH: That's my ticket for the journey.

INSPECTOR: I want the ticket by which you travel on the train.

DERVISH: This is the ticket by which I travel on the train.

INSPECTOR: Which train?

DERVISH: The main-line train.

INSPECTOR: What main-line train?

DERVISH: The main-line train which departed before this branch-line one. Don't you know that?

INSPECTOR: Listen. I don't understand such talk. Give me the ticket by which you're traveling on this train of mine.

DERVISH: And if I don't give you the ticket?

INSPECTOR: Proceedings will be brought against you.

DERVISH: And what are these proceedings?

INSPECTOR: Payment of the price of the ticket plus a fine.

DERVISH: And if I don't have any money?

INSPECTOR: I'll put you off the train at the first station and hand you over to the station master.

DERVISH: And what will the station master do with me?

INSPECTOR: He'll hand over to the police.

DERVISH: And what will the police do with me?

INSPECTOR: They'll file a case against you and send you to be tried.

DERVISH: And what will be the outcome of being tried?

INSPECTOR: You'll be sentenced to pay a fine.

DERVISH: And if I don't pay the fine?

INSPECTOR: You'll be put in prison.

DERVISH: And what shall I do in prison?

INSPECTOR: You'll do nothing.

DERVISH: I do nothing now.

INSPECTOR: You want me, then, to take proceedings against you?

DERVISH: And why should you take proceedings against me?

INSPECTOR: Because you're traveling without a ticket.

DERVISH: Do you want a ticket?

INSPECTOR: Yes.

DERVISH: One ticket?

INSPECTOR: Of course one—after all you're one passenger.

DERVISH: Here are ten tickets for you!

He stretches his hand out of the window into space and produces ten tickets which he hands to the INSPECTOR.

INSPECTOR [*in surprise*]: What's all this?

DERVISH: Examine them well—they're genuine, aren't they?

INSPECTOR [*scrutinizing the ten tickets in astonishment*]: Indeed. . . . Indeed, they're all genuine . . . but . . . but where did you get them from?

DERVISH: That's my business.

INSPECTOR: And what shall I do with all these tickets?

DERVISH: Didn't you ask for a ticket? Here are some then.

INSPECTOR [*returning nine of them*]: Just one's enough. What about the rest?

DERVISH: Distribute the rest among those passengers who haven't got one.

INSPECTOR: There was no one but you who didn't have a ticket.

DERVISH: Then you don't need the remaining nine?

INSPECTOR: No.

DERVISH: Give them back to me then.

The INSPECTOR *returns them to him in amazement.*

DERVISH [*throwing them out of the window*]: There you are, I've sent them back whence they came.

INSPECTOR: And where did they come from?

DERVISH: That's my business.

INSPECTOR: But that's remarkable!

DERVISH: It's exceedingly simple. Getting hold of tickets for this train of yours is a most simple matter. [*He laughs.*] Tickets for this train of yours?— nothing simpler.

INSPECTOR: You are a man blessed with powers from God. The veil of the invisible has been lifted from before you. Will you allow me to sit beside you for a while?

DERVISH: Don't put questions to me! You can, though, make any request of me you want.

INSPECTOR: Do you know what I ask of life?

DERVISH [*singing*]:

Oh tree climber bring me a cow with you
Milk it and feed me with a china spoon.

INSPECTOR: It seems you know.

DERVISH: He who knows doesn't need to be told.

INSPECTOR: Then there's no need for me to explain?

DERVISH: There in the suburb of Zeitoun . . . .

INSPECTOR: The suburb of Zeitoun?

DERVISH: There you will find . . . .

INSPECTOR: Find what?

DERVISH: The tree. In winter it produces oranges, in spring apricots, in summer figs and in autumn pomegranates.

INSPECTOR: A single tree?

DERVISH: A single one. Everything is one—there: the tree and the cow and venerable Lady Green. . . .

INSPECTOR: Lady Green?

DERVISH: Everything is green, everything is green.

INSPECTOR: Everything is green? Those are reassuring words.

DERVISH: Just for a time. . . .

INSPECTOR: Do you see something unpleasant?

DERVISH: Don't put questions to me! I told you: don't put questions to me!

INSPECTOR: There is a question I simply must put to you: will you permit me to be one of your disciples?

DERVISH: Why?

INSPECTOR: Because when I'm near you I feel a sense of security.

DERVISH: You're in no need of a sense of security. Anyone who takes a train without anxiously looking forward to the destination always has a sense of security.

INSPECTOR: That's true, but . . . .

DERVISH: But you look out of the window too much, and thus, when you do so, you see the trees fleeing by.

INSPECTOR: That's also true but . . . .

The train whistles.

DERVISH: Your work calls you, Mr. Inspector.

INSPECTOR: My work has begun to bore me. Thirty-five years on the railways. Aren't I entitled to be bored?

DERVISH: But the train doesn't get bored.

INSPECTOR: Because it doesn't know what boredom is.

DERVISH: It knows only locomotion . . . motion . . . motion . . . motion . . . motion. Wouldn't you be better off as a train?

INSPECTOR: I used to be a train.

DERVISH: When you were a child?

INSPECTOR: Yes.

DERVISH: And you didn't feel bored?

INSPECTOR: No.

DERVISH: Yes, how delightful were those days when we were trains!

INSPECTOR: We would hang on to each other's coat-tails and spend the whole day going along the roads, whistling and blowing out imaginary smoke from our small tireless mouths.

DERVISH: The train doesn't tire. It's the passengers who get tired.

INSPECTOR: And when we grew up we were no longer suitable for being trains.

DERVISH: And weariness set in and boredom too!

INSPECTOR: Yes.

DERVISH: Go off to your work, Mr. Inspector

INSPECTOR: Don't you want me to stay and talk to you?

DERVISH: Off to your work, Mr. Inspector! To your work!

The HUSBAND *to the* DETECTIVE.

HUSBAND: Why does this man get annoyed with me?

DETECTIVE: Be quiet and let me hear what answer you give him!

HUSBAND: But I shan't answer, I'm getting ready to go off to my work.

DETECTIVE: On the contrary, you're getting ready to speak. Look!

HUSBAND: Indeed, but what could I possibly say now?

DETECTIVE: That's something you don't know, but he knows—by which I mean that you do.

HUSBAND: I don't know it and yet I know it?

DETECTIVE: Here you are speaking.

HUSBAND: I haven't spoken. I have nothing to say.

DETECTIVE: There! Look! Look! You're speaking!

The INSPECTOR *speaks.*

INSPECTOR: Reverend sir, save me, for God's sake save me!

DERVISH: Save you?

INSPECTOR: Yes, save me from a person who upsets me.

DERVISH: He's always with you.

INSPECTOR: Yes.

DERVISH: Sometimes you don't understand what he wants.

INSPECTOR: I don't understand what he wants.

DERVISH: Yet he upsets you.

INSPECTOR: He upsets me and frightens me and I'm afraid one day he'll lead me astray.

DERVISH: Yes, I know.

The DETECTIVE *to the* HUSBAND.

DETECTIVE: Who is that person who upsets you and you're afraid will one day lead you astray?

HUSBAND: I don't know.

DETECTIVE: But it's you who are saying so.

HUSBAND: I don't know why I say it.

DETECTIVE: But as I see it the dervish knows.

HUSBAND: Doubtless he does.

DETECTIVE: What way is there of finding out about this point?

HUSBAND: I don't know the way.

DETECTIVE: If only we were able to ask this dervish.

HUSBAND: Do you want to ask him?

DETECTIVE: There's no doubt he's capable of shedding some light.

HUSBAND: He would be able to, certainly.

DETECTIVE: And where is he now?

HUSBAND [*pointing to a part of the train*]: In front of you—on the train.

DETECTIVE: And how can we get hold of him?

HUSBAND: If you want, let's summon him. But the train, as you see, is on the move.

DETECTIVE: And the solution?

HUSBAND: Let's wait a while till the train stops at the next station.

The DERVISH *to the* INSPECTOR *in the train.*

DERVISH: Why do you want to summon me to appear before the police?

INSPECTOR: I want to? There's no longer any necessity—you've got your ticket.

DERVISH: You still want to.

INSPECTOR: Why?

DERVISH: I don't know exactly—perhaps for the purpose of giving evidence.

INSPECTOR: Evidence?

DERVISH: Giving evidence in a case.

INSPECTOR: To do with me?

DERVISH: Yes, to do with you.

INSPECTOR: When would that be?

DERVISH: I don't yet know.

INSPECTOR: But I am now with you here.

DERVISH: Not here.

INSPECTOR: Where, then?

DERVISH: There, in the suburb of Zeitoun.

HUSBAND: The suburb of Zeitoun.

DERVISH: In your house, your wife's house.

INSPECTOR: My wife? But I haven't married yet.

DERVISH: There's no point in waiting for the train to stop at the next station. I'd better go to you there.

The DERVISH *rises from his place and goes out of the carriage, leaving the* INSPECTOR *astonished at his disappearance.*

INSPECTOR: Reverend sir. Reverend sir, where have you gone? Where have you disappeared to?

He leans out of the carriage window looking for him, but the DERVISH *is groping his way with fumbling steps to the side of the stage where the* DETECTIVE *and the* HUSBAND *are. At the same time the whistle and clamor of the departing train is heard, followed by the disappearance of the* INSPECTOR, *the window and the chair. Nothing remains but the* DETECTIVE, *seated before his table, and the* HUSBAND. *Then the* DERVISH *appears and slowly approaches them.*

DERVISH: Peace be upon you!

DETECTIVE: And upon you be peace and the mercy of God!

DERVISH: You asked for me to be summoned.

DETECTIVE: Yes.

HUSBAND: You came with the utmost speed, reverend sir.

DERVISH: I saw no point in keeping you waiting.

HUSBAND [*giving up his chair to the* DERVISH]: Please be seated, reverend sir.

DERVISH [*looking around him*]: Is this the house?

HUSBAND: Yes.

DERVISH [*turning in the direction of the garden*]: And the tree's over there?

HUSBAND: Yes.

DERVISH [*pointing to the* DETECTIVE]: And the gentleman's from the police?

HUSBAND: Yes.

DERVISH: It's a pleasure to meet you.

DETECTIVE: We are in need of your assistance.

DERVISH: I'm at your service.

DETECTIVE: Have you any information on the subject?

DERVISH: What subject?

DETECTIVE: His wife's disappearance?

DERVISH [*to the* HUSBAND]: You did it then?

HUSBAND: What do you mean?

DERVISH: You know what I mean.

HUSBAND: No. Please, reverend sir, we are in the presence of a detective and every word of yours could be interpreted in a way you don't intend.

DERVISH: You're right.

DETECTIVE: What did he do?

DERVISH: Did I say he'd done something?

DETECTIVE: You said to him "You did it then?" What did he do?

DERVISH: Don't put questions to me! Make any request you want, but don't put questions to me!

DETECTIVE: I'm a detective and in order to investigate I must inevitably put questions.

DERVISH: Your investigation is no business of mine. If you want something of me, request it, but don't put questions!

DETECTIVE: Then, I'd like your opinion about his wife's disappearance. That's a request and not a question.

DERVISH: His wife?

DETECTIVE: Yes, I'm requesting your opinion about her disappearance.

DERVISH: His wife—either he has killed her or else he hasn't yet killed her.

HUSBAND [*shouting*]: What's this you're saying, reverend sir?

DERVISH: Have you killed her?

HUSBAND: I? God forbid, sir!

DERVISH: Then you haven't killed her yet?

HUSBAND: What are you saying, man?

DETECTIVE: It is your opinion then, sir, that he killed her?

DERVISH: Either he has killed her or else he has not yet killed her.

DETECTIVE: In any event, then, her fate is to be killed?

DERVISH: Yes.

DETECTIVE: At the hands of this man, her husband?

DERVISH: Yes.

DETECTIVE [*to the* HUSBAND]: What have you to say now?

HUSBAND [*shouting*]: This man's a charlatan, a liar, a fraud and a windbag.

DETECTIVE: But up till this moment you had confidence in him, you wanted to be a disciple of his.

HUSBAND: He's accusing me falsely, without justification.

DETECTIVE: He must have some justification.

HUSBAND: None except that he bears me a grudge for having asked him for a ticket.

DETECTIVE: That's not a cause for a serious grudge—and even then he presented you with ten tickets instead of one.

DERVISH: Tell him, officer! Tell him!

HUSBAND: Why do you accuse me of killing my wife?

DERVISH: I don't accuse, I see.

HUSBAND: You see that I killed her?

DERVISH: If you haven't killed her, you will kill her.

HUSBAND: You see that?

DERVISH: Yes.

HUSBAND: And why didn't you inform me of this vision of yours when we met on the train?

DERVISH: I hadn't seen it then.

HUSBAND: But you saw the suburb of Zeitoun, you saw me with the tree and a wife?

DERVISH: Yes, I saw that.

HUSBAND: And you didn't see the killing?

DERVISH: The train had not brought me to where I could see further than I had seen.

HUSBAND: What train?

DERVISH: My train.

HUSBAND: You're muddled, reverend sir.

DERVISH: I only say what I see, and if I have seen then I say.

HUSBAND: And why should I kill my wife?

DETECTIVE: Permit me to say that it is no concern of a witness to answer that. The motives for the commission of a crime may be found at all times and in every form.

HUSBAND: I love my wife.

DETECTIVE: And you love the tree more than her.

HUSBAND: She used not to complain of that.

DETECTIVE: But the tree used to complain of being undernourished.

HUSBAND: What do you mean?

DETECTIVE: It was you who were saying so a little while ago.

HUSBAND: I don't understand what you're driving at?

DETECTIVE: Let's leave all that for now and talk about the characteristics of trees—and let's bring our reverend friend into the discussion. He no doubt knows a lot about them.

DERVISH: No, very little.

DETECTIVE: Your very little will do us fine, reverend sir. What if I were to ask you your opinion about a method by which an orange tree for example makes great growth?

DERVISH: It is said that there is a tree that gives oranges in winter, apricots in spring, figs in summer and pomegranates in autumn.

HUSBAND: One tree that gives all that?

DERVISH: Yes, one tree.

HUSBAND: One tree combining all these contradictions? Is that feasible? Could it possibly happen? I declare, officer, that this man is joking. Where would such a tree be found?

DERVISH: In any place you like—perhaps your tree is such a one.

HUSBAND: This tree of mine, this orange tree could do that?

DERVISH: Don't you know—didn't I tell you about it on the train?

HUSBAND: I thought you were joking and making fun.

DERVISH: I know nothing of joking and making fun.

HUSBAND: This tree of mine could give all these different fruits at the different seasons?

DERVISH: If you nourished it with the fertilizer you know.

HUSBAND: What fertilizer do you mean?

DERVISH: If the complete body of a human being were buried underneath it, then it would be nourished with all the contradictions it contains.

HUSBAND: I didn't know that.

DERVISH: But you did.

HUSBAND: Perhaps I heard something like that from him or someone else, but I paid no heed to it.

DETECTIVE: It's sufficient if some of it infiltrated into your being.

HUSBAND: Even so, what is the conclusion you want to arrive at?

DETECTIVE: I think the motive for the crime has begun to become apparent.

HUSBAND: Please be so good as to be explicit, officer.

DETECTIVE: There is no longer any need for being explicit. Confess—it's the best thing you can do.

HUSBAND: Confess what?

DETECTIVE: That you killed your wife and buried her under this tree.

HUSBAND: In order to nourish the tree with her so that in winter it might give oranges, in spring apricots, in summer figs and in autumn pomegranates?

DETECTIVE: After all, it's not a bad objective.

HUSBAND: Had I done that, do you think I could be regarded as being in possession of my full mental faculties?

DETECTIVE: The question of your mental faculties is the domain of the court. It's the court who'll examine that. My task is to investigate the crime and get your confession. The best thing you can do is to confess—especially after the witness's evidence.

HUSBAND: What witness?

DETECTIVE: This reverend gentleman.

HUSBAND: This man who came to us out of the air?

DETECTIVE: Whether out of the air or from outer space, he gave reliable evidence.

HUSBAND: That I killed my wife in order to nourish the tree? That's an absurd, fatuous motive. Could it occur to a man in our present age?

DETECTIVE: Have you some other motive worthy of our present age? I'm ready both to hear and adopt it.

HUSBAND: It's I who am ready to hear any reasonable motive, or at least one that isn't nonsensical, that would induce a man of our age to kill his wife. Then—fair enough—ascribe it to me.

DETECTIVE: You want to know why a man of our age should kill his wife?

HUSBAND: Yes. Tell me the most important motives and I'll choose the one that appeals to me.

DETECTIVE: Here they are then, sir. Firstly, marital infidelity.

HUSBAND: That's ruled out. I'm sixty-five and my wife's sixty and neither of us is any longer physically attractive.

DETECTIVE: Secondly: greed for wealth.

HUSBAND: That too is ruled out. She is poor and possesses nothing but this house which, as you can see, is very small. It would be ridiculous of me to kill her for it—there's no necessity at all for that.

DETECTIVE: Thirdly: incompatibility of temperament.

HUSBAND: That's no reason for murder.

DETECTIVE: On the contrary, it's one of the most important motives for modern murder. Haven't you heard of the murder case in which the husband strangled his wife because she always liked to ask him questions, and of the wife who poisoned her husband because he always refused to give an opinion about her hairstyle?

HUSBAND: My wife neither asks me nor I her about anything—you've seen for yourself. Neither does she nor I possess hair deserving of a style or the giving of an opinion!

DERVISH [*to the* HUSBAND]: Rest assured! Where you're concerned, murder is done for a very modern motive.

HUSBAND: That's really the limit, sir!

DERVISH: My sole aim is to put your heart at rest—your motive is in keeping with the philosophy of the age.

HUSBAND: The philosophy of the age?

DERVISH: Murder for philosophical motives is a common thing in our modern age.

HUSBAND: I killed my wife for a philosophical motive? That really was all that was missing, reverend sir!

DERVISH: Calm yourself! Calm yourself!

HUSBAND: I'm quite calm, but I'd like to draw your attention to the fact that I know nothing of the word philosophy, except for such things as are bandied about by ordinary people. Don't forget that I am no more than a ticket inspector. I've never read a book in my life except for the railway timetable and a few detective stories.

DETECTIVE: Detective stories?

HUSBAND: They come to hand sometimes. I find them left behind by mistake on a seat after some passenger has finished reading them.

DETECTIVE: Then you read detective stories?

HUSBAND: And what's wrong with that?

DETECTIVE: Nothing . . . nothing . . . . Everything's beginning to become clear.

HUSBAND: What's beginning to come clear? I don't deny . . . .

DETECTIVE: You don't deny . . . .

HUSBAND: Yes, I don't deny that I read detective stories, but I've never read philosophical books.

DETECTIVE: I'm not interested in philosophical books.

HUSBAND: But our reverend friend claims that I murdered for reasons of philosophy.

DERVISH: The philosophy of the age.

HUSBAND [*to the* DETECTIVE]: Did you hear? There he is repeating it.

DERVISH: The philosophy of the age is inherent in you, and the philosophy of the tree is inherent in it.

HUSBAND: The philosophy of the tree?

DERVISH: Yes.

HUSBAND: And what is the philosophy of the tree?

DERVISH: It gives fruit and doesn't ask questions. It produces flowers it doesn't smell and fruit it doesn't eat—and doesn't ask why. It is not tortured by a question to which it will never receive an answer.

HUSBAND: Certainly that's fine for the tree, but where do I come into all this?

DERVISH: You're not a tree.

HUSBAND: That's self-evident.

DERVISH: And so you will kill your wife if you haven't already done so.

HUSBAND: Have you understood a thing, officer?

DETECTIVE: Not really. In any event the important thing is that the reverend witness is firmly resolved that you killed your wife.

HUSBAND: You're really putting on the pressure to prove the charge against me!

DETECTIVE: The charge is proven by itself. The best thing you can do is to confess.

HUSBAND: That I killed my wife?

DETECTIVE: By the way, what did you kill her with? How was the murder done? With a sharp instrument? By poison or by . . . ?

HUSBAND: Anything you like—but not poison.

DETECTIVE: Never mind. Never mind. Calm yourself. The method of killing will be revealed by the forensic doctor at the autopsy. There's no need to mention it—I have respect for your feelings.

HUSBAND: If only you'd mentioned to me some rational motive to justify her being killed.

DETECTIVE: Forget about reasonable motives. All murders are justifiable in the eyes of those who commit them—be the motive rational or irrational.

HUSBAND [*suddenly laughing*]: Anything you like—but not a philosophical motive!

DETECTIVE: I'm not sold on that motive.

HUSBAND: But our reverend friend appears to be.

DETECTIVE: With due deference to the opinions of our reverend friend, I promise you in the report of the investigation I shall mention no motives that don't appeal to you. Agreed?

HUSBAND: Agreed.

DETECTIVE [*getting up*]: Then let's away!

HUSBAND: Where to?

DETECTIVE: To prison.

HUSBAND: Prison? I? Why?

DETECTIVE: Because, naturally, you're under arrest.

HUSBAND: Are you going to arrest me?

DETECTIVE: I'm afraid so. It's an inevitable step I must take.

HUSBAND: Are you really serious?

DETECTIVE: Of course I'm serious. Do you think I came here to joke with you or to perform my official duty?

HUSBAND: But I've done nothing deserving of imprisonment.

DETECTIVE: If you consider that a husband's murder of his wife is something that does not deserve imprisonment, it's an opinion that can perhaps be respected. It is, however, not the opinion of the law.

HUSBAND: But, officer, I . . . .

DETECTIVE: Enough! The investigation has gone on too long. The best thing for you to do is to place yourself with all calmness at the disposal of justice. That's the best advice I can give you.

HUSBAND: The best advice you can give me?

DETECTIVE: Yes. Please listen to my advice — give yourself up!

HUSBAND: Give myself up!

DETECTIVE: And without wavering — it's the best thing for you. Listen to my advice!

HUSBAND [*turning to the* DERVISH]: Happy about this, reverend sir?

DERVISH: Don't ask me! I told you not to put questions to me

HUSBAND: But this is unfair!

DERVISH: Shall I leave, officer?

DETECTIVE: If you wish. I'm much obliged to you.

DERVISH [*to the* HUSBAND *as he leaves*]: Till we meet again, Mr. Inspector. I'm going back to the train.

HUSBAND: God's curse be upon you and upon those who summoned you!

DETECTIVE: As you are still adamant in your attitude, I must take the necessary measures. [*He goes in the direction of the door and calls out.*] Constable!

POLICEMAN [*The sound of feet being brought to attention is heard, though the man is not seen.*]

DETECTIVE: Detain the accused at the police station and bring someone to dig under this tree to remove the body.

HUSBAND [*screaming*]: They're going to dig under my tree! They'll kill the tree! Murderers! . . . Murderers!

ACT TWO

The same place. From where the DETECTIVE *stands overlooking the garden he supervises the digging operations and addresses a digger who is not visible. On the other side the old* MAIDSERVANT *is talking to a milkman who is also not visible, doing so through a window overlooking the road.*

DETECTIVE [*to the digger in the garden*]: Of course under the tree!

DIGGER [*His voice is heard but one cannot make out what he is saying.*]

DETECTIVE: The direction? Now that's something I can't guide you on. Like you, I don't know.

DIGGER [*an incomprehensible question*]: ?

DETECTIVE: You're right. Maybe you're quite correct in your opinion. Dig round the whole tree. Don't begin by going very deep. Maybe you'll come across something to decide the direction you should take, and then . . . . What are you saying?

DIGGER: ?

DETECTIVE: Certainly. Certainly, with the shovel first, and be careful when using the spade in case you crush part of the body.

DIGGER: ?

DETECTIVE: No. No. Naturally—I've got faith in your experience.

DIGGER: ?

DETECTIVE: Yes. That's the way. Go on. Go on.

The DETECTIVE *follows the digging operations with movements of his head that keep time with those of the shovel.*

MAID [*to the milkman*]: Don't bring any milk after today. Who are you bringing it for?

MILKMAN [*incomprehensible sound from outside.*]

MAID: Isn't it so? Then you've learnt it all from the neighbors.

MILKMAN: ?

MAID: No one but the police—they're removing her body from the garden.

MILKMAN: ?

MAID: Yes, in prison.

MILKMAN: ?

MAID: No one knows why he killed her.

MILKMAN: ?

MAID: Nor do I. Perhaps he hated her. You can never tell with people, there's no knowing what goes on inside them.

MILKMAN: ?

MAID: Ah, that's simple. In the house there are all sorts of implements like spades and shovels and garden shears. A knock on the head from one of those would do it.

MILKMAN: ?

MAID: Honestly, he was kind-hearted—and so was she. You can never tell, though, with people.

MILKMAN: ?

MAID: Who told you that? No. It's lies—she hadn't any money for him to be greedy about.

MILKMAN: ?

MAID: No, and no jewelry.

MILKMAN: ?

MAID: Another woman! No, he wasn't of an age for gallivanting about. If it was a question of love, the only love he had was for his tree.

MILKMAN: ?

MAID: Confessed? Yes, he said during the investigation that he'd killed her and buried her under the tree.

MILKMAN: ?

MAID: What's to happen to the house? I heard the officer say that it would be locked up and sealed with red wax.

MILKMAN: ?

MAID: Me? . . . What will happen to me? I honestly don't know what will happen to me. . . . I hate domestic work. I was really lucky to find this place—no children or noise. The lady of the house used to do most of the work herself and only needed me for the washing and scrubbing the floors. When I finished my work she used to let me go back home, and so I've spent several years in complete contentment here. All houses, however, aren't like this one. In the end, though, even this house winds up with a crime and is locked and sealed with red wax!

MILKMAN: ?

MAID: What do you say? You've got work for me? Where?

MILKMAN: ?

MAID: No, I don't like working in hospitals. . . . A washerwoman at the Charity Hospital? God forbid! Spend all day washing disgusting clothes contaminated with all sorts of diseases. . . .

MILKMAN: ?

MAID: You're right—there's a God up above! Our Lord takes care of every one of us in His providence. What?

MILKMAN: ?

MAID: How much exactly?

MILKMAN: ?

MAID: Is the account in arrears?

MILKMAN: ?

MAID: I know nothing about it. The lady . . . I mean the late lady said nothing to me.

MILKMAN: ?

MAID: No, if you don't mind. The day before she was killed she told me the milk bill was paid up.

MILKMAN: ?

MAID: A hundred per cent. Sure—I heard her with my own ears. The very words she said to me were: "Take note that the milk bill is paid up—we've got no arrears."

MILKMAN: ?

MAID: And what should I want with your bill? Keep it with you—who's there to look into it now and argue with you?

MILKMAN: ?

MAID: I know no better than you do.

MILKMAN: ?

MAID: Look to God for your reward!

MILKMAN: ?

MAID: We're all in the same boat: I too haven't been paid for the remainder of the month. There's nothing, though, to be done about it. Who can I ask: the master who's in prison or the mistress who's buried under the tree?

MILKMAN: ?

MAID: The police? The government? As you well know you've got a long wait before the government does anything. Don't take it to heart. In any case our problem's nothing much—it could be a lot worse.

MILKMAN: ?

MAID: Goodbye.

The MAIDSERVANT *goes toward the* DETECTIVE. *He pays no attention to her and continues to follow the digging operation in the garden.*

DETECTIVE [*to the digger*]: Haven't you come across anything yet?

DIGGER: ?

DETECTIVE: What are you saying? Almost there? Are you sufficiently deep?

DIGGER: ?

DETECTIVE: Go on then—carefully.

MAID [*following the digging*]: Take it easy, please, so you don't mutilate her face with your spade. The dead have a sanctity.

DETECTIVE [*turning to the* MAIDSERVANT]: You were talking to someone from the window?

MAID: The milkman—he was in the street.

DETECTIVE: You were saying to him that the accused killed his wife with a blow of a spade, shovel or some shears. How did you know that?

MAID: I don't know anything and I haven't seen anything. It was all guess-work.

DETECTIVE: And why did your thinking and guessing direct themselves to that in particular?

MAID: And how would he kill her then?

DETECTIVE: Had he ever threatened her in front of you with any such implement?

MAID: Never, not even with words.

DETECTIVE: Then you consider that the natural way for him to kill her was by using one of these implements.

MAID: Because he always has them to hand and works with them in the garden every day, cleaning them himself as you saw.

DETECTIVE [*turning his attention to the digger*]: We shall in any case soon be finding out. The method of killing will be clearly evident on the body.

A knocking at the front door.

MAID: That's someone knocking at the front door.

DETECTIVE: Who could it be?

MAID: Perhaps the butcher or the grocer. Shall I go and see?

DETECTIVE: Please do so.

MAID [*answering the person knocking as she hurries to the door*]: Take it easy, I'm coming.

DETECTIVE [*turning to the digger*]: Go on digging. Go on.

The MAIDSERVANT *from outside gives a loud scream of terror.*

MAID [*rushing toward the* DETECTIVE]: It's her ghost. Save me!

DETECTIVE: What's the matter with you?

MAID: It's her . . . the murdered woman . . . my mistress.

The WIFE *appears in her outdoor clothes and in a state of amazement.*

WIFE [*to the* MAIDSERVANT]: What's this madness? What's the matter with you? What are you screaming like that for?

DETECTIVE [*in stupefied astonishment*]: Is it her?

MAID [*to the* DETECTIVE]: Yes, it's her all right.

WIFE [*to the* MAIDSERVANT]: What's happened? Who's this gentleman?

MAID [*to her mistress*]: So you weren't murdered?

WIFE: Have you gone mad? She's absolutely off her head.

DETECTIVE: Madam? [*Looks intently at her.*] Yes? Is it really you?

WIFE: I'm the owner of this house, and who would you be?

DETECTIVE: I'm the police.

WIFE: Police? Nothing wrong I trust? Has anything happened?

DETECTIVE: It's so happened that we . . . that you . . . .

WIFE: That I what? What would bring the police to our house? Where's my husband?

DETECTIVE: Your husband, Madam, is in . . . prison.

WIFE: In prison?

DETECTIVE: We thought you'd been murdered.

WIFE: Murdered?

DETECTIVE: Your disappearance aroused suspicions.

WIFE: My disappearance? I was certainly away, but do you suspect everyone who's away from home of being . . . ?

DETECTIVE: Then, you were merely away?

WIFE: Naturally.

DETECTIVE: But your husband . . . .

WIFE: My husband—where's my husband? You said he was in prison.

DETECTIVE: Yes, but allow me to put the mistake to rights immediately. . . . Without delay.

WIFE: This is a most extraordinary business! By what right was he put in prison? He's a good man, he never did anything wrong in his whole life.

DETECTIVE: I beg of you, please, just a moment. Where's the telephone?

He hastily makes his way to the telephone.

WIFE: How strange! It's all so strange!

DETECTIVE [*on the telephone*]: Hullo. . . . Hullo. Listen, I'm speaking from the house where the crime was committed. Yes, yes, the suburb of Zeitoun. Listen to what I say: There's been no crime. You must release the accused at once. . . . Of course. There wasn't a murder. Of course I'm certain, a hundred per cent. Certain . . . . My dear sir, there's been no murder. . . . Do you hear?. . . How am I certain? Because the murdered person is here in front of me alive . . . I mean the victim . . . I mean the person we thought . . . . Yes, yes, she was only away from home. . . . The point is, the husband must be released immediately—as quickly as possible. . . . Good. I'll be waiting here. [*He replaces the receiver.*]

WIFE [*to the* MAIDSERVANT]: Whatever's the matter with you? Tell me why do you look at me like that? It's extraordinary—I've never seen you in such a state before. What are you so pale about?

MAID: Please excuse me, Madam, I was . . . I was . . . .

WIFE: I don't understand. I still don't understand at all what's going on here.

DETECTIVE: I'll explain to you, Madam. Just relax a while and I'll explain to you.

DIGGER [*calling from the garden*]: Sir!

DETECTIVE: What?. . . Did you find anything?

DIGGER [*from outside*]: I haven't found her yet. Shall I go on?

DETECTIVE: No, stop—she's here now.

DIGGER: The body?

DETECTIVE: Sssh! Be quiet. Leave everything now and clear off! There's no need for that now. Clear off, please, quickly!

WIFE [*looking at the garden*]: Who's that man? What's he doing in the garden? How strange! Who's been digging under the orange tree? My husband'll be furious.

DETECTIVE: We are extremely sorry, Madam, but . . . .

WIFE: But why this digging under the orange tree?

DETECTIVE: We were engaged in a search.

WIFE: A search? What for?

DETECTIVE: For you—begging your pardon.

WIFE: For me? Looking for me under this tree?

DETECTIVE: We thought you were buried under it. Your being absent without telling anyone gave us doubts about this whole business.

WIFE: Buried under this tree?

DETECTIVE: We imagined you'd been murdered and buried there.

WIFE: And who would murder me and bury me like that?

DETECTIVE: Suspicion fell on your husband.

WIFE: My husband? My husband do that to me? But why should you think that?

DETECTIVE: Suspicion and circumstantial evidence—then there was his confession.

WIFE: His confession? His confession of what?

DETECTIVE: He didn't confess openly, but he did say things that could be taken as a semi-confession.

WIFE: A confession of what?

DETECTIVE: That he killed you and buried you under the tree.

WIFE: Did he say he killed me and buried me? Why should he lie? Why should he say something that didn't happen?

DETECTIVE: The fact is that this is something quite inexplicable.

WIFE: And what motive could make him think of . . . of murdering me?

DETECTIVE: We haven't actually arrived at a convincing motive.

WIFE: We're a most affectionate couple.

DETECTIVE: I know.

WIFE: We've never had a disagreement.

DETECTIVE: I know that too.

WIFE: How do you know?

DETECTIVE: He told me so himself.

WIFE: Told you we were affectionate and never had a disagreement?

DETECTIVE: Yes, he told me.

WIFE: And yet he said he'd killed me.

DETECTIVE: He didn't say so explicitly but I as good as understood from his words that he'd committed a crime.

WIFE: Wasn't it possible to understand something else from his words?

DETECTIVE: Something else?

WIFE: I always understand something else from his words.

DETECTIVE: Actually I . . . .

WIFE: Then you didn't properly understand what he was saying.

DETECTIVE: It's possible.

WIFE: Perhaps you understood him to be saying something he wasn't.

DETECTIVE: Maybe.

WIFE: Then he didn't say anything about killing and burying?

DETECTIVE: Maybe not.

WIFE: Then how was it that you came to arrest him and put him in prison?

DETECTIVE: Truly—how did it occur? But wait . . . wait . . . . There was the witness.

WIFE: What witness?

DETECTIVE: The dervish.

WIFE: Dervish? Who's he?

DETECTIVE: A man who knows everything and sees everything. He suggested that your husband killed his wife and buried her under this tree.

WIFE: He suggested that, suggested that he'd killed and buried me? And where did this man come from?

DETECTIVE: He came from the train.

WIFE: From what train?

DETECTIVE: From out of the air. I mean, he was in the train—with your husband in the train—then we called him and he left your husband in the train doing his inspecting and came and sat down with us here—with your husband and me—in this very place.

WIFE: What a muddle! Do you understand what you're saying?

DETECTIVE: No.

WIFE: Neither do I. I don't understand.

DETECTIVE: The fact is I don't understand what I was saying. It would appear to be quite meaningless.

WIFE: Of course.

DETECTIVE: And yet it happened. Everything happened. The dervish came along and said a lot of things your husband agreed about. He didn't agree about everything, naturally, but the suspicions and circumstantial evidence against him were strong.

WIFE: You have just admitted that what you said was meaningless, so how were the suspicions and circumstantial evidence so strong?

DETECTIVE: Actually, everything at that time seemed to have a meaning. I don't know why it's all collapsed now.

WIFE: Then had I not returned at the right time nothing would, in your view, have collapsed?

DETECTIVE: Naturally not.

WIFE: And my husband would have remained in prison.

DETECTIVE: Naturally.

WIFE: And he would have been tried and sentenced?

DETECTIVE: Naturally.

WIFE: And perhaps he would have been sentenced to death because of me, though I was still alive.

DETECTIVE: Maybe.

WIFE: And you would have remained your whole life contentedly believing that your suspicions and circumstantial evidence, your dervish and his suggestions and all that rubbish—begging your pardon—were real, meaningful things. Isn't that so?

DETECTIVE: Certainly.

WIFE: And you're happy about such an outcome?

DETECTIVE: It isn't altogether my fault, Madam—not really. Your husband is equally responsible. Yes, your husband himself helped me to build up this false picture of the incident.

WIFE: My husband himself helped you?

DETECTIVE: In an extraordinary fashion. At certain times there was almost co-operation between us—close co-operation in the investigation. After all, how could I have known about this dervish? It was he who brought him here.

WIFE: My husband hasn't met anyone for five years, ever since he left the service and retired.

DETECTIVE: I know that. However, he had met the dervish on the train when he was still in the service.

WIFE: And how did he bring him here to you now?

DETECTIVE: He called to him from here and while on the train he answered the call.

WIFE: He answered the call?

DETECTIVE: It seems he heard your husband's call from here, so he left your husband on his train inspecting the tickets and came to join in the conversation with your husband and me.

WIFE: Perfectly rational!

DETECTIVE: Isn't it? You find it rational then?

WIFE: Without a doubt. Have you any doubts?

DETECTIVE: No, but I was afraid you might be . . . disbelieving.

WIFE: What reason should I have for disbelief?

DETECTIVE: Perhaps, for instance, you find in such words . . . .

WIFE: A certain amount of confusion?

DETECTIVE: Something like that.

WIFE: As you insist that this happened . . . .

DETECTIVE: I swear to you it happened—I swear by the honor of my position!

WIFE: Don't do that—it really did happen.

DETECTIVE: It really happened? You are convinced then?

WIFE: Absolutely.

DETECTIVE: But a moment ago you were calling me a liar and accusing me of being confused.

WIFE: Because I was talking in accordance with my intellect.

DETECTIVE: And now?

WIFE: In accordance with what occurred.

DETECTIVE: Please be absolutely sure it did occur.

WIFE: I am sure. In fact I am now prepared to see everything you see, everything you and my husband saw. The train was over there—didn't the train pass on that side?

She points to where the train was.

DETECTIVE: Exactly!

WIFE: Yes, and you and my husband were on the other side.

She points to the place.

DETECTIVE: Exactly!

WIFE: And the dervish came to you from here.

She points in the direction.

DETECTIVE: Exactly!

WIFE: I see it all now.

DETECTIVE: Then everything was real?

WIFE: Naturally.

DETECTIVE: And it had meaning?

WIFE: Naturally.

DETECTIVE: Then nothing has collapsed, everything we built up is genuine.

WIFE: Naturally it's genuine. It's all genuine because it all happened. But there is something else that has also happened.

DETECTIVE: And what's that?

WIFE: I've returned, it so happens that I have now returned.

DETECTIVE: That has indeed happened. You returned, safe and sound. At that moment all this had to be changed; we had to do something else and that's just what I did without delay. Didn't I in fact get in touch by telephone for the immediate release of your husband? We'll be seeing him here soon.

WIFE: Is he on his way here now?

DETECTIVE: He should be.

WIFE: I'm afraid that prison may have affected his health.

DETECTIVE: He hasn't spent a long time there.

WIFE: The poor man was never previously in prison.

DETECTIVE: In any event imprisonment at our place is not all that irksome. Allowance is generally made for people like him and he would be put in a comfortable room.

WIFE: He's used to the open air.

DETECTIVE: There are windows in prison.

WIFE: The windows he used to gaze from look on to things that move.

DETECTIVE: But since he left the service and retired here he no longer saw anything that moved.

WIFE: He sees the tree moving.

DETECTIVE: Yes, the tree.

WIFE [*looking toward it*]: Why did you do that to it? He'll be extremely sad.

DETECTIVE: It was inevitable. However, I don't believe any harm has come to it—its roots are intact.

WIFE: I hope so, it's his life.

DETECTIVE: I know, I saw that with my own eyes.

WIFE: What did you see?

DETECTIVE: I saw him here talking with you—not so much talking with you as speaking about the tree.

WIFE: He? He has never spoken about the tree.

DETECTIVE: But I heard him with my own ears.

WIFE: Maybe you heard wrong, officer. It was I who was talking to him about the tree. I always talk to him about it because I know he loves it.

DETECTIVE: But you were talking about . . . your daughter.

WIFE: My daughter . . . really . . . but it's he who was talking about my daughter—he always talks to me about her.

DETECTIVE: That's extraordinary. I'm sure, though, about what I'm saying. It couldn't be that I was as muddled as all that.

WIFE: What you are saying is not possible. He always talks to me about things I like and I talk to him about things he likes. That's why we have such affection and understanding.

DETECTIVE: That's natural. This, however, is not what happened—I'm certain. It couldn't be that I was as muddled as all that. I'll go mad. I'll go mad in this house.

WIFE: Refresh your memory, officer.

DETECTIVE: My memory's fine. Why don't you yourself think back over the whole matter, Madam. You were sitting here knitting and talking about your daughter who had not been born. He was standing in front of you over there cleaning his shears and shovel. He was talking about the tree, its fruit and its growth.

WIFE: Not at all, he was talking about the fruit which had stirred within me and the way in which destiny had ordained it should grow.

DETECTIVE: But it was you, Madam . . . .

WIFE: No, he.

DETECTIVE: Do you want proof? You mentioned the party on the seventh day after birth. I heard it with my own ears, also the sound of the pounding of the mortar, then the song "Bargalatak . . . Bargalatak . . . ."

WIFE: Did you hear it?

DETECTIVE: Just as I heard the engine's whistle and the noise of its wheels and the voices of the pupils on the school outing singing "O tree climber fetch me a cow."

WIFE: And where were you?

DETECTIVE: I was sitting right here—in this very place.

WIFE: I didn't see you.

DETECTIVE: I don't think you did.

WIFE: And what were you doing in this place?

DETECTIVE: I was undertaking the investigation.

WIFE: The investigation?

DETECTIVE: Yes, into the question of your disappearance.

WIFE: But I hadn't yet disappeared, I hadn't left the house.

DETECTIVE: But I came here because you had left the house, had gone out and disappeared.

WIFE: Yet you had seen me here having a conversation with my husband.

DETECTIVE: Yes, I saw this with my own eyes and heard it with my own ears.

WIFE: This certainly must have happened, seeing that you are convinced you saw it with your own eyes and heard it with your own ears.

DETECTIVE: I'm absolutely convinced.

WIFE: But in as much as you saw me here with your own eyes and heard me with your own ears conversing with my husband, why did you proceed with the investigation into my having gone out and disappeared?

DETECTIVE: Because previous to that I had been informed of the matter of your disappearance.

WIFE: Who informed you?

DETECTIVE: I don't know exactly. It was a phone call to the police station from the house, from this house—from the maid or from your husband. I haven't yet investigated this point, and of course it's no longer necessary, is it?

WIFE: But it is necessary—I'm interested to know who it was who informed the police.

DETECTIVE: Seeing that you have turned up and no crime has taken place, it wouldn't be right for me to continue the investigation.

WIFE: Will you permit me to ask the servant?

DETECTIVE: Please do.

WIFE [*turning to the* MAIDSERVANT *who is standing near the entrance*]: Come along! As you've been listening to everything, answer me this question.

MAID: It wasn't I who got in touch with the police.

WIFE: Then it was my husband.

MAID: I didn't see him do so—I was busy in the kitchen.

DETECTIVE: Didn't he tell you he intended to contact the police?

MAID: No, he merely said to me: "How long does it take to buy a skein of wool and return?" I answered him that my mistress had said: "A period of half an hour." To which he had said: "When half an hour is up, tell me," and he left me and went with his spade to the garden. That was on the following day.

DETECTIVE: The following day?

MAID: Yes, a night had passed since my mistress had gone out.

DETECTIVE: And didn't he show any anxiety?

MAID: On the first day, no. He said to me: "Seeing that your mistress has not yet returned, the half hour is not yet up. She is precise in her reckoning, and I am more sure about her reckoning than I am about the rotation of the earth." And on the following day, the second night . . . .

DETECTIVE: What did he say on the second night?

MAID: He said: "It's possible that the earth has stopped rotating for a day, up to such time as your mistress appears at the appointed hour."

DETECTIVE: And on the third day?

MAID: On the third day he began to worry.

WIFE: Poor thing!

DETECTIVE: And what did he say?

MAID: He said: "The skein of wool your mistress bought has undoubtedly taken her round the earth's globe twice. But that one single skein should take her round three times—that's altogether too much."

WIFE: Indeed, he's quite right.

DETECTIVE: And what did he do?

MAID: Only then did I understand he would do something.

WIFE: It was he, then, who contacted the police?

MAID: There was no one else.

WIFE: What a pity! It's bad sign.

DETECTIVE: Does it upset you that he worries about you?

WIFE: I don't like him to be worried.

DETECTIVE: In such circumstances it is a duty to be worried.

WIFE: He has never known what it is to be worried—he shouldn't have to know.

DETECTIVE: That is proof of his deep feelings for you.

A knocking at the front door.

WIFE: That's him.

MAID [*hurrying to open it*]: Yes, it's him.

DETECTIVE: I stayed on here specially so that I could apologize to him.

MAID [*from outside*]: Master! Master!

The HUSBAND *appears; he looks tired.*

WIFE: My dearest husband!

HUSBAND: My dearest wife!

They embrace.

WIFE [*scrutinizing her* HUSBAND]: Are you all right?

HUSBAND [*scrutinizing her*]: And you?

WIFE: I'm fine, as you can see.

HUSBAND: And I too.

DETECTIVE: Will you allow me to go now? I waited specially so as to extend my apologies to you myself.

HUSBAND: Apologies? Why?

DETECTIVE: For this inconvenience.

HUSBAND: You mean the imprisonment?

DETECTIVE: I am extremely sorry.

HUSBAND: Don't be sorry. I personally am not sorry. Imprisonment has caused me no inconvenience, just the opposite.

DETECTIVE: Really?

HUSBAND: Be sure of that. I didn't imagine imprisonment had such advantages.

DETECTIVE [*in amazement*]: What advantages?

HUSBAND: Have you not experienced imprisonment?

DETECTIVE: Who? Me?

HUSBAND: Naturally you have never been imprisoned.

DETECTIVE: Naturally not.

HUSBAND: You've missed something important.

DETECTIVE: What's that?

HUSBAND: The feeling that you're a fetus which has returned to its mother's womb, feeding and breathing from within, and waiting for a hand to drag it out at some time or other.

WIFE: How nice it would have been had she returned to the womb and emerged alive.

HUSBAND: That's because there's no joy like that of the moment when one emerges.

DETECTIVE: Naturally the moment of release is always exhilarating for a prisoner.

HUSBAND: The moment when the seed emerges from the earth's womb green and alive.

WIFE [*repeating herself*]: How nice it would have been had she returned to the womb and emerged alive.

DETECTIVE: Thank God, you have emerged safe and in good spirits. The period of your imprisonment wasn't long. And now—let's shake hands. Once again my apologies and regrets. I'll take my leave now.

He shakes the HUSBAND *by the hand, then the* WIFE, *and departs.*

HUSBAND [*having returned from seeing the* DETECTIVE *to the front door*]: And now, my dearest wife, to work—to my shovel and spade.

WIFE: Are you going right away to your garden to exhaust yourself?

HUSBAND: Does one say to the newborn child at the moment it moves on emerging from its mother's womb: Don't exhaust yourself?

WIFE: No, I give trilling cries of joy.

HUSBAND: Then do so! Go on! [*He moves to the garden, looks at it and shouts*]: What disaster! What a disaster!

WIFE: What, my dearest?

HUSBAND: All this digging—what's all this digging? I didn't think they'd do all this amount of digging. It's a bad day for them and for me if they've brought any harm to the tree.

WIFE: I knew you'd be angry and sad.

HUSBAND [*disappearing into the garden*]: A bad day for them and for me! For them and for me!

MAID [*appearing*]: Why is Master shouting like this?

WIFE: It's the tree!

MAID: They were digging like madmen.

WIFE: Were you here all the time?

MAID: Yes.

WIFE: You may go home now and return tomorrow morning. I don't think we're in need of you today. It's enough that you stayed in the house and looked after it in our absence.

MAID: Thank you, Madam. Thank you. In fact my blind husband was poorly and is in need of me today. I leave you in good hands, Madam. [*She departs.*]

HUSBAND [*shouting from the garden*]: This is extraordinary! It's quite extraordinary!

WIFE [*leaning out*]: What has happened?

HUSBAND [*appearing*]: The lizard, the lizard's appeared. She's returned.

WIFE: She's returned?

HUSBAND: Yes, Lady Green has returned. I spotted her ambling along in her green dress on her way to her sanctuary. Then she stopped as though baffled, for she found an enormous hole awaiting her.

WIFE: Awaiting her?

HUSBAND: I wonder where could she have been?

WIFE: Without a doubt she was somewhere.

HUSBAND: What place could she have been in far away from her sanctuary all this time? Talking of which—where were you?

WIFE: I?

HUSBAND: Yes, you. Where were you all this time?

WIFE: I went off, as you know, to buy some wool.

HUSBAND: I know. For half an hour?

WIFE: Correct.

HUSBAND: But you didn't return after half an hour, you in fact returned after three days.

WIFE: Three days? Are you sure?

HUSBAND: Quite sure.

WIFE: Yes, quite so. You're right.

HUSBAND: You were without doubt somewhere during all those three days?

WIFE: Quite so—somewhere.

HUSBAND: What place could you have been in far away from your home all that time?

WIFE: Certainly this is a question that can be asked.

HUSBAND: That must be asked.

WIFE: Must? And why must?

HUSBAND: Because . . . because it . . . because I must know.

WIFE: Is it necessary for you to know?

HUSBAND: Very necessary. Don't you find it necessary I should know where you were all this time?

WIFE: And if I were not to tell you?

HUSBAND: And why not tell me? There is, then, some motive prompting you to keep it secret.

WIFE: A motive?

HUSBAND: A shameful motive most probably.

WIFE: Shameful?

HUSBAND: I say "most probably" because people generally only keep secret those motives that occasion shame, though this is not an inevitable condition in all cases.

WIFE: Especially with me.

HUSBAND: Especially with you. I thus regard as remote anything shameful having occurred.

WIFE: You make me laugh.

HUSBAND: I withdraw my words.

WIFE: Well done! We are in agreement, then, so let's talk about something else.

HUSBAND: Am I to understand from this that you're determined to remain secretive?

WIFE: I've never before seen you so insistent in your questioning.

HUSBAND: Because the situation invites the putting of questions. Perhaps the matter does not in truth require secretiveness, but it is your being secretive that alone impels me to discover the motive for it. Why be secretive? Were there something to be ashamed of I would understand, but seeing as how we have eliminated this motive, what other one is there?

WIFE: The other motive? What other motive?

HUSBAND: The motive that is not shameful.

WIFE: Shameful like what?

HUSBAND: I have no wish to give examples. Every motive you're ashamed to mention is shameful—that's what I mean; even if in everyone else's view it's quite innocuous. But be sure—I swear to you, although there is, as you know, no need for me to do so—that whatever the motives, whatever place you may have disappeared to, whatever the deeds done by you throughout those three days, none of all this will make me angry or change our relationship one to the other. You're convinced about that, are you not?

WIFE: Certainly I'm convinced.

HUSBAND: We are not at a stage of life when either of us can pass judgment on the other for any reason.

WIFE: That's right.

HUSBAND: The roof that gives us shelter together is all we have; after which there is nothing under it that can upset us.

WIFE: That's right.

HUSBAND: We no longer have time in life, nor energy, to spend on one of us taking the other to serious task on what should or should not be. Suppose that during these three days you perpetrated some serious crimes: you committed adultery, you stole, you murdered—or did things even more dreadful. . . .

WIFE: What's this you're saying?

HUSBAND: Just suppose! Suppose! What would you expect me to do? With me at my age and you at yours, if I didn't try to save you I would at least not be the cause of your downfall. Isn't that what you'd expect of me?

WIFE: Naturally.

HUSBAND: Then the one person you shouldn't be secretive with is me.

WIFE: Naturally.

HUSBAND: Have you anyone in this world but me?

WIFE: No.

HUSBAND: Then why are you being secretive with me?

WIFE: I hadn't thought of being so and it surprises me that you should talk all the time about my being secretive. I am not trying to hide anything. It has never occurred to me either to hide or not to hide anything from you. Where did you get that idea from?

HUSBAND: How extraordinary! You don't mean to be secretive after all? It's my own idea then?

WIFE: Of course it's your idea.

HUSBAND: Then the question's resolved.

WIFE: It's you who have complicated things.

HUSBAND: It would appear so. Things being as they are, then, everything is in excellent shape.

WIFE: Naturally.

HUSBAND: Then I shall be receiving from you answers to my questions?

WIFE: Are we going back to questions?

HUSBAND: How extraordinary! Haven't you promised to answer?

WIFE: I promised?

HUSBAND: Goodness gracious! Weren't you saying just now that you don't want to hide anything from me?

WIFE: Yes, I did.

HUSBAND: Tell me, then, where were you?

WIFE: I was somewhere.

HUSBAND: Naturally. Inevitably you were somewhere, because you cannot be nowhere. But where was this somewhere? At the house of one of your relations?

WIFE: No.

HUSBAND: At the house of one of your acquaintances?

WIFE: No.

HUSBAND: It was, at any rate, a house?

WIFE: No.

HUSBAND: A hotel?

WIFE: No.

HUSBAND: A hospital?

WIFE: No.

HUSBAND: A sanatorium?

WIFE: No.

HUSBAND: A prison?

WIFE: No.

HUSBAND: A boarding-house?

WIFE: No.

HUSBAND: A brothel?

WIFE: No.

HUSBAND: A dance-hall? A night club?

WIFE: No. No.

HUSBAND: A grocery. A herbalist? A hosiery?

WIFE: No. No. No.

HUSBAND: At a dressmaker's? A fashion house?

WIFE: No. No.

HUSBAND: An orphanage?

WIFE: No.

HUSBAND: A kindergarten?

WIFE: No.

HUSBAND: At a girl's school?

WIFE: No.

HUSBAND: At a fortune-teller's?

WIFE: No.

HUSBAND: At an exorcizer of devils?

WIFE: No.

HUSBAND: In a mosque?

WIFE: No.

HUSBAND: With the holy saints of God?

WIFE: No.

HUSBAND: With pimps and pickpockets?

WIFE: No.

HUSBAND: In a dahabiya on the Nile?

WIFE: No.

HUSBAND: In a houseboat?

WIFE: No.

HUSBAND: On a train?

WIFE: No.

HUSBAND: In a car?

WIFE: No.

HUSBAND: In an airplane?

WIFE: No.

HUSBAND: On a ship?

WIFE: No.

HUSBAND: In a submarine?

WIFE: No.

HUSBAND: On a country estate?

WIFE: No.

HUSBAND: In a tent in the desert?

WIFE: No.

HUSBAND: In a howdah on a camel?

WIFE: No.

HUSBAND: On a horse?

WIFE: No.

HUSBAND: On a donkey?

WIFE: No.

HUSBAND: On a motorcycle?

WIFE: No.

HUSBAND: On top of the Pyramids?

WIFE: No.

HUSBAND: On a roof terrace?

WIFE: No.

HUSBAND: On the pavement?

WIFE: No.

HUSBAND: On the grass?

WIFE: No.

HUSBAND: On the beach?

WIFE: No.

HUSBAND: In a bathing cabin?

WIFE: No.

HUSBAND: Under parasols?

WIFE: No.

HUSBAND: Under bridges?

WIFE: No.

HUSBAND: At a doctor's?

WIFE: No.

HUSBAND: At a midwife's?

WIFE: No.

HUSBAND: At a hairdresser's?

WIFE: No.

HUSBAND: With a lover?

WIFE: No.

HUSBAND: With a gangster?

WIFE: No.

HUSBAND: In a hashish den?

WIFE: No.

HUSBAND: At the vegetable market?

WIFE: No.

HUSBAND: At the fish market?

WIFE: No.

HUSBAND: At the second-hand market?

WIFE: No.

HUSBAND: At the arms market?

WIFE: No.

HUSBAND: In a factory?

WIFE: No.

HUSBAND: In a workshop?

WIFE: No.

HUSBAND: In a laundry?

WIFE: No.

HUSBAND: In an offal restaurant?

WIFE: No.

HUSBAND: At the warehouses?

WIFE: No.

HUSBAND: At the burial-grounds?

WIFE: No.

HUSBAND: Then where were you? Where were you? Where? Where? Where? My head will burst. I'll go mad.

WIFE: Why do you give such importance to where I was?

HUSBAND: Why have I given it such importance? Don't you see now how important it is? After I've taken you round every place in heaven and earth without coming across it?

WIFE: I don't see that it possesses any importance.

HUSBAND: You don't think so because you know where it was. As for me the matter has become one of prodigious gravity.

WIFE: Of prodigious gravity?

HUSBAND: Indeed I must know where this place is—this place which there is no means of knowing.

WIFE: Why don't you give your brain and mine a rest from this subject? Wouldn't that be better?

HUSBAND: Impossible. It's now impossible. Can you imagine this? Do you imagine it is possible . . . for me . . . to give my mind rest, to sleep, to work, to eat or to drink without turning this question round in my head time and time again?

WIFE: Do you doubt me so much?

HUSBAND: It's not doubt at all. The matter has nothing to do with doubting you, or of being critical of your behavior, or any such thing. I assured you of that before. You must understand me properly. The matter is now of more gravity than that.

WIFE: You're exaggerating—I don't see any gravity in it.

HUSBAND: Maybe. Maybe the thing's actually as you say. Maybe it's of extreme triviality, extreme simplicity, but the mere fact of not knowing about it . . . . Do you get what I'm driving at?

WIFE: No.

HUSBAND: The mere fact of leaving me without an answer to my simple question does not allow me to calm down. Now do you understand?

WIFE: It's that you doubt me.

HUSBAND: No. No, it's not that. It's something else. I don't know how to explain it to you.

WIFE: I don't really understand any longer. I've never seen you in this mood before.

HUSBAND: Because I haven't previously been faced with such a state of affairs—a simple question to which I find no answer and to which there's no way of knowing the answer.

WIFE: That's something that happens every day and doesn't call for being upset and worried.

HUSBAND: But not in this situation, not in circumstances such as ours. Listen and understand properly! Suppose we left this whole question and each went about his business, is it possible that I would stop asking: Where was my wife during those three days? In what place was she? Because you were certainly somewhere—this by your own admission. Indeed it is also self-evident—you couldn't be other than somewhere. We have now made the tour together of every place there could be and your answer has been that you weren't there. I do not for a moment doubt that you were telling the truth, for there is nothing to induce you to lie.

WIFE: No, I didn't lie.

HUSBAND: When you said "No" it was in truth "No."

WIFE: You may be sure of that.

HUSBAND: I am sure. However, you have yet to give an answer to the original question: Where is this place, this place you were in? But it is here that you maintain silence—absolute silence, frightening, terrifying, dreadful silence!

WIFE: You employ strange words.

HUSBAND: They are the simplest words with which to express what I now feel. I would have liked to have said "killing silence."

WIFE: Killing?

HUSBAND: Yes, you'll really kill me. Were I to be left for a further hour in my present state, I might well commit some crime.

WIFE: What's this you're saying?

HUSBAND: You talk so coldly and nonchalantly as though this matter were one of the utmost simplicity.

WIFE: Which in fact it is.

HUSBAND: For you, yes—because it would appear you want to torture me.

WIFE: It's you who are torturing yourself with this senseless talk.

HUSBAND: It's not senseless—it's something grave, very grave.

WIFE: I still don't understand you since your return from prison. I don't understand what you're saying.

HUSBAND: And was my imprisonment other than on your account?

WIFE: It was not on my account.

HUSBAND: Not on account of your disappearance?

WIFE: I hadn't disappeared.

HUSBAND: You were somewhere no one knows of—not even the police.

WIFE: The police are no concern of mine.

HUSBAND: And your husband too is no concern of yours?

WIFE: And what has it to do with you?

HUSBAND: They accused me of killing you—because you were somewhere no one knows of.

WIFE: That's the fault of those who accused you.

HUSBAND: And not yours?

WIFE: No.

HUSBAND: You didn't try to inform me about your absence by telephone, did you?

WIFE: No.

HUSBAND: You didn't think of the worry you might cause by being absent for three consecutive days?

WIFE: No.

HUSBAND: It didn't occur to you that this behavior of yours could have bad results?

WIFE: No.

HUSBAND: You went out determined to stay away for these three days?

WIFE: No.

HUSBAND: Then you went out and were met by circumstances that made you stay away without premeditation?

WIFE: No.

HUSBAND: Then you thought about staying away before going out?

WIFE: No.

HUSBAND: Listen and understand me well: the answer cannot be "no" in both instances. Either you thought of staying away or you didn't. Did you think of it?

WIFE: No.

HUSBAND: Then you didn't think of it?

WIFE: No.

HUSBAND: It's only too clear you're making fun of me. You want to make fun of me—isn't that what you're after now? That's what you're aiming at, isn't it?

WIFE: No.

HUSBAND: I can't bear this attitude of yours any longer. I'm warning you—do you want me to resort to violence?

WIFE: No.

HUSBAND: I have never been violent with you. The reins, though, may slip from my hands. I might do you some injury—or do myself some injury. Do you want me to do you some injury?

WIFE: No.

HUSBAND: Do you want me to do myself some injury?

WIFE: No.

HUSBAND: Then speak. Say something. My heart has begun to grow weary. What is your aim from this silence? Are you afraid that some harm will come to us by talking frankly?

WIFE: No.

HUSBAND: Why the silence, then? What's the sense of it? Perhaps you have some justification. Perhaps in your view it makes sense. Does this silence make sense to you?

WIFE: No.

HUSBAND: If, then, silence makes no sense to you and has neither purpose nor justification, what meaning has it? Does it possess any meaning for you?

WIFE: No.

HUSBAND: Speak, then! Aren't you able to speak?

WIFE: No.

HUSBAND: Why? You're not dumb, you've got a tongue that can speak, yet your tongue gets struck dumb when I ask you to answer me—because you don't want to answer me, you don't want to give an answer, that's all there is to it. You don't want to, do you?

WIFE: No.

HUSBAND: "No" in all circumstances. Aren't you going to stop this nonsense? Won't you cease this making fun of me? There's not a man alive who'd stand for it—not one. I've been far too patient with you. But I know how to compel you to speak—I'll compel you by very force. I'll make this tongue of yours utter. I'll show you how it'll give out an answer. [*He presses on her throat.*] Speak out!

WIFE: No. . . . No.

HUSBAND: I told you to talk! Speak!

WIFE: No. . . . No. . . . No.

HUSBAND: Don't force me to press tighter on your throat. Speak! Speak! Let your tongue give out an answer!

WIFE [*with a rattling in the throat*]: No. . . . No. . . . No. . . . No.

HUSBAND: You don't want to! Speak, I tell you! . . . Speak! I tell you—Talk! Say something! [*Her head is seen to drop forwards. He shakes her in terror as he sees that she has departed this life.*] Behana! Behana! My wife! My dearest! Behana! Behana! There is no power and no strength save in God. Did it necessitate my doing this? What's to be done now? What's to be done? I must do something. Hurry! Hurry! First of all I must inform the police and hand myself over—that's essential. I've killed my wife because she . . . because I . . . because she . . . .

He continues repeating these words as he moves to where the telephone stands on the table. However, he turns away from it and disappears inside for a moment, to return with a white bedspread with which he covers his dead wife, shifting her slightly so that she is out of sight. He then returns to the telephone, dials a number, and lifts the receiver to his ear. At that moment, on the other side of the stage, the DETECTIVE *comes into view. He is sitting at his desk and is lifting his receiver. A conversation takes place.*

HUSBAND: Hullo. Detective-Inspector?

DETECTIVE: Bahadir Effendi? I knew you from your voice.

HUSBAND: Yes, it's me.

DETECTIVE: Excellent! May I repeat to you once again my regrets. Well, sir, anything I can do for you?

HUSBAND: No, thanks. I'm talking now from home. It's about . . . .

DETECTIVE: About what?

HUSBAND: The fact is that I wanted . . . I want to . . . to report about . . . .

DETECTIVE: Go ahead, I'm at your disposal. Please don't hesitate—tell me what you want.

HUSBAND: The fact is that I thought it my duty to report . . . .

DETECTIVE: Report? Is your wife all right?

HUSBAND: No . . . my wife has . . . .

DETECTIVE: Don't say she's disappeared?

HUSBAND: In fact she has . . . she's disappeared all right, only . . . .

DETECTIVE: Again? Disappeared again?

HUSBAND: Yes, but . . . .

DETECTIVE: That's strange. Permit me to say that your wife's behavior is very odd! This repeated disappearing has become a sort of hobby with her!

HUSBAND: Indeed, but . . . .

DETECTIVE: Has she once again failed to tell you where she's gone?

HUSBAND: No, but . . . .

DETECTIVE: Perhaps she's gone to the same place as on the previous occasion?

HUSBAND: No, but . . . .

DETECTIVE: How do you know? Did she tell you so?

HUSBAND: She told me nothing.

DETECTIVE: You naturally asked her where she'd been on the previous occasion?

HUSBAND: I asked her . . . I asked her but she didn't want to tell me anything.

DETECTIVE: Then you're ignorant of her whereabouts?

HUSBAND: Utterly ignorant.

DETECTIVE: That's odd. She's gone off this time too?

HUSBAND: She went off, yes, she went off, but . . . .

DETECTIVE: She didn't tell you where?

HUSBAND: No, she said nothing, but . . . .

DETECTIVE: And what makes you think that this time too she has gone to where she went on the previous occasion?

HUSBAND: I don't know, but . . . .

DETECTIVE: Then you are wholly ignorant about her personal secrets?

HUSBAND: Completely ignorant.

DETECTIVE: And she doesn't want to tell you anything?

HUSBAND: No, she doesn't.

DETECTIVE: And she went off this time just like she went off on the previous occasion.

HUSBAND: Yes, she went off, but . . . .

DETECTIVE: Listen then! Listen to my advice: Don't upset yourself.

HUSBAND: Don't upset myself?

DETECTIVE: Under no circumstances. She'll return, just as she returned before.

HUSBAND: She'll return?

DETECTIVE: I'm sure of it. Don't worry about her.

HUSBAND: Not worry about her?

DETECTIVE: That's the best thing you can do. Calm yourself, don't be upset and go about your gardening. Let her do as she pleases. She'll return home when she wants to.

HUSBAND: That's your opinion?

DETECTIVE: Yes it is, and this is the best advice I can give you: let the matter be, don't upset yourself about it at all, keep silent and quiet and don't be disturbed!

HUSBAND: Keep silent and quiet and not be disturbed?

DETECTIVE: Exactly.

HUSBAND: And do nothing at all?

DETECTIVE: That's my advice to you—in all sincerity.

HUSBAND: Thank you. . . Thank you.

DETECTIVE: Don't mention it. I'm always at your disposal.

Each replaces his receiver. The DETECTIVE *disappears from view.*

HUSBAND: Seeing as how this is the police's advice, I'd better keep silent and quiet and not be disturbed. That really is the best thing I can do. But . . . the body? It must be buried. Where? How extraordinary! [*Looking toward the garden.*] There's her grave all ready—and it was the police who dug it! The police themselves! Thank you. Thank you. Then she may as well be buried in peace and quiet!

He moves to where he left the body and, putting it on his shoulder, bears it off toward the garden. At that moment, hearing a knocking, he hides the body where he is, and goes to open the door.

HUSBAND [*to the* DERVISH *who has appeared at the door*]: It's you?
DERVISH: Yes, it's me.
HUSBAND: What has just brought me to your mind?
DERVISH: I learnt that you had come out of prison.
HUSBAND: And is that of interest to you?
DERVISH: Naturally, I don't want you to come to any harm.
HUSBAND: I should hope not, but . . . .
DERVISH: Do you doubt my good intentions?

He looks around him like someone searching for something.

HUSBAND: Why do you look around like that? Who are you looking for?
DERVISH: They say your wife has returned.
HUSBAND: Yes.
DERVISH: She's here, then?
HUSBAND: Yes.
DERVISH: Asleep?
HUSBAND: Yes, asleep.
DERVISH: The quietness of the house would indicate so.
HUSBAND: Yes.
DERVISH: And the expression on your face indicates it.
HUSBAND: The expression on my face?
DERVISH: It shows that everything is quiet here. . . . I'm afraid, though, that my coming here now has upset you.

HUSBAND: No, not at all.

DERVISH: The tone of your voice indicates that you're upset.

HUSBAND: Actually I'm . . . I wasn't expecting your visit.

DERVISH: That's evident. My visiting you now has come as a surprise. I trust the surprise was not an unpleasant one?

HUSBAND: Why unpleasant?

DERVISH: A mere speculation. A visitor is always afraid to come at an inopportune time.

HUSBAND: Inopportune time? Why?

DERVISH: A mere supposition.

HUSBAND: There is no point in such a supposition.

DERVISH: Then I have not taken you away from any work you were engaged on before I came?

HUSBAND: No, not at all.

DERVISH: Thanks be to God. Then I can stay on a while with you with a clear conscience?

HUSBAND: But . . . .

DERVISH: But what?

HUSBAND: No. . . . No. . . . Nothing at all.

DERVISH: Please speak! Be frank with me!

HUSBAND: I was intending to work a little in the garden.

DERVISH: On the orange tree?

HUSBAND: Yes.

DERVISH: I would say you've found the fertilizer it requires for its extraordinary growth.

HUSBAND: You think so?

DERVISH: That's for certain.

HUSBAND: How did you know?

DERVISH: I've known—for a long time. But you've got a poor memory.

HUSBAND: In truth, you know many things.

DERVISH: Don't be upset! There's no point in your getting upset.

HUSBAND: Did I get upset?

DERVISH: Be sure that I wish you no harm. I have merely come in order to pay you a visit, to pay a visit to you and your lady wife.

HUSBAND: My wife?

DERVISH: She's asleep—you told me so.

HUSBAND: Yes.

DERVISH: And will her sleep last long?

HUSBAND: Maybe.

DERVISH: Yes, perhaps it will last longer than we think.

HUSBAND: What are you getting at?

DERVISH: Sleep. . . . Aren't there some people who sleep a long time?

HUSBAND: What do you mean by a long sleep?

DERVISH: Death, of course.

HUSBAND: Death? What's the connection?

DERVISH: Don't you see the connection?

HUSBAND: Then you know?

DERVISH: Of course I know. I told you previously, but you've got a poor memory.

HUSBAND: Certainly—you told me and here I've gone and done it.

DERVISH: Oh, yes. You've done it. Now you have.

HUSBAND: There's no witness against me but you. You alone can now put me in prison.

DERVISH: And who said that I want to bear witness against you, or put you in prison?

HUSBAND: You did so previously.

DERVISH: At your own request. It was you who conjured me out of the air to bear witness.

HUSBAND: And you bore witness against me.

DERVISH: I said what I knew, and if you asked me again I would say what I know.

HUSBAND: And if I didn't ask you?

DERVISH: I wouldn't say anything.

HUSBAND: Can I have confidence in you?

DERVISH: Every confidence. I don't move under my own volition, nor do I volunteer to speak unless you wish me to.

HUSBAND: I shall not so wish.

DERVISH: And I shall not speak.

HUSBAND: How can I be sure?

DERVISH: You can be. I'm confident about myself, it's you I'm not confident about.

HUSBAND: You're not confident about me?

DERVISH: Who is to know you won't change your mind and yourself ask me to come along and talk one day?

HUSBAND: I ask such a thing? Ask to be harmed? Ask to be ruined?

DERVISH: I don't guarantee you—I only guarantee myself. I shan't talk unless asked to by you. If I speak I shall say what I know.

HUSBAND: I am not concerned with what you know, what I'm concerned with is that you shouldn't talk. Let us go, then.

DERVISH: Where to?

HUSBAND: For you to help me a little.

DERVISH: Doing what?

HUSBAND: Burying her. Her grave is ready—the police themselves dug it.

DERVISH: God forbid!

HUSBAND: Do you refuse?

DERVISH: Of course I refuse.

HUSBAND: But you knew I'd kill her.

DERVISH: Knowledge does not imply approval.

HUSBAND: Then in your eyes I'm a criminal?

DERVISH: Is there any doubt about it?

HUSBAND: Be a little fair to me—please! Her murder was quite by chance, and it was she who drove me to it. Was it possible to live with such a woman?

DERVISH: You had already lived with her for many years.

HUSBAND: But in the end she had turned into something terrible—into a wall of silence.

DERVISH: Justification enough for destroying it!

HUSBAND: Don't make fun. Had you been in my place you'd have done exactly the same.

DERVISH: I wouldn't have been in your place.

HUSBAND: Then don't be unfair to me!

DERVISH: I pity you—you bring down all this trouble on yourself because of a question you didn't receive an answer to!

HUSBAND: I couldn't stop myself, it was beyond my power.

DERVISH: I know.

HUSBAND: Was it possible for me to pass my whole life in ignorance?

DERVISH: No, not for you.

HUSBAND: Then . . . .

DERVISH: Had you informed the police you would also have destroyed yourself.

HUSBAND: Yes.

DERVISH: And all this is one to you.

HUSBAND: It was inevitable I should do it. I told you so.

DERVISH: Yes, it was inevitable. Go and bury her, then.

HUSBAND: Will you help me?

DERVISH: Don't expect assistance from anyone. Carry her by yourself.

HUSBAND: So be it! I'll carry her by myself.

DERVISH: I have confidence in the strength of your arms.

HUSBAND: I shall carry her and I shall bury her under the tree. I regret nothing—her life was useless. Her fruit had fallen and she lived only on the illusion of being a mother.

DERVISH: It is not in vain, so long as you present her as delectable sustenance to your tree.

HUSBAND: You're quite right. From this point of view she's of use.

DERVISH: If there's any futility it's in the life of the tree.

HUSBAND: How? The tree?

DERVISH: It produces flowers it doesn't smell, colors it doesn't see, and fruit it doesn't eat. Yet it repeats this futile procedure every year.

HUSBAND: That is not in vain—it's a useful occupation.

DERVISH: In relation to yourself?

HUSBAND: Of course.

DERVISH: Admit, then, that what you call futility is in relation to yourself.

HUSBAND: You want to say that my wife's life had meaning?

DERVISH: The meaning of every being within its own framework—not within your own head!

HUSBAND: But for me she is without meaning except when I now present her as sustenance for the tree, and through her the tree grows enormously and produces its prodigious fruit.

DERVISH: Oranges in winter, apricots in spring, figs in summer and pomegranates in autumn.

HUSBAND: Yes. Yes.

DERVISH: Then go and prepare the banquet for your tree.

HUSBAND: I'm going, but . . . .

DERVISH: But what?

HUSBAND: Will the tree really give forth all these different fruits in the four seasons?

DERVISH: It's not me you should ask.

HUSBAND: Let us try! If the experiment is successful, what miracle will have been revealed!

DERVISH: What a miracle indeed!

HUSBAND: But a tree that gives forth all that won't be an orange tree.

DERVISH: Naturally it will not be called an orange tree.

HUSBAND: What can we call it, then?

DERVISH: Postpone the question of the name till later.

HUSBAND: You're right—let's postpone that till later. Who knows, perhaps it will be named after me, "Bahadir's tree?"

DERVISH: Or "the Bahadir tree."

HUSBAND: Truly, "the Bahadir" instead of "the orange"—"the Bahadir" is an appropriate name, isn't it?

DERVISH: Very appropriate.

HUSBAND: And it will find its way into books and dictionaries.

DERVISH: Of course, and it will be studied at universities.

HUSBAND: And they'll say this marvelous tree is one of the most important discoveries of the age of modern science!

DERVISH: Without a doubt. Scientists will make of the tree a subject for research.

HUSBAND: Research? Then the scientists will come to this garden?

DERVISH: Why, of course, and they'll go through every inch of it.

HUSBAND: Go through every inch?

DERVISH: Quite obviously—so as to find out the reasons for this miracle.

HUSBAND: Then they'll dig under the tree?

DERVISH: Right down to the very roots.

HUSBAND: But they'll come across the body.

DERVISH: Or its skeleton.

HUSBAND: Human remains in one form or another.

DERVISH: Naturally.

HUSBAND: And there'll be a lot of whys and wherefores?

DERVISH: Certainly there will.

HUSBAND: And the police will come into it.

DERVISH: Without a doubt.

HUSBAND: But the marvelous tree, the marvelous discovery, the benefit to science and mankind from all this?

DERVISH: Science and mankind will benefit from it all.

HUSBAND: They will benefit from "Bahadir's tree?"

DERVISH: Yes, they'll benefit from "Bahadir's tree," but Bahadir himself will be put in prison.

HUSBAND: What's that you're saying?

DERVISH: The law.

HUSBAND: The law will bring me to trial for this crime?

DERVISH: Naturally, because it is called the crime of murder.

HUSBAND: But I'll have made a useful discovery.

DERVISH: The law still calls it murder.

HUSBAND: Why doesn't the law change its name?

DERVISH: What should it call it? "The Bahadir crime"—instead of "the crime of murder?"

HUSBAND: Something like that. It shouldn't be punished but should be shelved.

DERVISH: Shelved for the public good!

HUSBAND: Indeed—exactly!

DERVISH: The matter will also require scholars on the law, jurisprudence and legislation!

HUSBAND: Why not?

DERVISH: And that would lead to changing the meanings of many things: murder for example—and the murderer and the murdered.

HUSBAND: Why not, let all that be changed! Let it be changed!

DERVISH: Yes, let it all be changed!

HUSBAND: Since the orange tree is no longer an orange tree, then everything must change its name and meaning.

DERVISH: Certainly, but . . . .

HUSBAND: But what?

DERVISH: But it is inevitable that a certain amount of time must pass before "prison" is called by some name other than prison's so that it may be possible to rescue you from between its bars.

HUSBAND: Do you think I'll really be brought to trial?

DERVISH: And you might be sentenced to death! Even so, though, what does a sentence of death matter to you?

HUSBAND: What does it matter to me?

DERVISH: Weren't you on the point of reporting the crime and giving yourself up?—unless at the time you weren't being serious.

HUSBAND: At the beginning I was certainly serious, but . . . .

DERVISH: You've changed your mind, then?

HUSBAND: The long and the short of it is that you now want to frighten me and make me back out.

DERVISH: I want you to see the matter clearly, to understand thoroughly what awaits you.

HUSBAND: The marvelous discovery means that my crime will be discovered!

DERVISH: Exactly.

HUSBAND: And the price will be paid!

DERVISH: Exactly.

HUSBAND [*thoughtfully*]: Then I must decide.

DERVISH: And take your decision after due deliberation.

HUSBAND: There is no need for deliberation—my decision is made and there is no going back on it. Nothing will make me be afraid or flinch, even though I be sentenced to death, for otherwise my life would be worthless!

DERVISH: What your decision?

HUSBAND: I want the marvelous tree.

DERVISH: Then go and take it its food.

HUSBAND: I'm going.

He moves toward where he has placed the body. Presently he is heard screaming and appears in a state of great agitation.

DERVISH: What's happened?

HUSBAND: The body! My wife! The body!

DERVISH: What about it?

HUSBAND: It's disappeared.

DERVISH: Disappeared—from its place?

HUSBAND: It's disappeared—it's not where I left it.

DERVISH: Perhaps it's in the garden?

HUSBAND: And who would have taken it? I hadn't yet taken it there.

DERVISH: In any case, go and have a look.

HUSBAND [*going*]: That's odd, very odd! [*He goes to the garden with the* DERVISH *watching him.*]

DERVISH: Found it?

HUSBAND [*calling from the garden*]: No, I haven't, but Lady Green . . . .

DERVISH: What about her? What about Lady Green?

HUSBAND: She's dead—lying in the hole.

DERVISH: Verily we belong to God and to Him do we return! I'm going off to the post office to send you a cable of condolence.

The DERVISH *disappears, at which the stage is left empty. Suddenly it is filled with the faint sounds of the party given seven days after birth: "Bargalatak, bargalatak," followed with equal suddenness by the sound of a train and its whistle, also the song of the school outing "O tree climber, bring me a cow . . . ." Then the two sounds merge: those of the party and the song of the train and its whistle, each blending with the other.*

CURTAIN

Translated by Denys Johnson-Davies

The Donkey Market

———∿∿∿———

Cast

TWO UNEMPLOYED MEN

FARMER

FARMER'S WIFE

SCENE ONE

Near the donkey market. From afar is heard the braying of donkeys. Outside the market sit two men whose ragged clothes and filthy appearance indicate that they are out-of-work loafers.

FIRST UNEMPLOYED [*to his companion*]: Are you able to tell me what the difference is between us and donkeys?

SECOND UNEMPLOYED: You can hear the difference with your own ears.

FIRST UNEMPLOYED: The braying?

SECOND UNEMPLOYED: Just so, the braying.

FIRST UNEMPLOYED: Couldn't this braying be donkey talk?

SECOND UNEMPLOYED: That's what it must be.

FIRST UNEMPLOYED: So they're talking now.

SECOND UNEMPLOYED: Maybe they're also shouting.

FIRST UNEMPLOYED: I wonder what they're saying?

SECOND UNEMPLOYED: You'd have to be a donkey to know that.

FIRST UNEMPLOYED: They talk to each other so loudly.

SECOND UNEMPLOYED: Naturally, don't they have to hear each other?

FIRST UNEMPLOYED: I thought donkeys whispered together.

SECOND UNEMPLOYED: Why? Why should they?

FIRST UNEMPLOYED: Just like us.

SECOND UNEMPLOYED: Don't worry . . . donkeys aren't like us.

FIRST UNEMPLOYED: You're quite right, donkeys are a civilized species.

SECOND UNEMPLOYED: What are you saying? Civilized?

FIRST UNEMPLOYED: Have you ever seen wild donkeys? There are wild horses and wild buffaloes and wild pigeons and wild cats, but ever since donkeys have been going around amongst us they've been working peacefully and talking freely.

SECOND UNEMPLOYED: Freely?

FIRST UNEMPLOYED: I mean aloud.

SECOND UNEMPLOYED: Talking about aloud, can you tell me why we aren't able to live decently, your goodself and my goodself?

FIRST UNEMPLOYED: Because your goodself and my goodself are broke.

SECOND UNEMPLOYED: And why are we broke?

FIRST UNEMPLOYED: Because no one gives a damn about us. If only we had a market like this donkey market, someone would buy us.

SECOND UNEMPLOYED: And why doesn't anybody buy us?

FIRST UNEMPLOYED: Because we're local merchandise.

SECOND UNEMPLOYED: What's wrong with that?

FIRST UNEMPLOYED: There's only money for foreign merchandise.

SECOND UNEMPLOYED: Why don't we go off and advertise ourselves?

FIRST UNEMPLOYED: How?

SECOND UNEMPLOYED: With our voices.

FIRST UNEMPLOYED: They wouldn't come out loud enough.

SECOND UNEMPLOYED: How is it that a donkey's voice comes out all right?

FIRST UNEMPLOYED: Because, as I told you, they're a civilized species.

SECOND UNEMPLOYED: You've got me interested. Oh, if only I were a donkey, like this one coming along! Look over there . . . the donkey being led along by the man who's taking it out from the market. I wonder how much he paid for it! Look how proud and cock-a-hoop he is as he takes it away!

FIRST UNEMPLOYED: I've had an idea.

SECOND UNEMPLOYED: What is it?

FIRST UNEMPLOYED: Would you like to become a donkey?

SECOND UNEMPLOYED: Me? How?

FIRST UNEMPLOYED: Don't ask questions. Would you like to or wouldn't you?

SECOND UNEMPLOYED: I'd like to, but how?

FIRST UNEMPLOYED: I'll tell you. You see the donkey that's coming toward us, being led by the man who bought it. Well, I'll go up to the man and distract him by chatting him up. At the same time you undo the rope round the donkey's neck without its owner noticing and tie it round your own neck.

SECOND UNEMPLOYED: That's all? And then what?

FIRST UNEMPLOYED: And then he'll lead you off and I'll lead off the donkey.

SECOND UNEMPLOYED: And where will he lead me off to?

FIRST UNEMPLOYED: I wouldn't be knowing, that's in the lap of the gods.

SECOND UNEMPLOYED: Are you talking seriously?

FIRST UNEMPLOYED: Isn't it you who want it this way?

SECOND UNEMPLOYED: I tie a rope round my neck and he leads me away?

FIRST UNEMPLOYED: And what's wrong with that? At least you'll have found yourself someone to guarantee that you get a bite to eat.

SECOND UNEMPLOYED: It won't be what you call a bite . . . more like a munch.

FIRST UNEMPLOYED: It's all the same . . . just something to eat.

SECOND UNEMPLOYED: As you say, it'll be a change from being hungry and without a roof over one's head. But how am I going to put myself over to the man?

FIRST UNEMPLOYED: That depends on how smart you are.

SECOND UNEMPLOYED: We'll have a go.

FIRST UNEMPLOYED: Hide yourself . . . the man mustn't catch sight of us together.

The two men part and the stage is empty. A man—he looks like a farmer—appears. He holds a rope with which he is leading a donkey. The FIRST UNEMPLOYED *approaches him.*

FIRST UNEMPLOYED: Peace be upon you!

FARMER: And upon you be peace!

FIRST UNEMPLOYED: Good God, man, is it that you don't know me or what?

FARMER: You . . . who would you be?

FIRST UNEMPLOYED: Who would I be? Didn't we break bread together?

FARMER: I don't understand. You mean to say we once broke bread together?

FIRST UNEMPLOYED: You mean you've forgotten all that quickly? No one but
a bastard forgets a good turn.

FARMER: Are you calling me a bastard?

FIRST UNEMPLOYED: May God strike dead anyone who said such a thing about
you. What I meant was that anyone who forgets his friends . . . but then,
thank God, you're a really decent and civil person, it's merely that it's just
slipped your mind what I look like. The point is that we met at night, over
dinner, and it just happened the moon wasn't out that night.

FARMER: The moon? When? Where?

FIRST UNEMPLOYED: I'll remind you. Just be patient till the knot's untied.

*He looks furtively at his companion who has slipped by unnoticed and is
engrossed in undoing the knot of the rope.*

FARMER: What's untied?

FIRST UNEMPLOYED: I'm tongue-tied. You've embarrassed me, you've made
me forget what I was saying. Give me some help. [*Stealing a glance at his
companion and urging him to hurry up.*] Get the knot untied and do me
the favor of getting me out of this.

FARMER: I can't understand a thing you're saying.

FIRST UNEMPLOYED: You'll understand soon enough . . . once the knot's untied,
which it must be . . . things have gone on for a long time . . . far too long.
Man, get it untied quickly.

FARMER: But what shall I untie?

FIRST UNEMPLOYED [*seeing that his companion has finished undoing the rope
and has tied it round his neck and let the donkey loose*]: Well, it's finally
got untied all right. It's the Almighty God Himself who unties and solves
things. Everything is untied and solved in its own good time. Everything

has its time, and seeing as how you don't remember me now I'll leave you time in which to think it over at your leisure. God willing, we'll be meeting up soon and you'll remember me and you'll give me a real warm welcome. Peace be upon you.

He leaves the FARMER *in a state of confusion. He goes behind the donkey, takes it, and moves off without being noticed.*

FARMER [*to himself*]: Where did I meet him? Where did we have dinner? The moon wasn't out? Could be . . . these days one's mind wanders a bit.

He pulls at the donkey's halter so as to lead it away, not knowing that the SECOND UNEMPLOYED *has taken the donkey's place.*

FARMER [*calling out*]: C'mon, donkey.

The SECOND UNEMPLOYED *imitates the braying of a donkey.*

FARMER [*looking round and being startled*]: Hey, what's this? Who are you?
SECOND UNEMPLOYED: I'm the donkey.
FARMER: Donkey?
SECOND UNEMPLOYED: Yes, the donkey you've just bought at the market.
FARMER: It's impossible!
SECOND UNEMPLOYED: Why are you so surprised? Didn't you just buy me at the market?
FARMER: Yes, but . . . .
SECOND UNEMPLOYED: But what?
FARMER: In the name of God the Merciful, the Compassionate!
SECOND UNEMPLOYED: Don't be frightened, I'm your donkey all right.
FARMER: How? . . . you're human.
SECOND UNEMPLOYED: It's your destiny, your good luck.
FARMER: Are you really human or are you . . .?
SECOND UNEMPLOYED: Yes, human, not a genie. Don't worry, it can all be explained. Just calm down a bit.

FARMER: I . . . I've calmed down.

SECOND UNEMPLOYED: Listen, then, my dear sir . . . the explanation is that my father . . . a nice fellow like your goodself . . . was, however, real stubborn and got it into his head to marry me off to a girl I'd never seen and who'd never seen me. I refused but he still insisted. I suggested to him that we talk it over and come to some sort of understanding, that it had to be discussed in a spirit of freedom. He got angry and said, "I won't have sons of mine arguing with me." I said to him, "I refuse to accept what you're saying." So he said to me, "You're an ass." I said to him, "I'm not an ass." He said, "I said you're an ass and you've got to be an ass," and he called upon God to turn me into an ass. It seems that at that moment the doors of Heaven were open and the prayer was answered and I was actually turned into a donkey. My father died and they found me in the livestock fold, having become part of his estate. They sold me at the market and you came along and bought me.

FARMER: Extraordinary! Then you are the donkey I bought?

SECOND UNEMPLOYED: The very same.

FARMER: And how is it that you're now back again as a human being?

SECOND UNEMPLOYED: I told you, it's your destiny, your good luck. It seems you're one of those godly people and the good Lord, may He be praised and exalted, decided to honor you. . . .

FARMER: Really! But what's to be done now?

SECOND UNEMPLOYED: What's happened?

FARMER: What's happened is that you . . . is that I . . . I don't know how to go about things. What I mean to say is that I've lost my money, I'm ruined.

SECOND UNEMPLOYED: You haven't lost a thing.

FARMER: How's that?

SECOND UNEMPLOYED: Didn't you buy yourself a donkey? The donkey's right here.

FARMER: Where is he?

SECOND UNEMPLOYED: And where have I gone to?

FARMER: You?

SECOND UNEMPLOYED: Yes, me.

FARMER: You want to tell me that you're . . . .

SECOND UNEMPLOYED: Wholly your property. You bought me with your money on the understanding I'm a donkey. The deal was concluded. Let's suppose that after that I turn into something else, that's no fault of yours. You've made a purchase and that's the end of it.

FARMER: Yes, I bought . . . .

SECOND UNEMPLOYED: That's it . . . relax.

FARMER: You mean to say you're my property now?

SECOND UNEMPLOYED: In accordance with the law. I'm yours by right. Right's right . . . and yours is guaranteed.

FARMER: Fair enough. Good, so let's get going.

SECOND UNEMPLOYED: At your disposal.

FARMER: Turn here, O . . . . Hey, what shall I call you?

SECOND UNEMPLOYED: Call me by any name. For instance, there's . . . there's Hassawi.* What d'you think of that for a name? Hassawi . . . come, Hassawi . . . go Hassawi!

FARMER: Hassawi?

SECOND UNEMPLOYED: It's relevant!

FARMER: May it have God's blessings. Let's go then. . . . Mr. Hassawi! Wait a moment, I think this business of the rope round your neck isn't really necessary.

SECOND UNEMPLOYED: As you think best.

FARMER: Better do without the rope . . . after all where would you go to? Wait while I undo it from round your neck.

SECOND UNEMPLOYED [undoing the rope himself]: Allow me. Allow me . . . if you'd be so good.

FARMER: Yes, that's right. Come along, let's go home, Mr. . . . . Hassawi.

SCENE TWO

Inside the farmer's house his WIFE is occupied with various household jobs. She hears knocking at the door.

WIFE: Who is it?

---

* Hassawi is a well-known breed of riding donkey in Egypt.

FARMER [*from outside*]: Me, woman. Open up.

WIFE [*opens the door and her husband enters*]: You were all this time at the market?

FARMER: I've only just got back.

WIFE: You bought the donkey?

FARMER: I bought . . . .

WIFE: You put it into the fold?

FARMER: What fold are you talking about, woman? Come along in, Mr. Hassawi.

WIFE: You've got a guest with you?

FARMER: Not a guest. He's what you might . . . I'll tell you later.

WIFE: Please come in.

FARMER: Off you go and make me a glass of tea.

The WIFE *goes off.*

HASSAWI [*looking around him*]: It seems I . . . .

FARMER: And what shall I say to my wife?

HASSAWI: Tell her the truth.

FARMER: The truth?

HASSAWI: Exactly . . . not a word more and not a word less. There's nothing better than plain-speaking.

FARMER: And where will you be sleeping in that case?

HASSAWI: In the fold.

FARMER: What do you mean "the fold?" Do you think that's right?

HASSAWI: That's where I belong. Don't change the order of things. The only thing is that if you've a mattress and a pillow you could put them down for me there.

FARMER: Fine, but what about food? It's not reasonable for you to eat straw, clover, and beans.

HASSAWI: I'll eat beans . . . just as long as they're broad beans.

FARMER: With a little oil over them?

HASSAWI: And a slice of lemon.

FARMER: And you'll go on eating beans forever?

HASSAWI: It's all a blessing from God!

FARMER: Just as you say. Donkeys have just the one food. They don't know the difference between breakfast, lunch, and dinner. It's straw and clover and beans and that's all.

HASSAWI: I know that.

FARMER: Fine, we've settled your sleeping and your food. Tell me now, what work are you going to do?

HASSAWI: All work donkeys do . . . except being ridden.

FARMER: Ridden?

HASSAWI: You can't ride me because you'd only fall off.

FARMER: And carrying things? For example I was intending taking a load of radishes and leeks on the donkey to the vegetable merchant.

HASSAWI: I'll do that job.

FARMER: You'll carry the vegetables on your shoulders?

HASSAWI: That's my business. I'll manage. I may be a donkey but I've got a brain.

FARMER: Brain? I was forgetting this question of a brain.

HASSAWI: Don't worry, this brain of mine's at your service. You can always rely on me. Just give me confidence and the right to talk things over with you freely.

FARMER: Meaning you can go on your own to the merchant with the produce?

HASSAWI: And agree for you the best price with him.

FARMER: We'll see.

WIFE [*from outside*]: Tea!

HASSAWI: If you'll excuse me.

FARMER: Where are you going?

HASSAWI: I'm going to inspect the fold I'm sleeping in.

FARMER: You'll find it on your right as you go out.

HASSAWI *goes out. The* WIFE *enters with the glass of tea.*

WIFE [*giving the tea to her husband*]: Your guest has gone out?

FARMER: He's not a guest, woman. He's . . . .

WIFE: What?

FARMER: He'd be a . . . a . . . .

WIFE: Be a what?

FARMER: He's a . . . a . . . .

WIFE: Who is he?

FARMER: You won't believe it.

WIFE: What won't I believe?

FARMER: What I'll tell you now.

WIFE: All right then, just tell me.

FARMER: He's . . . the donkey I bought.

WIFE: The donkey?

FARMER: Yes, didn't I go to the donkey market today to buy a donkey? He's the donkey I bought at the market.

WIFE: Man, do you want to make an utter fool of me?

FARMER: Didn't I tell you that you wouldn't believe me?

WIFE: But what shall I believe . . . that the market's selling human donkeys?

FARMER: He wasn't a human at the time I bought him . . . he was a donkey like the rest . . . and he was braying.

WIFE: He brays as well?

FARMER: Yes, by God, I swear by the Holy Book he was braying.

WIFE: And then?

FARMER: And then on the way home . . . I was leading him by the rope . . . I turned round and found that he'd changed into a human.

WIFE: God save us! . . . an afreet!

FARMER: No, woman, he's no afreet . . . he was transformed. Originally he was a human being, the son of decent folk like ourselves. He was then transformed into a donkey and they sold him off at the market. I bought him and God, may He be praised and exalted, decided to honor me so He turned him back into a human.

WIFE: Your omnipotence, O Lord!

FARMER: Well, that's what happened.

WIFE: But after all . . . .

FARMER: What? What do you want to say?

WIFE: Nothing.

FARMER: No, there's something you want to say.

WIFE: I want to say . . . what I mean is . . . is . . . what are we going to do with him now, with him being a . . . a human being?

FARMER: Do what with him? Exactly as with any other donkey . . . and in addition to that he's got a brain as well.

WIFE: I suppose we won't be able to ride him?

FARMER: Let's forget about the question of riding for the moment.

WIFE: And we'll talk to him as with other human beings?

FARMER: Yes, talk to him and call him by his name.

WIFE: He's got a name?

FARMER: Of course, what do you think? His name's Hassawi. We'll call him and say to him, "Come here, Hassawi; go there, Hassawi."

WIFE: And where will he sleep?

FARMER: In the fold. You can put a mattress out for him there.

WIFE: And what will he eat?

FARMER: Beans . . . but with oil.

WIFE: With oil?

FARMER: And lemon.

WIFE: And he drinks tea?

FARMER: Let's not get him used to that.

WIFE: How lovely! . . . we've got a human donkey!

FARMER: Be careful, woman, not to say such things to the neighbors or they'll be saying we've gone off our heads!

WIFE: And what shall I say to them?

FARMER: Say . . . say for example that he's a relative of ours from far away who's come to help us with the work during these few days just as we're coming into the month of Ramadan.

A knock at the door.

WIFE: Who is it?

HASSAWI [*from outside*]: Me. . . Hassawi.

WIFE [*to her husband*]: It's him!

FARMER: Open the door for him.

WIFE [*opens the door*]: Come in . . . and wipe your feet on the doorstep.

HASSAWI [*entering*]: I've cleaned myself a corner in the fold and spread it out with straw.

FARMER: There you are, my dear lady, he cleans up and makes his own bed . . . yet another advantage.

WIFE: Yes, let him get used to doing that.

HASSAWI: I was coming about an important matter.

FARMER: To do with what?

HASSAWI: To do with the vegetable merchant.

FARMER: The vegetable merchant? What about him?

HASSAWI: A man came on his behalf . . . I just met him at the door and he said the merchant was in a hurry to take delivery. I got him talking and understood that the prices of radishes and leeks would go up in Ramadan. I told him that you were still giving the matter your consideration because there's a new buyer who's offered you a better price. The man was shaken and immediately said that he was prepared to raise the price he was offering.

FARMER: He said so?

HASSAWI [*producing some money*]: I took a higher price from him. Here you are!

FARMER: God bless you!

HASSAWI: But I have a request to make of you.

FARMER: What is it?

HASSAWI: Would you allow me, before you decide definitely about something, to talk the matter over with you freely and frankly?

FARMER: I'm listening.

HASSAWI: Were you intending to hand over the whole crop to the merchant?

FARMER: Yes, the whole of it.

HASSAWI: Why?

FARMER: Because we need the money.

HASSAWI: Is it absolutely necessary at the present time?

FARMER: Yes it is. We're in dire need of money as we come up to Ramadan. Have you forgotten the dried fruits, the mixed nuts, and the dried apricot paste we need to buy?

HASSAWI: I've had an idea.

FARMER: Let's have it.

HASSAWI: We set apart a portion of the crop and have it for seed for the new sowing instead of buying seed at a high price during the sowing season.

FARMER: It's a long time until the new sowing.

WIFE: The Lord will look after the new sowing . . . we're living in today.

HASSAWI: As you say. In any event I've given you my opinion . . . I'm just afraid the time for the new sowing will come and you won't have the money to pay for the seeds and you'll have to borrow at interest or go off to a money-lender, and perhaps you'll be forced to sell me in the market.

FARMER: Let God look after such things.

WIFE: What's he talk so much for?

FARMER [*to* HASSAWI]: Have you got anything else to say?

HASSAWI: Yes, I'm frightened. . . .

FARMER: What are you frightened about? Tell us and let happen what may!

HASSAWI: Yes, I must say what I have in my mind and clear my conscience. As I was passing by your field just now I noticed that the feddans sown under radishes and leeks had at least ten kerats lying fallow because the irrigation water isn't reaching there.

FARMER: And what can we do about that?

HASSAWI: It needs one or two shadoofs.

FARMER: We thought about it.

HASSAWI: And what stopped you?

FARMER: Money . . . where's the money?

HASSAWI [*looking at the* WIFE's *wrist*]: Just one of the lady's bracelets. . . .

WIFE [*shouting*]: Ruination!

HASSAWI: By putting ten kerats under irrigation you'll get the price of the bracelet back from the first sowing.

FARMER: You think so?

WIFE [*beating her chest*]: What disaster! Man, are you thinking of listening to what that animal has to say? Are you seriously thinking of selling my bracelets?

FARMER: We haven't yet bought or sold anything . . . we're just talking things over.

WIFE: Talking things over with your donkey, you sheep of a man?

FARMER: What's wrong with that? Let me hear what he has to say . . . you too.

WIFE: Me listen? Listen to that? Listen to that nonsensical talk that gives you an ache in the belly? He's been nothing but an ache in the belly from the moment he came.

FARMER: He's entitled to his opinion.

WIFE: His opinion? What opinion would that be? That thing has an opinion? Are we to be dictated to by the opinion of a donkey in the fold?

FARMER: He's not like other donkeys.

WIFE: So what! I swear by Him who created and fashioned you that if that donkey of yours doesn't take himself off and keep his hands away from my bracelets I'll not stay on under this roof!

FARMER: Be sensible and calm down. After all, have we agreed to go along with his opinion?

WIFE: That was all that was missing . . . for you to go along with his opinion! All your life you've been master in your own house and your word has been law. Then off you go to the market and come back dragging along behind you your dear friend Mr. Hassawi, whose every opinion you listen to.

FARMER: His opinions and help have gained for us an increase in price from the merchant.

WIFE: An increase? He won't allow us to enjoy it. He wants to waste it all on his crazy ideas, just as we're about to have all the expenses of Ramadan . . . and then don't forget there's the Feast directly after Ramadan and for which we'll need cake. . . .

FARMER: And after the cake for the Feast we'll have to face up to the Big Feast for which we'll need a sheep.

WIFE: Knowing this as you do, why do you listen to his talk?

FARMER: Listening doesn't do any harm.

WIFE: Who said so? A lot of buzzing in the ears is worse than magic.

FARMER: What you're saying is that we should tell him to keep his mouth shut?

WIFE: With lock and bolt . . . and put a sock in it! He's a donkey and must remain a donkey and you're the master of the house and must remain master of the house. You're not some tassel on a saddlebag at this time of life. Have some pride, man . . . you, with your gray hairs!

FARMER: So I'm a tassel on a saddlebag?

WIFE: You're getting that way, I swear it. Your dear friend Hassawi is almost all-powerful here.

FARMER: How all-powerful, woman? I still have the reins in my hand.

HASSAWI [*to himself*]: The reins?

FARMER: All right, what are you waiting for? Why don't you put the bridle on him as from now?

WIFE: And what does it matter if we let him ramble on as he wants?

HASSAWI [*to himself*]: Ramble on?

WIFE: I'm frightened of all this rambling and rumbling of his.

FARMER: What are you frightened of?

WIFE: That he'll try to fool you and you'll believe him.

FARMER: Believe him? Why should I? Who said I was a donkey?

WIFE: The donkey's there in front of you and he's had his say.

FARMER: Talking's one thing and action's another.

WIFE: What action are you talking about . . . you've let the rope go.

FARMER: You're saying I should tie him by the neck?

WIFE: Like every other donkey.

FARMER: But he's human, woman.

WIFE: Originally he was a donkey. When you bought him from the donkey market, when you paid good money for him, he was a donkey, and so his place is out there in the fold and he mustn't enter the house or have a say in things. That's how it should be. If you don't like it I'll go out and call upon the neighbors to bear witness. I'll say to them: "Come to my rescue, folk . . . my man's gone crazy in the head and has bought a donkey from the market which he's made into a human and whose opinions he's listening to."

FARMER: Don't be mad, woman!

WIFE: By the Prophet, I'll do it. . . .

FARMER: All right, keep quiet . . . that's it!

WIFE: What d'you mean, "That's it?" Explain!

FARMER: We'll go back to how we were and relax. Hey, you, Hassawi, listen here!

HASSAWI: Sir!

FARMER: See, this business of my asking your opinion and your asking mine doesn't work. I'm the man with the say-so round here, and all you've got to do is obey. What I mean is that that mouth of yours mustn't utter a word ... understand? Go off to the fold while I arrange about your work.

HASSAWI: Certainly, but would you just allow me to say something ... one last word?

WIFE: What cheek! He's told you that you shouldn't talk, that you should keep your mouth closed and shut up. You really are a cheeky fellow!

HASSAWI: That's it, then ... I've closed my mouth and shut up. With your permission. [*He goes out.*]

Scene Three

Outside the door of the FARMER'*s house* HASSAWI *suddenly sees his companion, the* FIRST UNEMPLOYED, *approaching and leading the original donkey. The two friends embrace.*

HASSAWI [*to his companion*]: Tell me ... what did you do?

FIRST UNEMPLOYED: And you? How did you get on?

HASSAWI: I'll tell you right now. How, though, did you know I was here?

FIRST UNEMPLOYED: I walked along far behind you without your noticing. Tell me ... what happened with our friend the owner of the donkey?

HASSAWI: You're well rid of him. He's an idiotic man who doesn't know where his own good lies. And why have you now come back with the donkey?

FIRST UNEMPLOYED: We don't need it. Things are settled ... the good Lord's settled them.

HASSAWI: How's that?

FIRST UNEMPLOYED: We've found work.

HASSAWI: You've found work?

FIRST UNEMPLOYED: For you and me.

HASSAWI: Where? Tell me quickly!

FIRST UNEMPLOYED: After I left you and went off, I and the donkey, I found a large field where there were people sowing. I said to them: "Have you got any work." "Lots," they said . . . "for you and ten like you." I said to them: "I've got someone with me." "You're welcome," they said to me. "Go and bring him along immediately and start working." So I came to you right away.

HASSAWI: Extraordinary! There we were absolutely dying to get work, remember? People used to look at us and say, "Off with you, you down-and-out tramps, off with the two of you . . . we've got no work for down-and-outs!"

FIRST UNEMPLOYED: It seems that having the donkey alongside me improved my reputation!

HASSAWI: You're right. Don't people always say "He works like a donkey?" A donkey means work just as a horse means honor. Don't people say that the riding of horses brings honor, that dogs are good guards, and that cats are thieves?

FIRST UNEMPLOYED: Yes, by God, that's right. They saw me with the donkey and said to themselves, "He can't be a down-and-out tramp . . . he must be one for hard work," so they took me on my face value and you sight unseen . . . on the basis of my recommendation!

HASSAWI: Your recommendation or the donkey's?

FIRST UNEMPLOYED: The donkey's. It actually got the work for both you and me. Isn't it only fair that we should return it to its owner?

HASSAWI: That's only fair.

FIRST UNEMPLOYED: What shall we say to him?

HASSAWI: We'll tell him to take back his donkey.

FIRST UNEMPLOYED: And you . . . didn't you pretend to be his donkey and tie the halter round your neck?

HASSAWI: He'll now prefer the real donkey.

FIRST UNEMPLOYED: Look, instead of handing over the donkey to him and getting into all sorts of arguments, with him asking us where the donkey was and where we were, we'll tie the donkey up for him in front of his house and clear off. What d'you think?

HASSAWI: Much the best idea . . . let's get going.

They tie the donkey to the door of the house, then knock at the door and disappear from view. The door opens and the FARMER *appears.*

FARMER [*sees the donkey and is astonished and shouts*]: Come along, woman!

WIFE [*appearing at the door*]: What's up?

FARMER: Look and see!

WIFE: What?

FARMER: He's been transformed again . . . Hassawi's become a donkey like he was at the market. He's exactly the same as he was when I bought him.

WIFE: Thanks be to God . . . how generous you are, O Lord!

FARMER: Yes, but . . . .

WIFE: But what? What else do you want to say?

FARMER: But we're the cause.

WIFE: Why, though? What did we do to him?

FARMER: We did the same as his father did to him . . . he silenced him and turned him into a donkey!

WIFE: And what's wrong with him being a donkey? At least we can ride him.

FARMER: You're right. When he was a human with a brain he was useless for riding.

WIFE: And what did we need his brain for? What we want is something to ride, something that's going to bear our weight and take us from one place to another. Give thanks to the Lord, man, for returning your useful donkey to you.

FARMER [*gently stroking the donkey's head*]: Don't hold it against us, Hassawi! Fate's like that. I hope you're not annoyed. For us, though, you're still as you were . . . Mr. Hassawi.

WIFE: Are you still at it, man? Are you still murmuring sweet nothings to that donkey? Mind . . . he'll go back to speaking again!

The FARMER *leads his donkey away in silence toward the fold, while the* WIFE *lets out shrill cries of joy.*

CURTAIN

Translated by Denys Johnson-Davies

The Song of Death

—∿—

Cast

ASAKIR

MABROUKA

ALWAN, Asakir's son

SUMEIDA, Mabrouka's son

A peasant house in Upper Egypt. Two women are sitting by the entrance dressed in black: they are ASAKIR *and* MABROUKA. *A step or two away from them stand a calf and a goat eating grass and dried clover. The two women are sitting in silence with heads lowered. The sound of a train's whistle is heard.*

MABROUKA [*raising her head*]: That's the train.

ASAKIR [*without moving*]: D'you think he's on it?

MABROUKA: Didn't he say so in his letter which Sheikh Mohamed al-Isnawi, the assistant schoolmaster, read over to us yesterday?

ASAKIR: I hope, Mabrouka, you haven't told anyone he's my son.

MABROUKA: Am I crazy? Your son Alwan was drowned in the well at the water-wheel when a child of only two years. The whole village knows that.

ASAKIR: But they still can't quite swallow that story.

MABROUKA: Who are *they*—the Tahawis?

ASAKIR: Didn't your son Sumeida tell you what he heard in the market the other day?

MABROUKA: What did he hear?

ASAKIR: He heard one of them say, in a crowd of people, that either the Azizis have nothing but women left, or they are hiding a man to take vengeance—a man nearer to the murdered man than his cousin Sumeida.

MABROUKA: Yes, my son Sumeida did say that. Were it not for this rumor he wouldn't be able to walk about the village with raised head.

ASAKIR: Let them learn today that the son of the murdered man is still alive. There is no reason to fear for him now that he has attained manhood. It is no longer I who live in fear but those who cannot sleep at night for fear. Bring him quickly, train, quickly, for I have waited so long! Seventeen years! I have counted them up hour by hour. Seventeen years! I have milked them from Time's udders drop by drop just as the milk drips out from the udder of an old cow.

MABROUKA [*listening to the sound of a whistle*]: There's the train as it enters the station. He'll find my son Sumeida waiting for him.

ASAKIR [*as though talking to herself*]: Yes.

MABROUKA [*turning toward her*]: What's wrong, Asakir? You're trembling?

ASAKIR [*as though talking to herself*]: Sumeida's song will tell me.

MABROUKA: Tell you?

ASAKIR: About whether he's come.

MABROUKA: You told my son to sing as a sign that Alwan had come?

ASAKIR: Yes, as they approach together from the district office.

MABROUKA: Take heart, Asakir. Take heart. Much has passed, only little yet remains.

ASAKIR: What I feel now is neither fear nor weakness.

MABROUKA: The days of fear have gone never to return. I shall never forget that day I hid your son Alwan when he was two years old in the large basket of meal and carried him off by night, taking him out of the village to Cairo to put him with your relative who worked as a grinder in the perfume shop in the district of Sayyidna al-Hussein.

ASAKIR: I told him: bring him up as a butcher so that he can use a knife well.

MABROUKA: He didn't carry out your wish.

ASAKIR: No, he did—when he was seven years old he put him into a butcher's shop, but the boy ran away.

MABROUKA: To join al-Azhar University.

ASAKIR: Yes, and when I went to see him last year, I found him dressed in his turban and gibba, looking very dignified. I said to him: "If only your father could have seen you like this he would have been proud of you." But they didn't allow him to see his son grow up and know such joy.

MABROUKA: Wouldn't it have been better if he'd stayed on at the butcher's shop?

ASAKIR: Why do you say that, Mabrouka?

MABROUKA: I don't know, a passing thought.

ASAKIR: I know that thought.

MABROUKA: What is it, Asakir?

ASAKIR: It hurts you that my son puts a turban and gibba while yours goes on wearing a skullcap and peasant gown.

MABROUKA: I swear to you, by the soul of the departed, that such a thing never occurred to me.

ASAKIR: Then why do you hate Alwan being at al-Azhar University?

MABROUKA: By God, it's not that I hate it, only that I fear . . . .

ASAKIR: Fear what?

MABROUKA: That . . . that he does not know well how to use a knife.

ASAKIR: Have trust. Have trust, Mabrouka. When you see Alwan now that he has grown into a man you'll find that he has the strength of arm you know about in the Azizis.

MABROUKA [*listening to the whistle*]: The train is leaving the station.

ASAKIR: Let it leave to where it will just so long as it has brought us Alwan to take away the life of the murderer and leave him a rotting corpse for the farm dogs.

MABROUKA: And if he hasn't come?

ASAKIR: Why do you say that, Mabrouka?

MABROUKA: I don't know—just speculation.

ASAKIR: And what would prevent him from coming?

MABROUKA: And what is there to induce him to leave the civilization of Cairo and of al-Azhar to come here?

ASAKIR: It's his birthplace, it's where blood calls out to him for revenge.

MABROUKA: How far our village is from Cairo! Can the voice of blood reach
to the capital?

ASAKIR: Do you believe he won't come?

MABROUKA: I know no better than you, Asakir.

ASAKIR: And his letter which the schoolmaster read for us?

MABROUKA: Have you forgotten that he said in it: "Perhaps I'll come if circumstances permit." Who knows whether the circumstances have
permitted or not?

ASAKIR: Don't break my spirit, Mabrouka. Don't destroy the hope of someone
who heard the train whistles turn to trilling cries of joy in her heart as they
made it known that this long period of mourning was nearly at an end.
Alwan not coming? What would be my fate? Until when would I have to
wait for another time?

MABROUKA: The station is not far away and the district office is close by. If he
had come Sumeida would by now have started to sing.

ASAKIR: Perhaps they're walking leisurely and talking together. It's more than
three years ago since they met—the last time your son went off to Cairo
at the time of the birthday feast of Sayyidna al-Hussein.

MABROUKA: If he'd come my son would be so overjoyed he'd have burst into
song before reaching the district office.

ASAKIR: Perhaps he forgot about it.

MABROUKA: He couldn't forget.

ASAKIR [*listening*]: I don't hear singing.

MABROUKA: [*listening*]: Nor I.

ASAKIR: No one singing—not even a shepherd. Nothing singing—not even an
owl in some ruins. I believe, Mabrouka, that he has not come.

MABROUKA [*as though talking to herself*]: My heart tells me something.

ASAKIR: My heart, too, my heart that is as sealed as a tomb, as hard as rock,
has now begun to tell me things.

MABROUKA: What does it tell you?

ASAKIR: Of things that will happen.

MABROUKA: Tell me.

ASAKIR [*listening hard*]: Quiet! Listen! Listen! Do you hear, Mabrouka? Do
you hear?

MABROUKA: Sumeida's singing.

ASAKIR: Oh what joy!

They listen with all their attention to SUMEIDA's *song which is heard coming from outside more and more clearly.*

SUMEIDA [*singing outside in the dialect of Upper Egypt*]:

Friend, what excuses have we given,
What assurances that we'd repent?
And when your blame you yet continued
Our shirt and outer robe we rent.
When of the father I did hear
My shame no bounds did know,
And both mine eyes did open wide
And copious tears did flow.

ASAKIR: Has he come? Has Alwan come? Today I'll rend the garment of shame and put on the robes of self-respect.

MABROUKA: And we'll hold a funeral for the departed.

ASAKIR: And slaughter the goat and calf for his soul.

MABROUKA: Oh what joy! [*She is about to let forth trilling cries of joy.*]

ASAKIR [*stopping her*]: Not now, or things will be revealed before their time.

MABROUKA: From now, Oh Suweilam Tahawi, your hours are numbered.

There is a knock at the door. ASAKIR *hurries to open it.* SUMEIDA *appears carrying a bag.*

SUMEIDA: I've brought Sheikh Alwan.

He puts the bag on the ground and ALWAN *follows him in.*

ASAKIR [*opening her arms to* ALWAN]: My son, Alwan, my boy!

ALWAN [*kisses his mother on the head*]: Mother!

ASAKIR [*to her son*]: Give greetings to your aunt Mabrouka!

ALWAN [*turning*]: How are you, Aunt Mabrouka?

MABROUKA: Things are unchanged with us, Alwan. Our hopes lie in you.

SUMEIDA: Let us go now to our house, Mother.

MABROUKA: Yes, Asakir, the hour of release is near!

MABROUKA *goes off with her son* SUMEIDA. *Only* ASAKIR *and* ALWAN *remain onstage.*

ASAKIR: Aren't you hungry, Alwan? I have a bowl of curds.

ALWAN: I am not hungry, Mother, I ate some bread and eggs on the train.

ASAKIR: Aren't you thirsty?

ALWAN: Nor thirsty.

ASAKIR: No, you have not come for our food or our drink—you have come to eat of his flesh and to drink of his blood.

ALWAN [*like someone in a dream*]: I have come, Mother, for something great!

ASAKIR: I know, my son. I know. Wait while I bring you something you have never seen before. [*She hurries off into an inner room.*]

ALWAN [*looking round about him*]: My eye still sees in your houses these animals and their droppings, the filth of the water pitcher, and the lengths of firewood and maize stalks roofing over this tumble-down ceiling.

ASAKIR [*appearing from the room carrying a saddlebag which she throws down in front of her son*]: Seventeen years I've kept these things for you!

ALWAN [*looks at the saddlebag without moving*]: What's this?

ASAKIR: The saddlebag in which your father's body was brought to me, carried upon his donkey. In this pocket I found his head, in the other the rest of his body cut into pieces. They killed him with the knife he was carrying. They put the knife with his body in the saddlebag. Look, this is the knife. I kept it like this with the blood on it so that it's gone rusty. As for the donkey which brought your murdered father, making its way to the house it knew, its head lowered as though mourning its owner, I have been unable to keep it for you: it has died, unable to bear the long years.

ALWAN: And who did all this?

ASAKIR: Suweilam Tahawi.

ALWAN: How did you find out?

ASAKIR: The whole village knows.

ALWAN: Yes, you told me that. You mentioned his name to me dozens of times whenever you came to visit me in Cairo. I was young and unthinking and did not discuss things with you, but today my mind wants to be convinced. What proof is there? Was this crime investigated?

ASAKIR: Investigated?

ALWAN: Yes, what did the district attorney's office say?

ASAKIR: District attorney? For shame! Would we say anything to the district attorney's office? Would the Azizis do such a thing? Did the Tahawis ever do such a thing?

ALWAN: Didn't the district attorney's office question you?

ASAKIR: They asked us and we said we knew nothing and had not seen a body. We buried your father secretly at night.

ALWAN [*as though talking to himself*]: So that we might take vengeance into our hands.

ASAKIR: With the same knife with which your father was killed.

ALWAN: And the murderer?

ASAKIR: Alive and well. Alive. There is not a Sheikh's tomb in the district, not a shrine, not a saint at whose grill I have not clung, in whose dust I have not covered my head, at whose grave I have not bared my hair, praying that God might keep him alive till you, my son, bring about his death with your own hand.

ALWAN: Are you sure, Mother, that it is he?

ASAKIR: We have no enemies but the Tahawis.

ALWAN: And how are you to know that it's Suweilam Tahawi himself?

ASAKIR: Because he believes that it was your father who killed his father.

ALWAN: And did my father really kill his father?

ASAKIR: God knows best!

ALWAN: And what's the origin of this enmity between the two families?

ASAKIR: I don't know. No one knows. It's something from of old. All we know is that there has always been blood between them and us.

ALWAN: The origin could be that one day a calf belonging to one of our forefathers drank from a watering-place in a field of one of their forefathers!

ASAKIR: Knowledge about that lies with Him who knows the invisible. All that people know is that between the Azizis and the Tahawis rivers of blood have flowed.

ALWAN: They irrigate no vegetation or fruit.

ASAKIR [*continuing*]: They only stopped to flow after the death of your father—because you were so young. The years flowed by, dry like the days of high summer, till people began whispering and others spread false rumors. I twisted and turned on a fire of rage, suppressing my anger, waiting for this moment. And now it has come, so rise up, my son, and quench my fire, water my thirst for revenge with the blood of Suweilam Tahawi!

ALWAN: And has this Suweilam Tahawi a son?

ASAKIR: He has a son of fourteen.

ALWAN: Then I have no more than four or five years left.

ASAKIR: What are you saying?

ALWAN [*continuing*]: Until he becomes strong and does to me what I shall do to his father.

ASAKIR: Are you afraid for your life, Alwan?

ALWAN: And you, Mother, are you not afraid for it?

ASAKIR: God is my witness how afraid I am for every hair on your head!

ALWAN: You hold dear my life, Mother?

ASAKIR: And have I any life except through yours, Alwan? Have the Azizis any life except through you? For seventeen years we have all lived only by the breaths you draw.

ALWAN [*with lowered head*]: Yes, I understand.

ASAKIR: What feelings of humiliation we have had and how patiently we have suffered harm, yet no sooner does the specter of you cross our minds than our resolution is spurred on, our determination is strengthened and we look at each other in hope, a hope centered on you.

ALWAN [*with head lowered, like someone talking to himself*]: Truly you must have my life.

ASAKIR: Even your father's funeral waits for you, Alwan. These animals have been prepared for slaughter; my wailing, which I have imprisoned in my throat all these years, waits for you to burst forth; my gown that I have refrained from rending all this time bides your coming; everything in our existence is lifeless and stagnant and looks to you to charge it with life.

ALWAN [*as though talking to himself*]: Is it thus that you are charged with life?

ASAKIR: Yes, Alwan. Hasten the promised hour; hasten it, for we have waited too long.

ALWAN [*in surprise*]: The promised hour?

ASAKIR: I have forgotten nothing, not even the stone on which to sharpen the rusted knife. I have brought it for you and hidden it in that room.

ALWAN: And how shall I know this Suweilam, never having seen him in my life?

ASAKIR: Sumeida will lead you to him and will show you where he is.

ALWAN [*looking at his clothes*]: And shall I commit this act dressed as I am?

ASAKIR: Take off those clothes of yours. I have an aba of your father's, which I have kept for you. [*She moves toward the inner room.*]

ALWAN [*stopping her*]: There's no hurry, Mother. What's the rush?

ASAKIR: Every breath Suweilam takes with you here is a gift from you to him.

ALWAN: And what's the harm in that?

ASAKIR: It is taken from our own breaths, is deducted from our happiness. Despite ourselves we provided him with an extension of life that has almost put us in our graves. Look closely at your mother, Alwan! I was in my youth when your father died. Look at what these years have done to me! It is as though they were forty years, not seventeen! The sap of youth has drained away, the bones have lost their vigor, and no strength is left to me except the unforgettable memory, the unrelenting heart.

ALWAN [*as though talking to himself*]: How heavy is the price of revenge upon the person taking it!

ASAKIR [*not understanding*]: What are you saying, Alwan?

ALWAN: I am saying that the Mighty Avenger was merciful to us when He wanted to take from us this burden without paying a price.

ASAKIR [*in a suspicious tone*]: What do you mean?

ALWAN: Nothing, Mother. Nothing.

ASAKIR [*in a decisive tone*]: Take off your clothes and I'll bring you the aba. I'll sharpen the knife with my own hand.

ALWAN: Is there no mosque nearby?

ASAKIR: We have only a small prayer-room near to Sheikh Isnawi's school.

ALWAN [*making a move*]: I shall go to it to perform the sunset prayer.

ASAKIR: Now?

ALWAN: I think the sun has almost set.

ASAKIR: Do you want all the people of the village to see you there?

ALWAN: It is the best opportunity for serving my purpose.

ASAKIR [*staring at him*]: Are you mad, Alwan?

ALWAN [*continuing*]: This meeting with the villagers is for me one of the most important things. Did I not just tell you that I have come for something important?

ASAKIR [*sarcastically*]: I can't think you're going to tell the villagers what you've come for!

ALWAN: I must let them all know about it.

ASAKIR: Alwan! My son! What am I hearing from you! Are you being serious? Are you in your right mind? What will you say to them?

ALWAN [*like one in a dream*]: I shall tell them what I have come to tell them. For so long I have thought about my village and its people, despite my long absence. In the free time from lessons at al-Azhar, when fellow students gather together, when newspaper are read, and when we are overcome by yearning for the land where we have been raised, we ask ourselves longingly: when will our people in the countryside live like human beings in clean houses where the animals do not eat with them? When will their roofs be covered with something other than twigs from cotton bushes and maize stalks, and their walls be painted with something other than mud and animal dung? When will the water jar be replaced by clean running water, and electricity take the place of lanterns? Is that too much to wish for our people? Have not our people the same rights in life as others?

ASAKIR [*like someone who does not understand*]: What talk is this, Alwan?

ALWAN: This is what the villagers must know, and it is the duty of us who have been educated in Cairo to open their eyes to their rights in life. The attainment of this goal is not difficult for them if they unite and help one another and co-operate in setting up a council from amongst themselves which will impose taxes on those who can pay, and to form teams of the strong and the able who, during their long hours of free time, will set up bridges and construction works, instead of wasting it in dissension and squabbles. If they rallied round this idea and expended serious effort on this task, they could make a model village here, and it would not be long before all the villages in the countryside were copying it.

ASAKIR: This bookish talk is something to chat about later on with Sheikh Mohamed al-Isnawi, who will understand it. As for now, Alwan, we have more important things before us.

ALWAN [*brought up with a jolt*]: What is more important than that?

ASAKIR: Yes, leave off praying tonight in the prayer-room in case its spoils things. Pray here tonight if you want to. Get up and take off your clothes and I'll bring you some water from the jar to wash yourself with, then put on the aba and we'll sharpen the knife together.

ALWAN [*in a whisper with head lowered*]: Almighty God, grant me your mercy, your favor and your pardon.

ASAKIR: What are you saying, Alwan?

ALWAN [*raising his head*]: I was saying that I come only to open people's eyes to life; I bring you life.

ASAKIR: And this is what we have been waiting for patiently for all these nights—seventeen years with all the Azizis like the dead, waiting for you to come to bring them back life!

ALWAN [*in a whisper with head lowered*]: Oh God! What shall I do with these people?

ASAKIR: Why do you keep your head lowered like that? Get up and don't waste time. Get up.

ALWAN [*taking heart, he raises his head*]: Mother, I won't kill!

ASAKIR [*concealing her dismay*]: What do I hear?

ALWAN: I won't kill.

ASAKIR [*in a hoarse voice*]: Your father's blood!

ALWAN: It is you who have failed him by hiding it from the government—reprisal is for those in power.

ASAKIR [*paying no attention*]: The blood of your father!

ALWAN: My hand was not created to bring about someone's death.

ASAKIR [*half out of her mind*]: The blood of your father!

ALWAN [*alarmed at her state*]: Mother—what's happened to you?

ASAKIR [*as though unconscious of anyone being with her*]: The blood of your father . . . seventeen years . . . the blood of your father . . . seventeen years . . . .

ALWAN: Calm yourself, Mother. Certainly it is a shock but you must understand that I am not the man to murder with a knife.

ASAKIR [*whispering, like someone possessed*]: Seventeen years—revenge for your father—seventeen years.

ALWAN [*as though talking to himself*]: I know that you have suffered and endured for a long time, Mother. Were your patience and endurance for a worthwhile end I would have performed miracles for you, but you must understand. . . .

ASAKIR [*in a choking voice*]: The blood of your father!

ALWAN [*hurrying over to her in alarm*]: Mother! Mother! Mother!

ASAKIR [*rousing herself a little in his arms*]: Who are you?

ALWAN: Your son Alwan. Your son.

ASAKIR [*coming to her senses and shouting*]: My son? My own son? No, never, never!

ALWAN [*taken aback*]: Mother!

ASAKIR: I am not your mother. I do not know you. No son issued from my belly.

ALWAN: Try to understand, Mother.

ASAKIR: Get out of my house. God's curse be on you until the Day of Judgment. Get out of my house.

ALWAN: Mother!

ASAKIR [*shouting*]: Get out of my house or I shall call the men to put you out. We have our men, there are still men amongst Azizis, but you are not one of them. Get out. Get out of my house.

ALWAN [*taking up his bag*]: I shall go to the station to return whence I came. I ask God to calm your agitated soul and shall see you shortly in Cairo; then I shall explain to you my point of view in an atmosphere of calm far away from here. Till we see each other again, Mother!

He goes off, leaving ASAKIR *in her place, motionless. A moment later* SUMEIDA *appears, putting his head round the door and pushing it open gently.*

SUMEIDA: Was it you who were shouting, Aunt Asakir?

ASAKIR [*with determination, having recovered her senses*]: Come, Sumeida!

SUMEIDA [*looking around him*]: Where's your son Alwan?

ASAKIR: I have no son, I was not blessed with children.

SUMEIDA: What are you saying, Aunt Asakir?

ASAKIR: Had I a son he would take revenge for his father.

SUMEIDA [*looking round the room*]: Where has he gone?

ASAKIR: To the station in order to return to Cairo.

SUMEIDA: My mother was right! When she saw him just now she said, as we were going out: "This gentleman is not the one to kill Suweilam Tahawi."

ASAKIR: Oh that my belly had been ripped apart before bringing into the world such a son!

SUMEIDA: Take it easy, Aunt—there are men among the Azizis!

ASAKIR: Our hopes rest in you, Sumeida.

SUMEIDA: A cousin in place of a son.

ASAKIR: But the son is alive. It is he who should avenge the blood of his father. He is alive, alive and walking about amongst people.

SUMEIDA: Assume that he has died.

ASAKIR: Would that he had actually died as a child in the well of the water-wheel. We would not have waited these long years, squirming with pain on the coals of suppressed rage, waiting futilely. Would that he were dead—we could have lived with our excuse and we would not have had to clothe ourselves in shame. But he is alive and it has been spread abroad in the district, has been circulated in the market place that he is alive. What disgrace! What ignominy! What shame!

SUMEIDA: Take it easy, Aunt!

ASAKIR: Everything is easy to bear except this disgrace! After it life becomes impossible. How can I live in the village when the people know that I have such a son? Everyone will spit in disgust at the mere mention of his name. From every side voices will be raised saying: "What a failure of a belly that brought forth such a child!" Yes, this belly! [*She strikes at her belly with violent blows.*] All the women of the village will scoff at it, even the deformed, the dull-witted, and the barren. This belly! This belly!

SUMEIDA [*trying to prevent her striking herself*]: Aunt Asakir, do not hurt yourself in this way!

ASAKIR: Bring the knife, Sumeida—I'll rip it open with it!

SUMEIDA: Have you gone mad?

ASAKIR: Sumeida—are you a man?

SUMEIDA [*staring at her*]: What do you want?

ASAKIR: Ward off the shame from your cousin!

SUMEIDA: Alwan?

ASAKIR: And from his mother, your Aunt Asakir.

SUMEIDA: What am I to do?

ASAKIR [*taking up the knife from the saddlebag*]: Kill him with this knife!

SUMEIDA: Kill whom?

ASAKIR: Alwan. Plunge this knife into his chest!

SUMEIDA: Kill Alwan? Your son?

ASAKIR: Yes, kill him, bring him to his death.

SUMEIDA: Be sensible, Aunt!

ASAKIR: Do it, Sumeida—for my sake and for his!

SUMEIDA: For his?

ASAKIR: Yes, it is better for him and for me for it to be said that he was killed than that he shirked taking vengeance for his father.

SUMEIDA: My cousin!

ASAKIR: If you're a man, Sumeida, don't let him dishonor the Azizis! After today you will not be able to walk like a man amongst people; they will whisper about you, will laugh up their sleeves at you, will point to you in the market places saying: "A woman hiding behind a woman!"

SUMEIDA [*as though talking to himself*]: A woman?

ASAKIR: If there were such a son amongst the Tahawis, they would not have allowed him to stay alive for a single hour.

SUMEIDA [*as though talking to himself*]: "A woman hiding behind a woman!"

ASAKIR: Yes, you—if you accept to condone your cousin after what has happened!

SUMEIDA [*stretching out his hand resolutely*]: Give me the knife!

ASAKIR [*giving him the knife*]: Take it—no, wait, I'll wash off the rust and blood.

SUMEIDA [*impatiently*]: Give it here—before he makes his escape on the evening train.

ASAKIR [*giving him the knife resolutely*]: Take it, and may his blood wash off his father's blood that has dried on the blade.

SUMEIDA [*leaving with the knife*]: If his killing is brought about, Aunt, you will hear my voice raised in song from by the district office.

He goes out hurriedly. ASAKIR *remains alone, rooted to the ground like a statue, her eyes staring out, like someone stupefied. Then* MABROUKA *appears at the door, carrying a dish on her head.*

MABROUKA [*taking the dish from her head*]: A salted fish I brought for Sheikh Alwan.

ASAKIR [*turning to her slowly*]: Someone has died, Mabrouka!

MABROUKA: God spare you—who?

ASAKIR: Alwan.

MABROUKA: Your son?

ASAKIR: I now have no son, he has become one with the dust.

MABROUKA: What's this you're saying, Asakir? I left him with you just a while ago. Where is he?

ASAKIR: He went to the station to return whence he came and to flee from taking vengeance for his father.

MABROUKA [*with head lowered*]: That is what my heart told me.

ASAKIR: Your prediction was right, Mabrouka.

MABROUKA: Would that he had not come!

ASAKIR: Seventeen years we waited!

MABROUKA: And each year you would say, "He's grown older"—it was as if he were a maize plant that you were measuring each day with the span of your hand, until it had flourished and the corncob had properly ripened; you then tore off the covering only to find that it was empty of seed and fruit.

ASAKIR: If only he had grown up like some useless plant, it would have been easier to bear for we would not have expected to profit from him. As it was, we expected that he would restore our honor. How often, Mabrouka, did I feel proud of him within myself and boast of him in front of you, reckoning that I had produced a son who would wash clean the family honor. And lo! The son I have borne and whom I hid away, as one hides a treasure inside a clay jar, is nothing but a mark of shame that has befallen our tree, just as the blight attacks the cotton bush. A thousand mercies on your soul, O husband of mine whose blood has been spilt! I bore you the son who will make it possible for your adversaries to gloat and your enemies to rejoice.

MABROUKA: What degradation for the Azizis!

ASAKIR: Yes, were he to remain alive, but soon he will be buried in the ground!

MABROUKA [*turning round suddenly*]: Where is Sumeida?

ASAKIR [*listening carefully for the sound of a whistle*]: Quiet! There's the evening train entering the station!

MABROUKA: Where's Sumeida, Asakir?

ASAKIR [*listening carefully*]: Be quiet! Be quiet! Now at this moment, at this very moment . . . .

MABROUKA [*in surprise*]: What about this moment?

ASAKIR [*as though talking to herself*]: D'you think he has caught the train or has he been caught by . . . .

MABROUKA: So long as he's gone to the station as you said, he must have caught the train, and no good will come from all these pleas for perdition you heap on him.

ASAKIR: Do you really think he's caught the train, Mabrouka?

MABROUKA: And what will stop him?

ASAKIR [*unconsciously*]: Sumeida!

MABROUKA: Sumeida? Did he go after him to stop him from going?

ASAKIR: Yes.

MABROUKA: When did he go?

ASAKIR: Shortly before you came.

MABROUKA: I don't think he'll catch up with him.

ASAKIR [*taking a deep breath*]: Do you think so, Mabrouka?

MABROUKA: Unless he ran hard.

ASAKIR [*listening intently for the whistle*]: That's the train leaving the station.

MABROUKA [*staring at her*]: What's wrong with you, Asakir? Why's your face so pale?

ASAKIR: What does your heart tell you, Mabrouka?

MABROUKA: My heart tells me that he's gone.

ASAKIR: Gone, gone—where to?

MABROUKA: Whence he came.

ASAKIR [*staring*]: What do you mean?

MABROUKA [*looking at her*]: Why are you breathing so heavily, Asakir?

ASAKIR [*in a whisper, as she glances round distractedly*]: Gone to whence he came?

MABROUKA: Asakir, are you still hoping that some good will come out of him?

ASAKIR: No.

MABROUKA: Think of him as never having been.

ASAKIR [*as though talking to herself*]: Yes, his death is more of a secret than his life.

MABROUKA: Thank God that he is far away.

ASAKIR [*as though asking herself*]: Is he now on the train?

MABROUKA: Who knows? Perhaps Sumeida was able to catch up with him and to dissuade him from traveling and will return with him now.

ASAKIR [*as in a dream*]: Return with him now?

MABROUKA: Why not? If Sumeida really went like the wind he'd not miss the train.

ASAKIR [*in a whisper*]: Will he catch up with him?

MABROUKA: Maybe it won't be long before you see them coming along together again.

ASAKIR [*as though talking to herself*]: No, this time Sumeida will come by himself.

MABROUKA [*looking at her in alarm*]: Your face, Asakir, frightens me.

ASAKIR [*listening intently*]: Quiet! Listen! Listen! Do you now hear something?

MABROUKA: No, what should I hear?

ASAKIR: Singing.

MABROUKA [*listening*]: No, I don't hear singing.

ASAKIR [*breathing heavily*]: Nor I.

MABROUKA: Did Sumeida tell you he'd be singing?

ASAKIR [*in alarm, as though talking to herself*]: Perhaps he hasn't yet reached the district office.

MABROUKA: I would have thought he had.

ASAKIR [*breathing more heavily*]: Reached the district office and hasn't sung!

MABROUKA: Why is your face flushed, Asakir?

ASAKIR [*in a whisper*]: He hasn't caught up with him.

MABROUKA: You prefer, Asakir, that he does not return, that the train carries him far away from this village. I agree with you: it is better for him to return to Cairo, to his Sheikhs and his colleagues. He does not belong to us now nor we to him. He has done well to leave us quickly before he mixes with the people of the village and they discover what we have about him.

ASAKIR [*listens to a far-away sound*]

MABROUKA [*turning to her*]: You are not listening to me, Asakir. Is not what I'm saying right?

ASAKIR [*in a hoarse, frightening voice*]: No, I hear nothing!

MABROUKA [*listening*]: But that's Sumeida singing! [*She turns in terror to* ASAKIR.] Asakir! Asakir! What's happened to you? You're frightening me.

SUMEIDA [*singing from without in the dialect of Upper Egypt*]:

Friend, what excuses have we given,
What assurances that we'd repent?
And when your blame you yet continued,
Our shirt and outer robe we rent.
When of the father I did hear
My shame no bounds did know,
And both mine eyes did open wide
And copious tears did flow.

ASAKIR [*pulling herself together lest she collapse; even so a faint suppressed cry, like a rattle in the throat, escapes her lips*]: My son!

CURTAIN

Translated by Denys Johnson-Davies

from
Diary of a
Country Prosecutor

———〰〰———

hen we got back, it was time for the session to begin. Our car approached the court, where we saw people crowded like flies at the entrance. My assistant had slumped down at my side completely prostrate and I took no further notice of him. It did not occur to me to summon him in that state of fatigue to sit through a court session with me after attending an investigation. He was not yet accustomed to a twenty-four-hour day and the instructive night which he had just spent was quite enough for him.

So I decided to deal gently with him in the early period of his service; and as soon as we came to the court, I made the driver stop and ordered him to take my assistant home.

I bade farewell to the ma'mur and alighted from the car, clearing a path between the serried ranks of men, women, and children. When I entered the conference room the judge was already sitting. As soon as I saw him, my spirits dropped. There are two judges in this court and they work on alternate days. One of them lives in Cairo and travels up for the session by the first train. He always hears his cases with the utmost speed in order to catch the 11 o'clock train returning to Cairo. No matter how great the number of cases for hearing—this judge has never yet missed his train. The other judge is an excessively conscientious man who lives with his family in the district office. He is very slow in dealing with cases, for he is afraid of making mistakes through haste; and perhaps, too, he is eager to fill in time and enliven his boredom in this provincial outpost. Moreover he has no train to catch. So from early morning he sits at his desk as though he were inseparably nailed to it; and he never leaves it till just before noon. He generally resumes the session in the evening too. These sessions have always been a nightmare to me; they are a veritable sentence of imprisonment—as though I were condemned to be tied to my desk and remain immobile the whole day long. The red and green sash placed around my neck and under my armpit seemed like a yoke. Was it divine vengeance for all the innocent people whom I had inadvertently sent to prison? Or is it that the consequences of our professional mistakes recoil upon us, so that we pay for them some time in our life without knowing when?

I said nothing when I saw the judge. It was clear to me that I was in for a merciless session after a night of continuous toil. I don't know what can have blurred my memory and made me imagine that it was the turn of the brisk judge to preside this morning. . . .

I entered the court. First of all I glanced at the list and saw that we had to deal with seventy misdemeanors and forty felonies—quite sufficient to ensure an endless session with this particular judge. There were always more cases for him than for his colleagues; and the reason was quite simple. The conscientious judge never imposed a higher fine than twenty piastres for a misdemeanor, whereas his colleague raised the fine to as much as fifty piastres. People charged with misdemeanors had got to know this, and always took special care to escape from the expensive judge and patronize his more reasonably priced colleague. Today's judge had often complained and grumbled about the way his work increased in volume from one day to the next, and had never discovered the cause. I used to say to myself, "Raise your price and you'll have a pleasant surprise."

The usher began calling out the names of the accused from a paper which he was holding. Kuzman Effendi, the usher, was an old man with white hair and a white mustache, endowed with a presence and bearing fit for a Justice of the Supreme Court. Whenever he called anyone to the box, he was extremely majestic in his movements, gestures, and voice. He would turn to the court attendant with an air of supreme authority, and that worthy fellow would echo the name outside the chamber just as he had heard it from the usher, except that he would introduce a long-drawn-out chant and an intonation like that of a street-hawker. A certain judge had once noticed this resemblance, and said to him, "Come, Sha'aban, are you calling out the names of defendants in crime cases or selling potatoes and black dates?"

And the man replied, "Crime cases, potatoes, dates, it's all the same; it's all to make a living."

The first defendant took his place. The judge, who had plunged into his papers, now raised his head, adjusted a pair of thick spectacles on his nose and said to the man before him, "You have contravened the Slaughter of Animals Regulations by killing a sheep outside the slaughter-house."

"Your honor, we slaughtered the sheep—saving your presence—on a very special evening (may you be granted one like it)—it was the circumcision of our little son and . . . ."

"Twenty piastres fine! Next case!"

The usher called out a name. And so it went on—name after name—a whole succession of cases exactly similar to the first on which sentence had been pronounced. I left the judge to his verdicts and began to amuse myself by observing the people in the court. . . . They filled all the seats and benches and overflowed on to the floor and gangways, where they sat on their haunches like cattle gazing up humbly at the judge, while he pronounced sentence like a shepherd with a staff. The judge grew weary of the succession of identical cases and shouted, "What is all this about? Is there nothing in this court except sheep outside slaughter-houses?"

He glared at the crowd with eyes like little peas behind his spectacles, which bobbed up and down his nose. Nobody, not even himself, caught the implication of what he had said. The usher went on calling out names. The type of charge had begun to vary and we were entering a different world, for the judge was now saying to the accused, "You are charged with having washed your clothes in the canal!"

"Your honor—may God exalt your station—are you going to fine me just because I washed my clothes?"

"It's for washing them in the canal."

"Well, where else could I wash them?"

The judge hesitated, deep in thought, and could give no answer. He knew very well that these poor wretches had no wash basins in their village, filled with fresh flowing water from the tap. They were left to live like cattle all their lives and were yet required to submit to a modern legal system imported from abroad.

The judge turned to me and said, "The legal Officer! Opinion, please."

"The state is not concerned to inquire where this man should wash his clothes. Its only interest is the application of the law."

The judge turned his glance away from me, lowered his head, shook it, and then spoke swiftly like a man rolling a weight off his shoulders: "Fined twenty piastres. Next case."

A woman's name was called. It was the village prostitute. She had blackened her eyelashes with the point of a match and smeared her cheeks with the glaring crimson color which can be seen painted on boxes of Samson cigarettes. On her bare arm was tattooed the picture of a heart pierced by an arrow. She was wearing on her wrist several bracelets and armlets made of metal and colored glass.

The judge looked at her and said, "You are charged with having stood at the entrance of your house. . . ."

She put her hand on her hip and shouted, "Well, darling, is it a crime for someone to stand in front of his house?"

"You were doing it to seduce the public."

"What a pity! By your honor's beard, I've never seen this Public—he's never called in at my place."

"Twenty piastres. Next case."

Kuzman Effendi summoned the next defendant. He was a middle-aged farmer of some prosperity, to judge from his blue turban, his kashmir gallabiya, his cloak of "imperial" pattern, and his elastic boots of screaming yellow tint. As soon as he appeared, the judge sprang the accusation upon him: "You, sir, are charged with not having registered your dog within the statutory period."

The accused coughed, shook his head, and mumbled as though reciting a religious formula, "A fine age we're living in—dogs have to be 'registered' like plots of land, and a great fuss is made over them!"

"Twenty piastres fine. Next case . . . ."

The hearing of the misdemeanors continued, all in the same vein. Not a single one of the defendants showed any sign of believing in the real iniquity of whatever he had done. It was merely that fines had fallen upon them from heaven, whence all disasters proceed; they had to be paid, for so the law required. I had often tried to convince myself of the purpose of these sessions. Could one claim that these judgments had a deterrent effect when the delinquent had not the least idea of what fault he had committed?

We got through the misdemeanors and the usher called out, "Cases of Felony." He glanced at the list and shouted, "Umm as-Sa'ad, daughter of Ibrahim al-Jarf."

An old peasant woman walked slowly down the center of the room until she reached the dais, where she stood in front of Kuzman Effendi the usher. He directed her toward the judge, at whom she gazed weakly for a while. Soon she turned away from him and stood once more with her eyes fixed on the aged usher.

The judge buried his face in the papers and asked, "Your name?"

"Umm Sa'ad, sir."

She appeared to address this reply to the usher, who made a sign directing her once more to face the dais. The judge questioned her: "Your profession?"

"Woman, your honor!"

"You are charged with biting the finger of Sheikh Hasan Imara."

She left the dais and addressed the usher again: "I swear to you, by the honor of your white hair, that I haven't done any wrong—I swore, I gave a sacred oath that my daughter wouldn't be married for a dowry of less than twenty gold pieces."

The judge raised his head, adjusted his spectacles, looked at her, and said sharply, "Now then, speak to me. I'm the judge here. Did you bite him? Answer yes or no!"

"Bite him? God forbid! I've got a temper, I admit—but I don't go as far as biting people!"

"Call the witness," the judge said to the usher.

The victim appeared—his finger bound in a sheath. The judge asked him his name and occupation, made him swear that he would tell nothing but the truth, and asked him to elucidate what had happened.

"Your honor, I wasn't on one side nor on the other, and the matter arose because I generously offered to mediate."

He relapsed into silence, as though he had completely clarified the whole matter.

The judge glared at him in repressed anger, and then upbraided him and ordered him to recount in detail what had happened. The man made a full statement to this effect:

The accused woman had a daughter called Sitt Abuha; she was wooed by a peasant named Horaisha, who offered a dowry of fifteen gold pieces. The mother refused and demanded twenty. The matter stood there until one day the suitor's brother, a young boy called Ginger, came along on his own accord and informed the bride's family, quite falsely, that the suitor had accepted their terms. He then went back to his brother and told him that the girl's family had agreed to reduce the dowry and to accept his offer. As a result of this cunning joke played on both parties, a day was appointed for reciting the Fatiha at the bride's house, and the bridegroom deputed Sheikh Hasan and Sheikh Faraj to be his witnesses.

Everybody came together and the girl's mother killed a goose. Scarcely had the meal been made ready and served to the guests when the dowry was mentioned and the trick was revealed. It was evident that the deadlock had not been solved and a quarrel flared up between the two parties. The girl's mother began to shout and wail in the yard: "What a dreadful calamity! How our enemies would rejoice. By the life of the Prophet, I will not let my daughter go for less than twenty gold pieces." The woman, half-crazed, rushed in amongst the menfolk to defend her daughter's interests, fearing that the men would settle the matter in an unsatisfactory way. Sheikh Hasan was moved by the spirit of devoted zeal and did not touch the food. He began to argue with the woman, vainly trying to convince her, while his colleague, Sheikh Faraj, stretched out his hand toward the goose and began to guzzle it avidly, without entering into the impassioned dispute. It appears that the enthusiasm on each side went beyond the limits of verbal discussion, and soon Sheikh Hasan saw that his hand was not in the plate of goose but in the woman's mouth. He let forth a resounding shriek and soon the whole house was turned upside down in chaotic confusion. Sheikh Hasan grabbed his companion, pulled him violently away from the goose, and went out, gnashing his teeth with rage. His companion, who had not said a single word, had been rewarded with an excellent meal; whereas he, after all his zeal, had left the banquet hungry, with his finger bitten by the old woman. . . .

The plaintiff went on at great length. Suddenly the judge was seized with agitation. His conscientious scruples had come to life, and he interrupted the witness, saying, as though in a soliloquy, "I wonder if I made the witness take the oath!"

He turned to me and inquired, "Prosecuting Counsel, did I make the witness take the oath?"

I tried hard to remember, but the judge could not banish his doubts. He shouted at the witness, "Take the oath, sir. Say: 'By Almighty God, I swear to speak the truth!'"

The man swore the oath—whereupon the judge called out, "Begin your evidence from the beginning!"

I saw that we would never finish the session. I was utterly bored and sank, yawning, into my seat. Sleep began to play with my eyelids and there elapsed an interval the length of which I cannot surmise. Suddenly I heard the judge's voice calling to me: "Prosecution! What is the request of Prosecuting Counsel?"

I opened a pair of bloodshot eyes which requested nothing but sleep and was informed by the judge that he had just studied the medical report, which said that the injury had left a permanent infirmity—the loss of the medial parallax of the third finger. I sat up in my seat and immediately demanded a ruling of *ultra vires*. The judge turned to the old woman and said, "The case has become a felony and within the jurisdiction of the Criminal Court."

The old lady showed no sign of understanding this subtle distinction. In her view, a bite was a bite. How could it suddenly be transformed from a misdemeanor into a felony? (What an accursed law it is—far beyond the comprehension of these simple folk!)

The next case was called. It dealt with a violent quarrel, leading to blows, which had broken out between the father of Sitt Abuha and the family of the husband, Sayyid Horaisha—for eventually the marriage had taken place. The bridegroom had sent some of his relations with a camel to take the bride from her father's house, but her father had received them with sharp abuse, shouting in their faces, "What? A camel? My daughter leave here on a camel? Not likely! There must be a Toumbeel."*

The two parties began to argue about who was to pay for this newfangled device provided by modern scientific development. The argument led to the raising of sticks and the effusion of a few drops of blood—quite inevitable in a situation of this kind. Finally, a well-intentioned person produced a banknote from his pocket and hired one of the taxis which plied on the country roads.

The judge gave his ruling on the dispute, and remarked, "Thank heavens, we've finished with the joys of matrimony. Next case."

The usher called out with his deep, full voice, "Cases of detained persons!" He then recited a name. There was a clang of chains, and from a crowd of people dressed in regulation prison garb a man got up. The guard removed his fetters. From the lawyer's bench a fat effendi, with a stomach like a full water-skin, arose and said, "I represent the defendant."

"A case with an advocate." I reflected in silence—he won't leave us alone before unloading all his ideas upon us—in the name of freedom of defense. I may as well close my eyes, for my head is sorely in need of rest after being awake all night.

I heard the judge addressing the prisoner: "You are accused of having stolen a kerosene stove."

"It is true that I found a kerosene stove at the shop entrance, but I certainly didn't steal it."

His honor turned to the usher and called for the first witness. A man appeared, dressed in a white cap and a sleeveless tunic. He took the oath and described how he had lit a kerosene stove to make coffee for some of the customers sitting inside his shop. He was a little country grocer who sold sugar, tea, and tobacco. Sometimes people would assemble in his shop as though it were a sort of café. He had put the stove, already lit, at the threshold of the door and had gone inside to bring a pot. When he emerged, he saw the accused carrying off the stove, light and all, and running away with it. The witness went on at inordinate length, invoking the confirmation of those who had been present and had joined him in chasing the thief. The judge was silent and downcast, and I knew by his demeanor that he was thinking of something

---

* Automobile.

else. Suddenly he looked at me and said, as though speaking to himself, "Did I make the witness take the oath?"

I could endure no more and I snapped back in annoyance, "Good heavens, I heard him with my own ears take the oath!"

"Are you sure?"

I thought I was going to collapse. I muttered in a low whisper, "Do you want me to swear that he swore the oath?"

The judge was somewhat reassured and listened to the remaining witnesses in silent attention. But the defendant could no longer contain himself, and suddenly burst out in an imploring voice, "Your honor, is there any thief in the world who would steal a lit kerosene stove?"

The judge silenced him with a wave of the hand. "Are you asking me? I've never worked as a thief, so how should I know?"

He turned to the defending counsel's box. The advocate rose, saying, at the top of his voice, "Mr. President, we have neither encountered nor perceived nor passed in the vicinity of a kerosene stove. The entire accusation is fabricated from beginning to end."

He was about to proceed in this vein, but the judge interrupted him: "Excuse me, my learned friend. The defendant himself confesses that he did find the stove at the entrance of the shop."

The lawyer banged his fist on the desk and said, "It is bad defense on the part of my client."

"Does counsel imply that I should accept his excellent defense in preference to the truth pronounced by his client in open court?"

Counsel protested and raised his voice. It seemed that his only interest was to make his voice reverberate through the court, to flow with sweat and wipe it away with his handkerchief, looking at his client as if to demonstrate the trouble he was taking and the interest he was devoting in his cause. Weariness, boredom, immobile captivity at my desk—all this had made me unconscious and oblivious of what was going on around me. I buried my head in one of the files and surrendered myself to deep slumber.

Translated by Abba Eban

Miracles for Sale

T he priest woke early as was his wont, preceded only by the birds in their nests, and began his prayers, his devotions, and his work for his diocese in that Eastern land whose spiritual light he was and where he was held in such high esteem by men of religion and in such reverence by the people. Before his door there grew a small palm tree planted by his own hands; he always watered it before sunrise, contemplating the sun as its rim, red as a date, burst forth from the horizon to shed its rays on the dewy leaves, wrapping their falling drops of silver in skeins of gold.

As the priest finished watering the palm tree that morning and was about to return inside, he found himself faced by a crowd of sad and worried-looking people, one of whom plucked up the courage to address him in beseeching tones:

"Father! Save us! No one but you can save us! My wife is on her death-bed and she is asking for your blessing before she breathes her last."

"Where is she?"

"In a village near by. The mounts are ready," replied the man, pointing to two saddled donkeys standing there waiting for them.

"I am willing to go, my sons," said the priest. "Wait a while so that I may arrange my affairs and tell my brethren and then return to you."

"There's no time!" they all said as one voice. "The woman is dying. We may well reach her too late. Come with us right away if you would be a true benefactor to us and a merciful savior to the dying woman. It is not far and we shall be there and back before the sun reaches its zenith at noon."

"Well, then, let us go at once!" the priest agreed with enthusiastic fervor. He went up to the two donkeys, followed by the crowd. Mounting him on one of them while the husband of the dying woman mounted the other, they raced off.

For hours on end they pounded the ground with the priest asking where they were bound for and the men goading on the donkey, saying, "We're almost there!" It wasn't till noon that the village came into sight. They entered it to the accompaniment of barking dogs and the welcome of its inhabitants, and they all made their way to the village hall. They led the priest to a large room where he found a woman stretched out on a bed, her eyes staring up at the ceiling. He called to her, but no reply came from her, for she was at death's door. So he began to call down blessings upon her, and scarcely had he finished when she heaved a great sigh and fell into a deep fit of sobbing, so that the priest thought she was about to give up the ghost.

Instead her eyelids fluttered open, her gaze cleared, and she turned and murmured:

"Where am I?"

"You are in your house," answered the astonished priest.

"Get me a drink of water."

"Bring the pitcher!" shouted her relatives around her. "Bring the water jar!"

They raced off and brought back a jug of water from which the woman took a long drink. Then she belched heartily and said:

"Isn't there any food? I'm hungry!"

Everyone in the house set about bringing her food. Under the astonished gaze of those around her the woman began devouring the food; then she got up from her bed and proceeded to walk about the house completely fit and well again. At this the people prostrated themselves before the priest, covering his hands and feet in kisses and shouting, "O Saint of God! Your blessing has alighted on the house and brought the dead woman back to life! What can we possibly give you as a token of the thanks we owe you, as an acknowledgment of our gratitude?"

"I have done nothing that deserves reward or thanks," replied the priest, still bewildered by the incident. "It is God's power that has done it."

"Call it what you will," said the master of the house, "it is at all events a miracle which God wished to be accomplished through your hands, O Saint of God. You have alighted at our lowly abode, and this brings both great honor and good fortune to us. You must let us undertake the obligations of hospitality in such manner as our circumstances allow."

He ordered a quiet room to be made ready for his guest and there he lodged him. Whenever the priest asked leave to depart the master of the house swore by all that was most holy to him that he would not allow his auspicious guest to go before three days were up—the very least hospitality which should be accorded to someone who had saved his wife's life. During this time he showed him much attention and honor. When the period of hospitality came to an end he saddled a mount and loaded it up with presents of home-made bread, lentils, and chickens; in addition he pressed five pounds for the church funds in the priest's hand. Hardly had he escorted him to the door and helped him on to the donkey than a man appeared, puffing and out of breath, who threw himself down beside the priest.

"Father," he pleaded, "the story of your miracle has reached all the villages around. I have an uncle who is like a father to me and who is at death's door. He is hoping to have your blessing, so let not his soul depart from him before his hope is fulfilled!"

"But, my son, I am all ready to return home," the priest replied uncertainly.

"This is something that won't take any time—I shall not let you go till you've been with me to see my uncle!" The man seized the donkey's reins and led him off.

"And where is this uncle of yours?" asked the priest.

"Very near here—a few minutes' distance."

The priest saw nothing for it but to comply. They journeyed for an hour before they reached the next village. There he saw a house like the first one with a dying man on a bed, his family around him veering between hope and despair. No sooner had the priest approached and called down his blessing on the patient than the miracle occurred: the dying man rose to his feet calling for food and water. The people, astounded at what had occurred, swore by everything most dear that they must discharge the duties of hospitality toward this holy man—a stay of three full days.

The period of hospitality passed with the priest enjoying every honor and attention. Then, as they were escorting him to the gates of the village loaded down with gifts, a man from a third village came along and asked him to come and visit it, even if only for a little while, and give it the blessing of one whose fame had spread throughout all the district.

The priest was quite unable to escape from the man, who led the donkey off by its bit and brought the priest to a house in his village. There they found a young man who was a cripple; hardly had the priest touched him than he was up and about on his two feet, among the cheers and jubilation of young and old. All the people swore that the duties of hospitality must be accorded to the miracle-maker, which they duly did in fine style; three nights no less, just as the others had done. When this time was up they went to their guest and added yet more presents to those he already had, until his donkey was almost collapsing under them. They also presented him with a more generous gifts of money than he had received in the former villages so that he had by now collected close on twenty pounds. He put them in a purse which he hid under his clothes. He then mounted the donkey and asked his hosts to act as an escort for him to his village, so they all set off with him, walking behind his donkey.

"Our hearts shall be your protection, our lives your ransom," they said. "We shall not leave you till we have handed you over to your own people: you are as precious to us as gold."

"I am causing you some inconvenience," said the priest. "However, the way is not safe and, as you know, gangs are rife in the provinces."

"Truly," they replied, "hereabouts they kidnap men in broad daylight."

"Even the government is powerless to remove this widespread evil," said the priest. "I was told that gangs of kidnappers waylay buses on country roads, run their eyes over the passengers, and carry off with them anyone at all prosperous-looking so that they can afterwards demand a large ransom from his relatives. Sometimes it happens with security men actually in the buses. I heard that once two policemen were among the passengers on one of these buses when it was stopped by the gang; when the selected passenger appealed for help to the two policemen they were so scared of the robbers that all they said to the kidnapped man was: 'Away with you—and let's get going!'"

The people laughed and said to the priest, "Do not be afraid! So long as you are with us you will dismount only when you arrive safely back in your village."

"I know how gallant you are! You have overwhelmed me with honor and generosity!"

"Don't say such a thing—you are very precious to us!" They went on walking behind the priest, extolling his virtues and describing in detail his miracles. He listened to their words, and thought about all that had occurred. Finally he exclaimed, "Truly, it is remarkable the things that have happened to me in these last few days! Is it possible that these miracles are due solely to my blessing?"

"And do you doubt it?"

"I am not a prophet that I should accomplish all that in seven days. Rather is it you who have made me do these miracles!"

"We?" they all said in one voice. "What do you mean?"

"Yes, you are the prime source."

"Who told you this?" they murmured, exchanging glances.

"It is your faith," continued the priest with conviction. "Faith has made you achieve all this. You do not know the power that lies in the soul of the believer. Faith is a power, my sons! Faith is a power! Miracles are buried deep within your hearts, like water inside rock, and only faith can cause them to burst forth!" He continued talking in this vein while the people behind him shook their heads. He became more and more impassioned and did not notice that they had begun to slink off, one after the other. It was only when he reached the boundaries of his village that he came back to earth, turned round to thank his escort, and was rendered speechless with astonishment at finding himself alone.

His surprise did not last long, for he immediately found his family, his brother priests and superiors rushing toward him, hugging him and kissing his hand, as tears of joy and emotion flowed down their cheeks. One of them embraced him, saying, "You have returned safely to us at last! They kept their promise. Let them have the money so long as they have given you back, father! To us, father, you are more priceless than any money!"

The priest, catching the word 'money,' exclaimed: "What money?"

"The money we paid to the gang."

"What gang?"

"The one that kidnapped you. At first they wouldn't be satisfied with less than a thousand pounds, saying that you were worth your weight in gold. We pleaded with them to take half and eventually they accepted, and so we paid them a ransom of five hundred pounds from the Church funds."

"Five hundred pounds!" shouted the priest. "You paid that for me!—They told you I'd been kidnapped?"

"Yes, three days after you disappeared some people came to us and said that a gang kidnapped you one morning as you were watering the palm tree by your door. They swore you were doomed unless your ransom was paid to them—if we paid you'd be handed over safe and sound."

The priest considered these words, recalling to himself all that had occurred.

"Indeed, that explains it," he said, as though talking to himself. "Those dead people, the sick, and the cripples who jumped up at my blessing! What mastery!"

His relatives again came forward, examining his body and clothes as they said joyfully, "Nothing is of any consequence, father, except your safety. We hope they didn't treat you badly during your captivity. What did they do to you?"

In bewilderment he answered: "They made me work miracles—miracles that have cost the Church dear!"

Translated by Denys Johnson-Davies

Satan Triumphs

——⟋⟍——

S ome people began worshiping a tree. A pious man, who believed devoutly in God, heard about this. Picking up an axe, he set off to chop down the tree. When he approached it, the devil appeared between the man and the tree and shouted, "Stay where you are, man. Why do you want to cut down this tree?"

"Because it's leading the people astray."

"Why should you worry about them? Let them go astray."

"How can I? It's my duty to guide them."

"It's your duty to grant people the freedom to do what they want."

"They're not free . . . not while they're listening to Satan's whispered suggestions."

"Do you want them to listen to your voice instead?"

"I want them to listen to God's voice."

"I won't allow you to cut down this tree."

"I must cut it down."

Satan grabbed the man by the throat, and the ascetic caught hold of Satan's horn. They wrestled with each other for a long time until the struggle concluded with the pious man's victory. The ascetic threw Satan to the ground, sat on his chest, and taunted him: "Now you see my strength."

The defeated devil complained in a broken voice, "I didn't think you were this powerful. Let me go. You can do whatever you want."

The ascetic released Satan, but the effort he had expended in the fight had left him exhausted. So he went back to his cell to rest for the night.

The following day he took this axe and went off to chop down the tree. Jumping out from behind it, Satan shouted, "Have you come back today to cut it down?"

"I've told you: I must do this."

"Do you think you'll be able to beat me again today?"

"I will continue to battle with you to advance the cause of truth."

"Then show me how strong you are."

Satan took him by the neck and the ascetic grabbed the devil by the horn. They wrestled and fought until finally Satan fell at the feet of the man, who plopped himself on the devil's chest and asked, "What do you say about my strength now?"

"It certainly is amazing," Satan replied in a troubled, trembling voice. "Let me go and do whatever you want."

Releasing the devil, the ascetic returned to his cell and stretched out, for he was weary and exhausted. The next morning he took his axe and went to the tree. Satan appeared to him and shouted, "Won't you give up, man?"

"Never! This evil must be eradicated."

"Do you think I'll let you?"

"If you try to stop me, I'll defeat you."

Satan thought about this for a while and realized that he would never triumph over this man by physical combat, for nothing is more powerful than a person fighting for principle or belief. The only way Satan would be able to defeat him would be by subterfuge.

Pretending to befriend the ascetic, Satan advised him in a sympathetic tone, "Do you know why I don't want you to cut down this tree? I oppose that only because of my compassion and concern for you. If you chop it down, you'll expose yourself to the wrath of the people who worship it. Why should you bring down such misfortunes upon yourself? Leave it alone, and I'll give you two gold coins each day. Use them to defray your expenses, and you can live in peace, comfort, and security."

"Two gold coins?"

"Yes. Every day. You'll find them under your pillow."

The ascetic bowed his head and asked, "Who will guarantee that you'll be true to your word."

"I pledge it to you. You'll see that I keep my word."

"I'll give you a try."

"Yes. Try me."

"It's a deal."

Satan extended his hand to the man, and they sealed their pact with a handshake. The ascetic returned to his cell. When he woke each morning, he thrust his hand under the pillow and pulled out two gold coins. But one day, a month later, his hand found nothing under the pillow. Satan had cut off the allowance of gold, and the ascetic was furious. He rose, picked up his axe, and went to chop down the tree. Satan confronted him on the way and shouted, "Stay where you are! Where do you think you're going?"

"To the tree. . . to chop it down."

Satan scoffed bitterly, "You'll cut it down, because I cut off your gold."

"No. I'll do it to destroy a temptation to sin and to light a torch for the people's guidance."

"You?"

"Are you making fun of me, accursed one?"

"Excuse me . . . you look funny. That's all."

"Are you the one to talk, you wily liar?"

The ascetic pounced on Satan and grabbed his horn. They wrestled for a time, and the battle ended with the ascetic under Satan's hoof. Cocky and arrogant, the victorious devil straddled the man's chest and asked, "Fellow, where's your strength now?"

A cry like a death rattle emerged from the throat of the vanquished ascetic, who said, "Tell me: How were you able to defeat me, Satan?"

The devil replied, "When you were angry for God's sake, you defeated me. When you were angry for your own sake, I won. When you fought for your beliefs, you beat me. When you fought for yourself, I triumphed."

Translated by William M. Hutchins

Azrael the Barber

ife is stronger than death. Anyone considering the events of a single
day in his life will realize the truth of this, for death haunts us at
every step. All the same, we ward it off and usually escape, skipping
over its snares. Life's guiding hand rescues us. Life and death have been playing the selfsame game together from the beginning of time without variation
. . . the game children call blind man's buff. Life and death take turns. One
hides and waits anywhere he chooses, while the other calls out, "I see you and
know where you are." The lives of us poor human beings hang by all sorts of
threads, even totally trivial ones: a fly's feet, a mosquito's sting, the hands of
the driver or pilot operating a car, train, or airplane. You may even find that
the string binding you to life has been brutally plucked and shaken by the fingers of the barber, who receives you for a shave and a haircut when you are
as far as possible from suspecting any evil or danger.

At the beginning of summer I went to the barber for a shave. I felt joyfully optimistic about life and had a song in my heart. I listened to the
farmers sing as they led a line of camels bearing watermelons down the fan-
ciest streets of Cairo. Sinking back in the chair, I surrendered my head to
the barber, closed my eyes, and retreated into sweet reveries, welcoming
with my face the artificial breeze of an electric fan. As the barber lathered
my chin, I felt fully at ease. He then set about honing the razor until its
blade gleamed.

Taking my head in his hands, he whispered to me in a strange voice, "I hope you don't mind me saying that I've been scrutinizing you—and my hunches are never wrong. I have a small request for you."

He lifted the razor from my temple expectantly, and I quickly responded, "Go ahead."

Grasping my head and starting to shave me, he asked, "Sir, do you know anyone in the mental hospital?"

I was astonished but calmly replied, "If your hunches, which are never wrong, disclosed on the basis of your scrutiny that I've been a resident of such an establishment, then thanks."

He hastily apologized: "Sorry, sorry! I didn't mean that. I only wanted to say that my scrutiny showed you to be a benevolent and influential person who might know one of the doctors at the hospital."

"Why?"

"I have a crazy brother I want released."

"Crazy? Has he been cured?"

"He was never seriously ill. It was a trumped-up charge by the hospital. As you well know, sir, they are always locking people up by mistake. All it amounts to is that he occasionally suffers from certain delusions and imagines harmless and unobjectionable things. There's never been any wild or unruly behavior, no shrieking or bellowing, no assaults or violence. He has never caused the kind of tumult and uproar that the insane people confined in that hospital instigate."

"Amazing! What did he do then to deserve being put away?"

"Nothing, sir. The matter is a simple one: This brother of mine was a barber like me. He was working one morning, in fine shape. It was summer, and you well know that the heat makes one thirsty. My brother had his hand on the head of a customer no different from you. His delusions made him imagine that the head of his client was a watermelon. He had the razor in his hand and wanted to split it lengthwise."

I shuddered and yelled out at once, "Split what?"

"Split the watermelon . . . I mean the customer's head." The barber said this in a placid, natural tone of voice.

The blood froze in my veins. At that moment my head was in his hand,

and the sharp, glistening blade was gliding down my neck. I held my breath in fearful apprehension. I soon regained my composure and to please him and to reassure myself suggested in a gentle, kindly way to him, "Of course this brother was the exception in your family. . . ."

His razor against my throat, he replied as calmly as ever, "The truth is that the whole family is like this. I myself occasionally imagine strange things, especially in watermelon season. I'll tell you in confidence that my brother is not to blame."

A strange gleam, like that of the razor blade poised at my throat, shone in the barber's eyes. Certain I did not have long to live, I recited the Muslim credo and asked God's mercy for my soul.

Closing my eyes I gave myself up—not to sweet reveries this time—but to my imminent death and my spirit's departure. I did not open them until I heard cologne splashing against my face and the barber saying, "Congratulations."

I shook myself and rose like someone born anew. I paid, and the barber called after me, reminding me of his brother and the need to negotiate his release. I did not heed him or pay any attention. The moment I set foot in the street, I sighed deeply and swore that during watermelon season I would shave myself or at least never patronize this barber.

Translated by William M. Hutchins

from
The Prison of Life

T he academic year ended, the examination was held, and—by an act of Providence and despite my artistic involvements—I was admitted to the fourth and last year, the one leading to the *licence*. I left *The Seal of Solomon* in the hands of my colleague Mustafa, and headed for Alexandria to spend the summer there.

On arrival and at my first look at our blessed home, I was almost thunderstruck. What was that I saw before me? It was no longer a house, but a strange structure of which I could not tell the front from the back. One wall had been pulled down here, another built up there, a staircase had been ripped out, the entrails of a room were on view, the roof had been decapitated, and there were other mutilations of the same kind.

I soon learned the reason. It had occurred to my parents to carry out some improvements to the house, and to add a story to it. Cotton had sold at a high price that year, so they had made a fair amount of money. They chose to use it not in paying off the mortgage on either the land or the house, but on alterations to the house. I do not know which of them, my father or my mother, gave birth to this luminous idea, but I do know that the first hole made by pick-axes in the walls of this house was destined not to be refilled by all the money on earth—not by my father's salary, which by then was considerable, and not by the loans which they got from banks and from usurers.

Building and demolition in our house became something natural and continuous, like eating and drinking. For months, for years, it never stopped. For my father had decided to be his own architect, contractor, and master of works. He hired masons, carpenters, and blacksmiths, and would tell them, "Cut a new passage here. Pull down that wall over there. Block this window here. Fit a door over there." No sooner had they done what he commanded than it was found that the door opened not on the hall but on the water closet, that the wall that had been removed merged the kitchen with the lounge, and so on and so on.

My father would then command them to block what they had opened and rebuild what they had demolished. Next he would turn to another wall and order it torn down, only to find that it supported the ceiling of another room which was now sagging, so there was more rebuilding. All along, he was absolutely determined to rely on himself and his own expertise, and not to bring in an architect.

I was not only an observer of what was going on but also a victim, incommoded by having to sleep for a long time in rooms of which the windows had been ripped out and replaced by blankets. I would ask my father, "Why don't you employ an architect to take charge of all this, and give yourself a rest?" He would answer mockingly, "You are a fool! Does anybody but a fool employ an architect? What will he do but draw on blue paper a few elegant lines with a ruler and a compass and say, 'Here is a room, there is a hall?' What he will say we already know. We are far the best judges of what we want."

The ultimate result was quite simply that masons, carpenters, and painters became permanent residents with us. They arrogated to themselves a room near the garden gate, where they settled, stayed overnight, held parties, and received immediate members of the family, kinsmen, and friends as guests. From the house, a regular supply of coffee and tea and lunches and dinners was sent down. They even acquired a voice in what was cooked and presented them day by day. They would say, "We are tired of *mulukhiyya* and okra. Make us some *kushari* today!" Sometimes they would suggest, "Pickle us some cucumbers and green peppers," and they would even prescribe the way they liked the pickling to be done and the ingredients to be mixed. And in a corner of the garden they planted radishes and leeks and watercress. They thoroughly enjoyed this comfortable, soft life.

What with rooms minus walls, windows minus glass, and hammering and demolition taking place above our heads in the new story, my younger brother and I found life unbearable. Yet when I asked the workmen when the work was to be finished, they replied, "Never—it is like Goha's waterwheel! What we build in the morning we demolish in the afternoon. It's the Bey's orders."

And in truth it seems to me that my father had belatedly found his greatest hobby and entertainment in this building venture, and that he had come genuinely to believe that he knew all there was to know about architecture and building. He did occasionally consult his old friend Yusuf if he happened to meet him in Cairo, but such encounters were rare, for my father had taken up residence and settled in Alexandria as President of its court. When he came back from a session tired and exhausted, his first action was not to go in for a meal, but to head straight to the masons and carpenters to inspect what they had done, and check whether they had followed the instructions he had explained at length in the morning before he went out to work.

This had become his routine. He would summon the masons and carpenters and painters before him every morning to explain to them what they were to do during the day. This he called "the lesson" which he had to get into their heads. He would also expound to them what he called the daily 'duty roster.' Before leaving, he would make a point of asking them, "Have you learned the lesson?" They would answer with one voice, "We have learned it." He would stress, "And is the duty roster understood?" They would confirm, "Understood." Furthermore, it was his custom whenever he issued an order or instruction to anybody to require him to repeat what was requested word for word to avoid confusion and misunderstanding.

And yet when he returned shortly before the afternoon prayer, what we heard from him was uproar and shouting and reprimand. He would say, "These masons and painters are asses. They have not understood a word of what was explained to them!" And he would fall upon what they had built, tearing it with his own hands and kicking at it, shouting, "Tear it down at once! Everything is to be pulled down. The work is all wrong, from beginning to end!"

He would measure the walls with the walking stick he always carried instead of with a meter stick. If one of the tradesmen objected and told him, "Measure with the meter stick, your Excellency. It is right here!" he would shout at him, "My stick is more accurate than your meter. I have measured it against the original architectural meter in the Survey Department. It is exactly ninety centimeters."

His interest in architecture reached such a pitch that sometimes when we were walking together in the street he would suddenly stop in front of a house and tell me, "Wait while I measure this façade," and he would do so with his stick. If I asked him, "Why? Are we about to buy it?" he would answer, "Not at all. Just a matter of knowing." At other times we might again be walking in a street discussing important matters when he would interrupt the conversation and turn to me asking, "How wide would you say this street is?" And without waiting for an answer, he would brandish his stick and measure it, while I inwardly thanked God that there were no passers-by! I asked him what the point of this was, and he said, "Silly boy! The point is that we have to be knowledgeable about all these things, so the Municipality should not one day claim that our street is one of those on which it has decreed such-and-such in local taxes."

He also carried an old, cheap, metal pocket watch which he set back ten minutes, and if asked why he would say, "So that I always have ten minutes to spare for emergencies."

For all these peculiarities, my father possessed a quality that I regret I did not inherit, for it would have helped me a great deal, especially in the narrative arts. This was his inclination to dig deep into the minute details of anything in life, whether of immediate relevance to him or not. The amount of knowledge he accumulated on all things was truly amazing. He knew exactly how many bricks were needed to build a room so many meters by so many, how many measures of seeds were needed to plant so many acres with clover or cotton or maize, how many times a particular crop needed to be irrigated. If you were to question him on the law and its complicated procedures, or on the distinctive qualities of people engaged in different occupations, on medicine and pharmacology, on language and its grammar, on poetry and its meters, on blacksmithing or carpentry, or even on perfumery, you would find that he was master of fine and strange details.

I on the contrary can take things in only in their broad outlines, their main significations and not their details. I am also inclined to rid myself of anything I can dispense with. I have never carried a watch. I have never tried to acquire any curio or *objet d'art*. I eat only what is strictly necessary. This is why drama suits me as a medium of expression, for—unlike the novel which concerns itself with details—its proper scope is concepts and essences.

Yet for all his abundant knowledge of the finest details in any matter, my father no sooner turned to thinking about an actual project and carrying it out than he fell into laughable failure. With him knowledge was one thing, execution was another. Or could it be a clash between the imaginative and the practical tendencies in the same individual? My parents were of a practical turn of mind, but they were also imaginative. They would think about a practical project in a practical way, but then imagination intervened and swept them off to a ridiculous situation.

The building work in the house eventually came close to an end. The resident masons and carpenters and plasterers were getting ready to leave and end the era of occupation when a new idea struck my parents. They noticed that some of the higher neighboring houses overlooked the garden at the back, so they said, "Let us block their view. Let us build a wall." Then the notion of the wall developed into something else, a new idea. They reasoned, "Since we are going to build a wall, which costs money, why not build a second wall parallel to it, and we would then merely have to roof the space between them to have an independent addition to the property, suitable for living in or for renting?"

They set about carrying out the project. The masons, the carpenters, and the plasterers returned to their room. In time, the new wing was completed. Having brought it to a happy conclusion, they peered at it and pondered, "It would be nice if we could connect it to the original building by an elevated passageway or a bridge." Such a construction was unique, and odd-looking in a dwelling. But it was completed. They looked again and said, "Why leave the bottom of the new wing bare and exposed to the dust of the garden? Should we not have a terrace separating the wall from sand and dust?" This also was done. It stretched all the way along the wall of the wing, a matter of thirty meters at least, and it was paved with floor tiles that cost a fortune. Its surface and its dimensions made it look, as one of our visitors said, as if it had been designed for roller-skating.

One would surmise that things would come to an end at this point, and that the masons and carpenters and plasters would up and bundle their belongings in preparation for departure. So they did in fact. But then the gardener appeared asking for manure for the garden—sacks upon sacks of horse manure needed for the fruit trees and the lawn. He also spoke of the necessity of bringing in this manure at regular intervals to ensure the blossoming of the garden.

My parents thought about this with their customary genius and came up with a luminous idea: they should buy a horse, and use its droppings as manure. That would save them the cost of the manure to be bought, to say nothing of the cost of transport saved by the carriage that the horse would draw. That made sense. But were was the horse to live? Of course a stable would have to be built for it. That was natural. And at the far end of the garden was a suitable space. But would the stable be built in the fashion of all the stables in God's creation? Oh, no! An original design had to be produced by the genial architect, namely my father. And he did order the erection of an extraordinary stable on three levels. The top level was for the coachman to occupy, for he had to have living quarters; the middle level would accommodate the horse, and the bottom level its droppings, which were to slide down a hole and accumulate.

My father was very proud of this wonderful idea, and urged the masons and painters and carpenters to execute it right away. So they laid bricks and built up and whitewashed, and the stories rose one upon the other. And the building remained towering and empty for years, never graced by coachman or horse or manure.

That was because thinking had quickly shifted to something else: the exploitation of this large house, which thanks to successive brainwaves had outstripped the needs of the family. Why should it not be let to holidaymakers during the summer? Why, that was wisdom itself. The income from that would at least pay the mortgage installments. But then they pondered some more: if we are to let to holidaymakers, why not a third story?

This time the idea was my mother's, and as soon as my father went away to Cairo on business, she set about realizing it. And since the art of architecture was as easy to master as it had proved to be, why should she not rival my father in it? So she issued her orders to the team of masons and painters and carpenters. As soon as my father was back and saw the new story beginning to rise, he also rolled back his sleeves and returned to action, giving his 'lesson,' subjecting all to his 'duty roster,' and pulling down at night what was built during the day.

My father's reputation as a builder had spread in the city thanks to his purchases of bricks, floor tiles, Swedish timber, laths, steel girders, lime, and oils. Some of his colleagues in the judiciary who wanted to have a house built in the city or some quarters in the countryside came to him to receive instruction. I remember one consultant magistrate who shortly afterward became a minister, who used to come every afternoon to sit on a chair in the garden drinking the coffee that was brought to him, watching wide-eyed as my father went up and down the scaffolding, measuring walls with his stick, issuing orders and prohibitions, advising, counseling, scolding, shouting. . . . This consultant magistrate intended to have a small house built on an estate of his, and did not know how to go about it. When he saw my father dashing hither and thither in that great sprawling building, he muttered his admiration and esteem, then turned to me and said in a tone that bespoke sincerity, "Your father is an incomparable master of the art of architecture!"

At last all the building operations were over—God only knows after how long—and no ideas were left in the quiver for adding or subtracting anything. At that point my parents turned against the house and took to cursing it, especially as the idea of letting it had failed, for holidaymakers were beginning to favor the sea and the house's poor location was putting off prospective tenants. The cost of protracted building operations had weighed on my parents, debts were proving burdensome, and the price of cotton was dropping. Their thoughts were now directed to one aim: getting rid of the house. But how?

My father envisaged two possibilities: either selling it or exchanging it for land. He had recourse to brokers. And the dealings with brokers became no less involved than those with masons and carpenters.

He had become a consultant magistrate then left the service because he had reached the age of retirement. To be more accurate, he had accepted a golden handshake from the Ministry of Justice which had discovered that he and a number of other senior magistrates had been clever at tinting or dyeing their hair and mustaches and had sat on undisturbed, so it reminded them that, by any reckoning they chose, they had long before slipped past the age of retirement unawares. Agreement was reached to everybody's satisfaction, and along with those colleagues my father left the service. For the remainder of his life he could give his undivided attention to his private affairs, and he had no concern other than the sale or exchange of the house.

One day he came out with a new idea: loading the house with heavier mortgages. His reasoning was strange. It was that the more heavily indebted a piece of property was, the easier it would be to dispose of it or exchange it. That reasoning we could not follow. We kept telling him, "How can that be? Does it make sense? It is the opposite that is true." He answered as if pitying us for our ignorance, "What makes sense is what I have been saying. For who is it who offers his land in exchange for a house? Obviously one whose land is mortgaged. Naturally, he does not expect to have it exchanged except for a house that is equally mortgaged. For where is the idiot who would sacrifice a deed unburdened by any mortgage in return for mortgaged property? Since it's a matter of mortgage for mortgage, why should we give up a house and surrender it clean with its minimal mortgage to someone who will present us with land heavy with calamities?" Some logic!

From then on, my father was seen only in the company of brokers. He would be either walking in the street along with a broker or sitting in a café talking to a broker. Somebody once related to me that he had seen my father sitting at a café table on the pavement, waiting for a broker. Whenever the waiter came and made a show of wiping the table to get an order, my father would say, "Wait a little longer, my good man." The waiter would hold back a little, then come forward and wipe the table again. My father got annoyed, so he left the table and stood waiting at the edge of the pavement. When the waiter came once more to wipe the table he found it empty. He looked around and saw my father standing at the end of the street, looking daggers at him and saying, "Do you want something from me even here?"

I myself once saw him in the street as I was about to enter the Trianon Café in Alexandria, when I was already a functionary. He stopped me and said, "You are a fool to go in there. They charge three piastres for a cup of coffee." He left me and went to another café near the Stock Exchange called the Albyn, where the cup of coffee cost a piaster and a half. Yet I heard that he used to spend nearly twenty piastres a day there on the many cups of coffee consumed by brokers who got to hear about what he was after, and used to come one after the other raising his hopes and fostering his dreams.

My father's wish to dispose of the house outlived him. We did in fact exchange it for fallow land not reached by water; but God willed that that should not happen in his lifetime. He gave him the grace of dying in that house of his, or more correctly that his funeral should go out of that house, although in that respect I nearly committed an unforgivable error of judgment.

I was in Cairo in charge of the Directorate of Investigations in the Ministry of Education when I got news that he was ill and had been taken to the French Hospital in Alexandria. I went there immediately and found him in declining health, attended by an old Jewish nurse who used to come to the house regularly to administer injections, so my mother had entrusted her with constant attention to the patient.

Translated by Pierre Cachia

Modern Arabic Literature
from the American University in Cairo Press

Bahaa Abdelmegid *Saint Theresa and Sleeping with Strangers*
Ibrahim Abdel Meguid *Birds of Amber* • *Distant Train*
No One Sleeps in Alexandria • *The Other Place*
Yahya Taher Abdullah *The Collar and the Bracelet* • *The Mountain of Green Tea*
Leila Abouzeid *The Last Chapter*
Hamdi Abu Golayyel *A Dog with No Tail* • *Thieves in Retirement*
Yusuf Abu Rayya *Wedding Night*
Ahmed Alaidy *Being Abbas el Abd*
Idris Ali *Dongola* • *Poor*
Rasha al Ameer *Judgment Day*
Radwa Ashour *Granada* • *Specters*
Ibrahim Aslan *The Heron* • *Nile Sparrows*
Alaa Al Aswany *Chicago* • *Friendly Fire* • *The Yacoubian Building*
Fahd al-Atiq *Life on Hold*
Fadhil al-Azzawi *Cell Block Five* • *The Last of the Angels*
The Traveler and the Innkeeper
Ali Bader *Papa Sartre*
Liana Badr *The Eye of the Mirror*
Hala El Badry *A Certain Woman* • *Muntaha*
Salwa Bakr *The Golden Chariot* • *The Man from Bashmour* • *The Wiles of Men*
Halim Barakat *The Crane*
Hoda Barakat *Disciples of Passion* • *The Tiller of Waters*
Mourid Barghouti *I Saw Ramallah* • *I Was Born There, I Was Born Here*
Mohamed Berrada *Like a Summer Never to Be Repeated*
Mohamed El-Bisatie *Clamor of the Lake* • *Drumbeat* • *Hunger* • *Over the Bridge*
Mahmoud Darwish *The Butterfly's Burden*
Tarek Eltayeb *Cities without Palms* • *The Palm House*
Mansoura Ez Eldin *Maryam's Maze*
Ibrahim Farghali *The Smiles of the Saints*
Abdulaziz Al Farsi *Earth Weeps, Saturn Laughs*
Hamdy el-Gazzar *Black Magic*
Randa Ghazy *Dreaming of Palestine*
Gamal al-Ghitani *Pyramid Texts* • *The Zafarani Files* • *Zayni Barakat*
The Book of Epiphanies
Tawfiq al-Hakim *The Essential Tawfiq al-Hakim* • *Return of the Spirit*
Yahya Hakki *The Lamp of Umm Hashim*
Abdelilah Hamdouchi *The Final Bet*
Bensalem Himmich *The Polymath* • *The Theocrat*
Taha Hussein *The Days*
Sonallah Ibrahim *The Committee* • *Zaat*
Yusuf Idris *City of Love and Ashes* • *The Essential Yusuf Idris* • *Tales of Encounter*
Denys Johnson-Davies *The AUC Press Book of Modern Arabic Literature* • *Homecoming*
In a Fertile Desert • *Under the Naked Sky*
Said al-Kafrawi *The Hill of Gypsies*
Mai Khaled *The Magic of Turquoise*
Sahar Khalifeh *The End of Spring*
The Image, the Icon and the Covenant • *The Inheritance* • *Of Noble Origins*
Edwar al-Kharrat *Rama and the Dragon* • *Stones of Bobello*

Betool Khedairi *Absent*
Mohammed Khudayyir *Basrayatha*
Ibrahim al-Koni *Anubis* • *Gold Dust* • *The Puppet* • *The Seven Veils of Seth*
Naguib Mahfouz *Adrift on the Nile* • *Akhenaten: Dweller in Truth*
Arabian Nights and Days • *Autumn Quail* • *Before the Throne* • *The Beggar*
The Beginning and the End • *Cairo Modern* • *The Cairo Trilogy: Palace Walk*
Palace of Desire • *Sugar Street* • *Children of the Alley* • *The Coffeehouse*
The Day the Leader Was Killed • *The Dreams* • *Dreams of Departure*
Echoes of an Autobiography • *The Essential Naguib Mahfouz* • *The Final Hour*
The Harafish • *Heart of the Night* • *In the Time of Love*
The Journey of Ibn Fattouma • *Karnak Cafe* • *Khan al-Khalili* • *Khufu's Wisdom*
Life's Wisdom • *Love in the Rain* • *Midaq Alley* • *The Mirage* • *Miramar* • *Mirrors*
Morning and Evening Talk • *Naguib Mahfouz at Sidi Gaber* • *Respected Sir*
Rhadopis of Nubia • *The Search* • *The Seventh Heaven* • *Thebes at War*
The Thief and the Dogs • *The Time and the Place* • *Voices from the Other World*
Wedding Song • *The Wisdom of Naguib Mahfouz*
Mohamed Makhzangi *Memories of a Meltdown*
Alia Mamdouh *The Loved Ones* • *Naphtalene*
Selim Matar *The Woman of the Flask*
Ibrahim al-Mazini *Ten Again*
Samia Mehrez *The Literary Atlas of Cairo* • *The Literary Life of Cairo*
Yousef Al-Mohaimeed *Munira's Bottle* • *Wolves of the Crescent Moon*
Eslam Mosbah *Status: Emo*
Hassouna Mosbahi *A Tunisian Tale*
Ahlam Mosteghanemi *Chaos of the Senses* • *Memory in the Flesh*
Shakir Mustafa *Contemporary Iraqi Fiction: An Anthology*
Mohamed Mustagab *Tales from Dayrut*
Buthaina Al Nasiri *Final Night*
Ibrahim Nasrallah *Inside the Night* • *Time of White Horses*
Haggag Hassan Oddoul *Nights of Musk*
Mona Prince *So You May See*
Mohamed Mansi Qandil *Moon over Samarqand*
Abd al-Hakim Qasim *Rites of Assent*
Somaya Ramadan *Leaves of Narcissus*
Kamal Ruhayyim *Days in the Diaspora*
Mahmoud Saeed *The World through the Eyes of Angels*
Mekkawi Said *Cairo Swan Song*
Ghada Samman *The Night of the First Billion*
Mahdi Issa al-Saqr *East Winds, West Winds*
Rafik Schami *The Calligrapher's Secret* • *Damascus Nights* • *The Dark Side of Love*
Habib Selmi *The Scents of Marie-Claire*
Khairy Shalaby *The Hashish Waiter* • *The Lodging House*
The Time-Travels of the Man Who Sold Pickles and Sweets
Khalil Sweileh *Writing Love*
Miral al-Tahawy *Blue Aubergine* • *Brooklyn Heights* • *Gazelle Tracks* • *The Tent*
Bahaa Taher *As Doha Said* • *Love in Exile*
Fuad al-Takarli *The Long Way Back*
Zakaria Tamer *The Hedgehog*
M. M. Tawfik *candygirl* • *Murder in the Tower of Happiness*
Mahmoud Al-Wardani *Heads Ripe for Plucking*
Amina Zaydan *Red Wine*
Latifa al-Zayyat *The Open Door*